Hermione Hoby grew up in London. After working for the *Observer*, she moved to New York. She writes for publications including *The New Yorker*, the *Guardian*, the *New York Times*, and the *Times Literary Supplement*. She has interviewed hundreds of actors, writers, pop stars and other cultural figures. *Neon in Daylight* is her first novel.

Praise for *Neon in Daylight*

'Hoby's descriptive language is spectacular, like that of Elif Batuman with a freer spirit or Eve Babitz . . . The book is irresistible' *Los Angeles Review of Books*

'Hoby's skill on the sentence level – along with a keen eye for detail – will catapult her to stardom' *Chicago Review of Books*

'Hoby channels the spirit of Joan Didion and the keen observational eye of Ben Lerner to show us the here and now, made luminously real' Alexandra Kleeman

'In language so vivid that readers could break a sweat in an igloo, Hoby brings to life the seamy underworld of bright, bored people during a suffocating New York City summer, demonstrating the sure hand seen in works by Bret Easton Ellis and Tama Janowitz' *Library Journal*

'Highly propulsive reading' *Booklist*

NEON IN DAYLIGHT

HERMIONE HOBY

W&N

WEIDENFELD & NICOLSON

First published in Great Britain in 2018
by Weidenfeld & Nicolson
an imprint of The Orion Publishing Group Ltd
Carmelite House, 50 Victoria Embankment
London EC4Y 0DZ

An Hachette UK Company

1 3 5 7 9 10 8 6 4 2

A CIP catalogue record for this book is
available from the British Library.

ISBN (Mass Market Paperback) 978 1 4091 8462 1
ISBN (eBook) 978 1 4091 8463 8

Printed in Great Britain by Clays Ltd, Elcograf S.p.A.

www.orionbooks.co.uk

For my parents

Impossible to remember what she thought it would be, what she'd imagined it looking like, now that she was here. The door was brown, and Kate stood staring at it in a kind of paralysis, winded after three flights of stairs, a confusion of keys splayed heavy in her palm. Much like the new suitcase at her feet, these keys seemed to be an ugly prop, an aid to some kind of performance.

The apartment was owned by her mother's onetime best friend, off on the postdivorce cliché of an around-the-world, Thailand et cetera trip. A week ago Kate had stared at this stranger's face on a Skype screen, a face fussed with earrings and silk scarves, glitching in the sputtering Wi-Fi, exclaiming: "Oh, honey, I can't *believe* you've never been to New York!" And then: "Oh my god, your mom and I had such adventures when we were your age. Because you gotta travel! You gotta *live*, you know?" And Kate didn't know. Didn't know what *live* meant, in this context. She suspected, though, that it meant something you'd see on a Pepsi commercial: jumping into a waterfall in your underwear, piling into an open-top car to the beach, that sort of thing. But she'd said *"Absolutely"* into the screen like she knew, like *yeah*, she totally knew. As though she were the kind of person who was *up for it* and *down for it*. The kind of person who wouldn't be troubled, for instance, over how those two semantically opposed phrases could have come to mean, in essence, the exact same thing.

It was only now—a master's degree completed dutifully, pointlessly; a commitment to a Ph.D. made miserably, uncertainly—that she realized the world truly did not give one single shit whether you'd done your homework. This skyline, for example: the extent of its indifference was operatic. She'd watched it through the window of the cab and heard blooming Gershwin and an earnest voice in her head, subsumed by its own parodies, saying, "He *adored* New York City, he *idolized* it all out of proportion." The Empire State Building on the right, the Freedom Tower on the left, with its central spear naked on top. In the days before, Kate had nervously clicked her way around virtual maps, zooming in and out to learn the sequence of the bridges up the East River: Brooklyn, Manhattan, Williamsburg. Doing her homework. But she hadn't zoomed close enough to see that the struts of the Williamsburg Bridge were pink. Who paints a bridge pink? Those struts had come at her too fast, a metronome assault of pink flashes on blue.

And now, here, these keys, this door. Its spyhole's

beady avidity. Too easy to imagine an eyeball pressed up to the other side, watching. The keys worked, a minor astonishment, and then the door opened. The apartment was small and cluttered, a sofa overpopulated with the kinds of throws and cushions that people describe as "ethnic." Kate wondered what "Caucasian" cushions might look like, and the answer of course was these, because they were from IKEA, not Rajasthan, turquoise and purple and stuck all over with white cat hair, tufts of it spindled around the cheap sequins.

Somewhere in here was a cat to be sat. She couldn't bring herself to call the cat's name. The name embarrassed her, but it was more than that. Speaking anything out loud, alone in this other woman's apparently empty apartment, seemed like an audacity. Speaking anything anywhere, in fact, had come to feel like that. Lately, she could think the words fine, could sense their calm gray delineations in her mind, neutral and precise, but when she began to say them, to actually shape them into sounds to propel out of her mouth, the whole project seemed to fail.

On the large bed under the window, a bed almost as big as the room itself, the cat was waiting for her, facing her, staring at her, paws tucked under itself, the pose prim and a little censorious. When she moved closer and reached her hand toward its head, it flinched to sniff at her fingers, then made a couple of twitches of its whiskers and looked away, disdainful.

It didn't need her. The self-sufficiency of cats! Their

implacability! To be a cat. But then, she remembered they were sociopaths—scientists had said so. There seemed to be a problem with applying the human construction of "sociopath" to a nonhuman species. Wouldn't that make everything nonhuman sociopathic, in human eyes? Could that be right? It seemed quite arrogant. The thing to do was to assert, both to herself and to the cat and to the apartment itself, that this was her bed now, her territory. When she placed her hands on the creature now it seemed to entrench itself further, as if suctioning its soft underside to the sheets. She wobbled it feebly from side to side, trying to get a grip without hurting it. The cat looked both offended and embarrassed for her.

"Please," she said in a voice barely getting beyond a whisper. Steeled herself and said it: "Joni. Joni Mitchell."

As if she had been holding out to hear her name, the cat leaped, slipped out of her hands and onto the floor, where it paused to flick its tail once, like an indignant flamenco dancer. Then the cat turned and stalked away, tail straight and high above a puckered, evil-looking anus.

She put her hand on the warm patch it had left behind and lay down on the bed.

△▽△

The street was three floors down but the sounds she woke to were so rude and immediate that it seemed as though all the sidewalk tables of the café had levitated—that the whole tableau of chairs, plates, glasses was suspended right outside this window, with freshly showered men and women dining while their feet dangled happily in the air. That bright percussion of knives on plates, overlaid on the swell of voices, and this light through the window of a still-warm evening, reminded her of being small: British summertime in the suburbs, the plangent chimes of an ice-cream van several streets away. And now a female shriek from the sidewalk so loud that she flinched. Then a man's voice, booming unbelievably, urgent with his own humor, going, "No, no, no, but that's *before* he even met her!" and then laughter, outraged and delighted, slapping all the tails of these words. How weird that she could hear these people, hear their every syllable, and they had no idea she was up here, listening, or if they did, they simply didn't care.

She turned on her phone and watched it cast around for a signal, struggling. Eight thirty here, the evening just beginning, and one thirty a.m. in London, so late that it was already tomorrow. George would be asleep and oblivious. And her mother. Everyone, in fact, everyone who knew her was asleep right now.

Everyone needs a plan. That was the sort of thing George would say, something he'd wield from his well-ordered arsenal of maxims. He was doing a law conversion, and she hoped he would not be converted, but suspected it was already too late. He'd made his decision. Like always, it had been made simply, swiftly, confidently, irrevocably.

"You're being crazy," he'd said when she'd told him not to come, that she was going on her own. His words had an air of sensible finality, the genial confidence of putting this thing to bed: "You don't want to do this."

And that did it. That was perfect. In telling her that she did not want to do something, in the laughably egregious condescension of telling her what it was she did not want to do, he had succeeded only in letting her know that she had no choice but to do it. What could she do but smile a weird, wide smile at him and, robotically, make the series of mouse clicks that meant a flight to JFK, purchased with her dead grandmother's money.

She'd buy a pack of cigarettes. That'd be a thing to do, a new prop to hold—one that would be less ugly than the suitcase and the keys—some kind of shortcut to poise or personality. This was a thing the living did—smoked. It was a way to know you existed as a person in the world: blackening up your lungs with nicotine and tar.

As a kid she'd had nightmares of witches. She would wake up and smell them on her pillow, a sour yellow reek. Loneliness, too, had a smell, she thought, and it was almost the same, that witchy reek. As she walked out into the world she feared she was trailing it behind her.

In the deli on the corner Beyoncé was singing on the in-store radio and a young man was grabbing a beer from one of the chiller cabinets, a practiced, swinging ease to the motion. As she touched an enormous bag of pretzels, pretending to be interested in it, some shift happened, some subatomic shuffle. She looked up before she could think.

A girl was standing in front of the counter, peeling off

dollars. The bleached and frayed denim cutoffs she wore were butt-skimmingly short, cut high on the outer thighs and belted tight at her waist. A loose black top hung low from her shoulders, the upper part of her back gleaming with sweat.

"American Spirit," she said. Her voice made Kate think of caves, their smooth, dry walls. "Yellow."

As the man reached up behind him for the cigarettes the girl tilted her head and swept her hand across her hair, twisting it into one rope that she slung around her shoulder, a movement so fluent that Kate understood it to be habitual to the point of definitive. There was a worldly impatience to it, as though this length of hair were a wearisome but welcome thing. Kate thought of the way a mother hoists her kid on her hip, proprietorial pleasure humming through the sigh of it. She could almost feel it, the luxury of gathering up those black lengths, a musky smell rising from the weight of them.

A line of muscle stretched the length of the girl's brown thigh, and it strobed as she cast her weight onto her right hip and began tapping her foot. She was shoeless! And the piston-pedal made by those tensed and naked toes scandalized Kate. To be barefoot, in a shop—store—to walk across all the hot dirt of the city on the skin of your soles.

The tapping of her foot seemed less like agitation and more like an expression of optimism and energy, a hunger for things. Its regularity seemed almost practical, as though this foot pedaled the engine that powered the girl's world and she was simply keeping it going, pushing it forward, an impatient maintenance.

Kate stared, her fingers going a little slack around the pretzel bag. Maybe she was overthinking again.

But the girl's jawline, the silhouette of it, somehow had the same merciless quality as the skyline seen out the window of the cab a few hours earlier. It was this detail in particular that drove a new conviction in Kate: if she were ever to get to know this girl, she'd fail her. She saw the girl throwing a basketball at her, *blam*, fingers outspread from the center of her chest as if to mime an explosion—*catch it!*—but instead of catching it Kate would flinch, fumble, drop it. She felt her blush begin to rise at this imagined incompetence.

And then, finally, the girl turned her head and looked straight down the aisle at her, black rounds of sunglasses set on a symmetry so perfect that it induced a kind of terror. Kate's stomach fell. The girl began to withdraw her sunglasses with a sort of poisonous languor, and Kate jumped back to the pretzels before eye contact. This start, she knew, only underscored the gawking it was meant to conceal.

"Happyforth!"

Kate couldn't have responded anyway—stones choking up her throat—but the girl was already walking out the door, giving rhythmic slaps to the base of the cigarette packet with the heel of her hand. The bottoms of her feet were filthy; every step was a flash of grimed black sole.

It had been, what, nine seconds? Nothing. It was the

black-bottomed feet that filled her mind now, the sight of them as she'd walked away. A wolfish pang of wondering where she was going. The pretzels were still in her hand and she looked at them. An enormous bag. She put them back.

At the cooler cabinet were something like a hundred different waters. Fluoro-crystal-colored ones, glowing in the spaceship hum of refrigeration. Ones to energize you, ones proclaiming "Focus" and "De-stress," infusions named Immuno-defense and Activate and Balance. There was even, my god, Arouse. And yet no one, as far as she knew, had managed to manufacture and market a water that would tell you who you were and what you should do and where you should be in the future. No isotonic called "Drink This and You'll Know If Your Relationship Is Over and How to End It."

At the counter, she parroted the girl's words: "American Spirit." The guy made an irritable wince at her and she repeated herself, repeating the girl, but the stones were back, throat-cluttering, and the words came out tremulously.

"Eh?" he said.

She swallowed, blinked, indicated the packets behind him, and made her third attempt: "American Spirit cigarettes? Those yellow ones?"

He dropped his wince and laughed. She had no idea what was happening. Finally, she realized she was being teased. He chuckled, reached for the cigarettes, and slapped them down on the counter with the lovely largesse of a bet well won. With a pinch and a flourish, he added a lighter to the pile—bright yellow, the same shade as the cigarette packet. "American Spirit for English girl!"

She thanked him.

He seemed to expect a little more, a chat or a joke.

She smiled weakly and could say nothing. His joy faded. With his palms on the countertop, he seemed to recede into himself.

"Thanks," she mumbled again, pocketing the cigarettes.

When he slowly raised his hand to wipe sweat from his brow there was something mournful in the movement. It was a kind of sad salute goodbye. He continued to look at her, wordless, as she left.

She walked to Tompkins Square Park, which that evening was still nameless for her, just a park that smelled of scorched grass and dust and hot air threaded through with notes of marijuana. A low-slung sun burned all the day's dirt into gold. There were so many faces here that for a moment Kate felt she was trespassing on a party. There was a consensus to their leisure, she could feel it, luminous and weird, a common sentience, as if all these people might turn in unison, any moment now, to look to her silently with wondering frowns—not exactly hostile, but certainly puzzled—that would ask who she was and what she was doing here. Friends and strangers were enacting their social lives all over this public space.

A trio of African American teenage boys, popping and flexing beside a miniature portable sound system, began to draw a crowd who clapped and nodded with an expansive, self-congratulatory indulgence, a great open willingness to be entertained. She became one of the crowd too, put her body between the shoulders of other people, one of the spectators watching torsos jerking, arms jolting out of sockets and swinging lifeless, eyes rolling back in heads. The performers' faces displayed exaggerated expressions of astonishment at their own virtuosity. The crowd cheered again. Kate moved away.

Across the park a tiny old woman, humpbacked and sinewed, was shadowboxing and jogging feebly on the spot. She was dressed in Barbie-pink satin boxing shorts and a bomber jacket, and a blond wig bounced on her skull, threatening to jerk itself loose. To Kate she was unignorable, spectacularly so, and yet everyone ignored her.

Kate followed the park's paths, the sensible curves of them prescribing the way. She had no idea how to be a body in space, of where to put herself and how and why. Along the benches homeless men were stretched out shirtless, heaving as they snored. Time had faded their tattoos and sun had darkened their skin so much that the two—inked flesh and unmarked flesh—were almost indistinguishable. Beyond them, on the grass, small groups of young white women in sunglasses and scanty floral dresses had arranged themselves around mini-picnics of hummus pots and carrot sticks, and even the prostrate among them seemed to have configured themselves in ways that would flatter them in photographs, on their fronts with their chins in their palms and their ankles crossed in the air, Lolita-ish, or erect with their knees tucked to one side, pulling waists lean and long. Some of them were tattooed, too, but these were discreet and pretty little concessions to the act: a childish star on an ankle, or some bird, any bird, on a wrist. The kind of tentative adornment that they hoped lovers would remember, even fetishize, so that even if they were one body in a lifetime of many, he might say, years later, *Oh yes! The girl with the star on her wrist.* As if there weren't galaxies of them.

The light was fading and the color of the sky began to find its way into her—the whole gathering night, unknowable, mushrooming in indigo and violet. Limbs gleamed with sweat all around her; the laughter seemed louder and her anxiety rose. This city, this time, this massive stupid gift of a free apartment, demanded something of her: a grandness, an expansiveness, some kind of vision, bold acts. And she was already failing with thoughts like these; dropping all the basketballs, butterfingered, dribbling apologies.

She'd made it up the three flights of stairs and had closed a series of doors behind her when she heard an obscene rupturing of sound, a noise splitting the air. The cat was crouched under the kitchen table, and Kate lurched toward it, but it yowled—a horrible, unheimlich noise—and shot away, seeking refuge without her. And now she was just a human cowering under a stranger's table. Within the panic there was a small space for one thought, a sickly little pocket in which she was able to realize that if she survived, she'd be able to say the words "I arrived in New York the night of a terrorist attack." A grim little tale to treasure forever. *Where were you?* people would ask, and she'd never not remember.

But now the sound of sky breaking had rumbled down quieter, like sonic rubble, and she crawled to the window to see signs of panic. There were none. She lifted the window with fumbling, frightened fingers. First an inch, then two, then all the way, and the heat rushed in, bringing the smell of cordite. On a rooftop, blocks away, she could see figures moving, ecstatically, looping wands of light in the air that left trails and sparks like tiny comets. She stared, stupefied. And then the word for those things came to her: *sparklers.* And then this knowledge, slow and steady: that people don't dance on rooftops in the middle of a terrorist attack. Through the sputtering light trails, she began to see the words the girl had shouted to her in the bodega, forming sense in the spaces.

Happy *Fourth.*

She'd arrived in a city celebrating its independence from her nation. Fireworks sound the same as bombs. Or as imagined bombs. On the bed, weak and ridiculous, foolish with tears, she let relief claim her.

2

Inez was photographing the mirror and Dana was watching. This was often how it was: she did things, and Dana watched.

"No one's going to buy it," Dana was saying, softly, to the ceiling.

She'd sat on the end of Inez's bed, then flopped backward, so that her feet were still planted, and her palms were upturned by her sides. Her body seemed to announce, with a certain fatalism, that it would never move from this position.

"I wished this girl in the bodega a happy Fourth," Inez said, tossing her the cigarettes, "and she looked like I was about to *shoot* her."

The cigarettes lay where they landed, on her friend's belly.

"Well," Dana said dully. "Sometimes you have that effect on people."

"You saying I'm scary?"

"Can't you just put it out on the street?" Dana said. "I don't know why you can't just put it out on the street."

Inez could put the mirror out on the street, sure. She could also—and this would be much more spectacular—toss it out one of the windows of the loft's main space and watch it cartwheel down to smash on Broadway. But there was something far more appealing about selling off a piece of childhood, about having the object taken off your hands and out of your life for cash. Her plan to sell the mirror was, to her mind, both hygienic and ruthless.

Around the mirror's corners were the scarified white patches of stickers stuck there in clusters, then scraped away at a later date. She hadn't noticed these patches until now, the gummy blight of them, and she scratched at them ineffectually, feeling Dana's gaze on her all the while. The real blight, of course, was the mirror itself. It hung low on the wall in its cheap molded plastic pink frame, at a height right for a seven-year-old, the one she'd been twelve years ago. As she stood in front of it now in her bare feet, her reflection was neatly guillotined.

How to photograph a mirror? With her phone raised at her hip she took another picture and studied the image. There they were, her skinny hips cocked, and her head cropped out, a small blare of flash around the top of her phone and her fingers. She scowled at this image of the object, then at the object itself, looking between the two, and at herself, looking. You could see the white patches in the photo. Maybe someone would consider the thing "distressed."

"Why," Dana said, "now?"

Inez began half humming, half singing, as she typed "Craigslist" in the screen's search bar.

"Are you singing the Bee Gees?" Dana asked, apparently amused.

"Aaliyah!" Inez said. "Fucking sacrilege! *Bee Gees.*"

She resumed the tune but as she clicked into the blurry photographs and banality of for sale > furniture, the humming lost its will. Ugly furniture was all the same. All the cheap Billy bookcases. All the bland dorm-room desks. People, though, that was a whole other thing. She strayed within seconds to personals > miscellaneous romance. The pink mirror faded and was forgotten.

"Miscellaneous romance." That phrase was funny: *romantic* like the posts in > m4w, with their anxious, explicit wondering over anatomical parts? "Do you have cute feet?" they asked the ether. "Do you have big labia?" Or *romantic* like the messages posted beneath lewd requests that rang with something more plaintive than filthy—with need, rather than desire? "Will you spit in my mouth?" "Will you spoon me?" One message ended with the question "Does that make sense to you?"

She clicked and read and clicked and read, wound out of herself so thoroughly that when Dana spoke again Inez jumped slightly, just slightly, probably not enough for her to notice.

"Did you post it? Can we finally go now? We'll miss the fireworks."

"You know the fireworks will be lame, Gabe firing off one pathetic little rocket or something. Okay, listen to this," she said, and she began to read aloud in a goofy voice, gulping each word: "'Let's play Doctor! I've got all the equipment for your erotic sensual exam. About me: open-minded, kicked out of medical school—wonder why, lol?—semi-sane and lots of fun in the exam room.'"

With reluctance, Dana sat up, dislodging the cigarette packet.

"Wonder why, lol!" Inez crowed.

"We're never going to get to this party," Dana said.

Charged with glee now, bent over the laptop balanced on her crossed legs, Inez said, "He calls himself a regular guy."

"Maybe he is," Dana said.

"'Seeking young woman, slim, attractive, to be locked in closet for an hour, maybe more. Generous financial donation. Regular guy, nothing funny.'"

A small silence grew in the room. Like an oily bubble blown for a child, it suggested wonder as much as absurdity, the two states overlaid and glistening. The bubble swelled, wobbled, popped. Inez looked up. Dana's expression was heavy with warning.

"I'd totally do that," Inez mouthed.

"You wouldn't."

"I would. I'm going to."

"You're not."

"I am. Dare me."

"Absolutely not. No."

"Hey, Dana, am I slim?"

"Shut up."

"Attractive?"

"I will not endorse this. I am *not* daring you to do this."

"Generous financial donation."

"No. You're not doing this."

"I dare me. I double dare me, I—"

"You need to triple shut up."

"I'm doing it."

"Then I'm going."

"Oh, come on."

But Dana was actually getting up, actually gathering her things, frosty and fumbling.

"I'm going to e-mail him," Inez sang, "I'm e-mailing him now."

She felt the look, felt her friend waiting there, and kept her waiting. She could sense Dana stooped and motionless in the doorway, backpack slung over her shoulder, gripping its front strap tight, as if it were a parachute harness, a fist over her heart. Pull in case of emergency. Inez faked something conclusive—a forefinger's smack of the return key.

"Sent!" she whispered, lying.

"I really," Dana said, "*really* don't think you actually want to do this. I mean, I think you're fucking with me. Which is whatever . . ." Dana's voice was shining now and she blinked a few times, fast. "Oh, just do whatever you want—get yourself killed."

Inez had learned the trick this summer, doing it into her iPhone's camera, reversed so the screen mirrored her face: a minuscule muscle tensing. That shrinking of her eyes' lower corners that made them loom larger and lovelier, made some mystery out of them. And then, if you tipped your head forward a little too, so you had to raise your gaze just a few extra millimeters . . . She willed the radiation of hot, grave attention into Dana's waiting gaze.

"What?" Dana blurted, shifting her bag's strap.

"I have to ask you for a favor," she said.

"What?"

"When I go missing," she said, and now she felt her own smirk breaking through and cracking her solemnity with something she hoped was wicked, "you have to make sure the *Post* uses a really hot picture of me."

And then, a private flourish, she conjured the sight of her own strangled body dredged from the East River, eyes open and sightless, lips parted, her face shaded beautiful lifeless blues. Laura Palmer in *Twin Peaks*.

"Oh, fuck you," Dana said bitterly. "Seriously, fuck you. I'll see you on the roof. Or not."

And she left, knuckles tight on the backpack strap.

One further line of the ad that Inez hadn't read aloud was this: "Include the word 'real' in your e-mail subject line." This instruction seized her in a way she couldn't explain. It set off a warped thrill, the idea of declaring her reality, over e-mail, to some stranger.

Creating another e-mail address, xmariaforeverx@ gmail.com (Maria was her grandmother's name, but also just a name, millions of people's name), turned out to be the easiest thing in the world. And when, from an in-box empty but for the rote welcome note, she clicked COM-POSE and typed the words "I'm real . . ." everything in her quickened. It was a kind of salivation, strung through with a taste of something bitter. There'd been a line in a movie she'd seen: something about how the best perfumes always had something rotten in them.

△▽△

He'd replied in ten minutes, and she was astonished to be at his door fifty-seven minutes later, watching her own finger move toward his door buzzer. It sounded inside—a harsh and angry blare, all tired wires and ill will—and her muscles jumped to run as the door opened.

He nodded at her, uttered her grandmother's name as a question.

"Hey, show me your passport," she blurted back.

He faltered. "I don't have one." A small voice, nondescript.

"ID, then."

And, silently, he complied, shuffling off to a nightstand to find his wallet, to draw out his driver's license and come back to hand it to her. She felt him watching, without comment, as she took a picture on her phone and texted it to Dana: *if I'm not there in three hours lol.* She handed his ID back, told him what she'd done, and watched him slide it into his back pocket.

"Nothing funny," he said, quite softly.

"Right."

He wasn't a monster; there are so few. He was, however, creepy-looking. A pointed face, a snaggle tooth, and, visible as he turned, a greasy braid that snaked, dwindling, down the back of his neck to end in a curled tuft held by a rubber band. It made her think of the My Little Ponies she'd played with as a kid, the meagerness of their synthetic manes and tails, the gorgeous clunk of the scissors, and then the lurch as you knew that what had been cut would not grow back.

If she and Dana passed this man on the street he would, Inez knew, bring to bear a pause between them. And the pause would be Inez waiting the one beat until he'd passed, just out of earshot, or sometimes not, to say to her friend, her friend who was gay, her friend who she knew already sensed these words coming, "Why'd you ignore your boyfriend?" And however many times Inez made the joke, applying it to whichever passing stranger qualified as sufficiently mad or stinking, Dana could never quite manage to not smile. Inez knew this, that she would always make her laugh. Even when the joke was cruel. Especially when the joke was cruel.

His apartment was one room that smelled of mold mingled with weed and incense. Tattered dream catchers hung in the grimed windows, trailing dusty feathers caught by cactus spines. Damp shoe boxes with bulging sides and collapsed lids were piled up against the walls.

With his gaze settling somewhere around her knees, he said: "Hold out your wrists."

Not gentle, not gruff either. He had a tie, an ugly,

paisley tie, with which he noosed her hands, knotting it tepidly, frowning with concentration, like a parent readying a child for school. There was a queasy tenderness to the process that made Inez snap her attention to one of those dream catchers in the windows and fix her stare on it. Nothing in the world but a dream catcher, twisting sickly, as if it were feeling out the contours of her fear—which was here now, sudden and too late, hammering.

When he opened the door to the closet she saw there was a fat pillow in there for her, an archipelago of stains—tea stains?—across one corner. He still didn't meet her eyes as he murmured, softly, as if he hardly wanted her to hear it, "Just you try and get away now." And then she was inside and as she looked up the door was shut and he was locking it with a fleet, efficient twist. She heard his face against it, muttering, in a tone almost kindly, "Now you just stay there till I'm done with you."

Which would be precisely one hour later, the time stipulated, agreed, and paid for already in two fifty-dollar bills inside an envelope with "Maria" written on it in pencil.

Her eyes drank in the darkness, concentrating it to yield shapes and gradations, while her heartbeats became so violent that she wondered if some kind of permanent cardiac damage might be likely. With her back against one wall of the closet and her feet against the other, the hems of his shirts and jackets grazing the top of her head, she breathed in their marijuana residue as she listened for the inevitable sound.

He never did do anything. Or if he did, it was done silently somewhere, unseen. She hardened her jaw, swallowed, ran her tongue around her teeth, behind her upper lip, and thought about how in a few hours she'd be on the roof. She'd be there telling Dana she'd done it. Maybe she'd actually fling the bills in the air, make it rain. Rap video.

Her headphones rested around her neck, a silent, protective noose, and she slipped her wrists out of the tie—shackles like slips of cloud—took out her phone, and switched it to vibrate. Brightness thumbed right down low, in case light through the door-crack ruptured whatever illusion it was that he needed. She willed someone to text her and ask where she was so that she could reply, fingers electric with the relish of it, "Tied up in the closet of some guy's basement apartment." No one did. In her iMessages, the thumbnail image of a stranger's driver's license, delivered to Dana. His hollowed cheeks, a gaze that seemed to register some kind of exhaustion or disappointment (*this again?*), like most mug shots do. Reaching up into the jackets, she fingered a pocket in the darkness and pulled out a piece of paper, a ragged envelope, folded in half, a shopping list written in pencil in the same cramped and irregular letters that spelled out her grandmother's name on the envelope he'd given her: "milk, oranges, oreos." Something about this list made her feel shame. The intimation of the smallness of a life. She put it back quickly, as if it were infectious, as if something bad might seep into her fingertips.

And then, ridiculously, she heard the sound of a

guitar. And *singing*! So softly, to himself, as if she weren't there. As if maybe he'd forgotten that he'd locked her in his own closet. If she squinted through the chink she could just make him out, a sliver, in profile, strumming, eyes closed, chin raised: "where have all the flowers gone, long time passing." If Dana had been there too it would have been funny.

It occurred to her that he could forget about her. That nothing was stopping him walking away and leaving her locked up. Her pulse picked up the pace again and her heart felt tiny, a stuffed animal flung around inside a dryer.

Part of Inez had believed Dana when she'd said, her voice all embarrassing as it wobbled with the threat of tears, that she was going to die if she did this reckless thing. Maybe not quite die, but come right up close to the silvery edge of it. It was almost disappointing, then, how much this guy didn't seem like the strangling type. But then what did a strangling type look like? She studied the photograph of his license again, the photograph of his photograph. He stared back at her, and the longer she stared, the sadder and stranger his face looked.

She checked the time again: just five minutes. Willed herself not to check it again. This would be the challenge, not to look.

And she did it. She checked only when he was ostentatiously noisy about the process of release—and there it was, a perfect hour. Clearing his throat, shuffling over to the closet, rattling the latch open slowly, perhaps so as not to surprise her, or to wake her if she'd fallen asleep.

"I hope you've learned your lesson," he said, straining and failing to sound stern, and she nodded a bit, mute, not quite sure whether she was still meant to be in character at this moment. Maybe *character* wasn't even the right word for whatever she was. Was she a specific someone to him, or a re-creation of someone now gone, a body for a ghost? Or just a girl, any girl, tied up, in his house. She told herself she didn't care. Didn't care if he wondered about who she was, what her life was, what she did when she wasn't occupying this small dark space of his closet, knees under her chin. He helped her up, awkward and tender. This—him taking her tied hands to pull her up—was the only touch they shared, and it embarrassed them both.

"See you next week," he said, the necessary words of termination. He lifted his hand in a stiff and small sort of wave. She made a noncommittal noise, shook the feeling back into a leg, stamped the numbness out, and then it was over and she was walking out into the currents of downtown Manhattan with a hundred dollars packed tight against her skinny rump.

The evening seemed to have grown bigger, every-thing enlarged, as if it were impressed with her, as if it were opening its mouth in some wide "woah" of appreciation. She realized her hands were shaking slightly, that her body felt hot and cold, but that this feeling was the opposite of weakness. There was a laugh inside her, a laugh at nothing. She felt it on her lips, an uncontrollable smirk. She hoicked up the noose of her head-phones to clamp them down over her ears and turned up the volume, Atlanta rap juddering through her skull, ear to ear.

She walked south down Bowery with such swagger that oncoming men opened their mouths and said things at her, things to be ignored, their walks widening into parentheses, a force field around her.

Here was the New Museum with its stupid massive red rose, like something shoved there by a giant teenage boy, and, beside it, the homeless mission. An African American man was sprawled sideways on the pavement on a flattened packing box, singing. His clothes, which were layered and many despite the heat, were the saturated noncolor of the chronically unwashed. *Proper homeless*, she thought. Not like the twenty-something crusties with their gross dreads and brutish, ugly dogs, sitting outside the Strand with cardboard signs lettered prettily enough for five-dollar greeting cards. If they could put all that effort into their signs, she'd once said to Dana, couldn't they put a little more effort into getting a job? And Dana had told her that she was a terrible human being. This guy had no sign or serifs, just a force field of smell. One eye seemed not to see, screaming its glistening white, and the other eye swiveled and caught her. She pulled off her headphones.

"Spare dollar, miss."

She had never given a homeless person money before. It wasn't callousness, exactly. Or maybe it was. But Inez could still feel her mother's hand in hers, the strong grasp more reproving than protective as they'd walked fast past a man and his upraised Dunkin' Donuts cup one day, muttering to her that it was better to donate to homeless charities than to give to individuals in the street.

Well, fuck you, Mom, she thought cheerfully. *Hello, individual-in-the-street.* This would be a first, a bold new act, and as she peeled a fifty—a fifty!—from the envelope she felt herself swell with her own munificence and the massive craziness of having been locked in that tiny space. She handed it over casually, a wave of a note, and he grabbed it like a man killing a fly, scrunching it into his fist without looking or halting his singing. She stared at him.

"It's a *fifty*, dude," she said.

He kept singing.

"God bless, God bless," he sang in his madness, ignoring her words.

Fuck God, she thought, *thank* me.

"I just gave you a *fifty*," she said, loudly, but he wasn't listening.

Surely fifty dollars was huge—day-changing, week-changing. And he didn't even notice. She slammed her headphones back on, thumbed the volume higher, and now she was singing deaf and loud, tripping down the subway steps that would take her east into Brooklyn, oblivious to the premature fireworks, the first whine and burst of them in the still-light sky.

3

Bill woke up, stared into total darkness, and for a half second of hot terror he thought, almost calmly, *Oh, here it is.* That it had finally happened: he was in one of those black holes of boozed memory loss, actually *inside it.* Bullshit, of course. He was conscious, albeit with no idea where he was or how he'd got here. Gradually he began to make out very small lights above him, acknowledged that those lights were *stars,* that the ground beneath him was damp grass, that below that was solid earth, and that this was, yes, the real living world of Earth. With these discoveries made, it was time to roll onto his side, vomit voluminously, and then wipe his face on the ground like an animal, prostrating himself on his elbows. The bright tang of grass cut through the puke stench. And night air! Good, clean, glorious night air that he took in eagerly as he made his way onto his knees.

Taking its time, the world began to calibrate itself around him, tilting all its planes until they finally aligned. Okay, Prospect Park. He'd woken up in Prospect Park, and in this sick-drunk, fucked-up state, the name of the place struck him as hilarious. Prospect Park, in the dark. What prospects. Ha.

Time to piece it together. He'd been at the rooftop barbecue of an eminent former magazine editor—a pewter-haired, old-world fox, more scribbled sketch of a figure than man. There'd been mini lobster rolls, clam chowder served on ranks of porcelain spoons, and everyone drinking the same elaborate geranium-scented cocktails—his insides protested now at the memory—ostentatiously shaken by gym-bunny men in tight white shirts. Later, that party in the garden of a Park Slope brownstone. A small group of young teenage boys staring at him from a garden corner bright with fairy lights, brown eyes steeped in reproach, faces hushed like tiny monks. Shorts and ashy knees, baggy T-shirts and bony elbows.

And then? Fuck knows. But here he was.

He was clothed, at least, although barefoot. The darkness continued softening into gradations. Stars on the ground there—reflected, yes—a lake. He was near the lake. He patted his pockets to find, yes, familiar lumps of keys-phone-wallet. But no shoes. And the part of his mind that should explain to him where and why and when he'd taken his shoes off was miraculously missing.

"Where are my shoes?" he said out loud to the lake, a madman mumble. His feet were stuck all over with black wet bits of grass.

As he got closer to the lake, the dank reek of weeds and duck shit rose up and rolled toward him. But there was the moon on the water, the little rippling sonnet of it.

He stood there, hearing the susurrus of the crickets, and thought about how he might possibly be the only human being in the park right now. One man, alone, in a massive dark park. The clock on his phone said 03:33. He also had this thing on it, an app costumed with a quaint rendering of an old-fashioned compass, which quavered and found north when he asked it to. This way, then, northwest. He tried to think of himself as intrepid.

Small pinecones underfoot, pieces of twigs, dry and crumbled leaves, damp cool grass, and then the cold metal serration of something, an upturned beer bottle top, so quick and vicious that he yelped, came down in a clumsy drop, took his foot in his hand, and pulled it toward him for inspection. Like a cookie cutter in dough, the bottle top had left an indented ring on the mound of his flesh and he rubbed it, mute and dumb.

Sitting there, on the damp ground, holding his own naked foot in his hand like some kind of forsaken mental patient, he became aware of a thing glowing against the base of a tree in front of him, a bright shape that he didn't understand. His vision and his mind ran over and around it, but still the thing didn't yield itself. He stood and limped closer and the shape became brighter. It had legs, four slender legs tucked beneath its body, like an image of motion suspended, a perfect Muybridge gallop, but the space where its head should be was empty. This was what his mind had struggled with, that missing piece; it was a goat, a baby goat, but also couldn't be, because it was headless. There was something medieval in the image, but here it was, lying tenderly at the foot of a tree in Brooklyn.

There had been local news items about the mauled corpses of domestic animals. The mutant wildcat theory was popular, he remembered—some ungodly offspring of an escaped zoo beast and a stray. More plausible, and more ghoulish, too, was the psychopath theory, that some sick, sad human being captured the pets of moneyed Park Slope families and dismembered them here in the middle of the night. The headless kid seemed like a warning light. It said the space he moved in was just one layer, that there were so many more layers through which he moved obliviously, and that he'd just trespassed into a domain that was not his, like the sudden opening of elevator doors onto the wrong floor, into the wrong world.

Feeling foolish and afraid, he drew his phone out, held it up, and took a picture. As he did so every tree screamed with the assault of the flash, their branches like lightning rods in its sterile strobe, and he was suddenly hot with shame, as if he'd committed a dreadful impiety. He ran, an undignified scrabble, fueled by a boy's fear of monsters, sprinting now, belting in bare feet until he hit Prospect Park West. The low stone wall marked park from street like a mythical boundary, separating nature from the realm of emptied trash cans and functioning streetlights and alternate-side parking rules. It was a relief to feel smooth paving stone underfoot, to look up and see stately, pale apartment buildings gazing out placidly over the darkness behind him.

He checked his phone for the photo, wanting to see that headless kid, wanting to know if he'd really seen it. The image was just a blare, a white blare. He stared, just one second, then deleted it.

He retched viscous bile onto the clean sidewalk and wiped some cold streaks of bird shit from his feet. With a stitch in his side, he began to shuffle northeast, to Grand Army Plaza, where beneath the huge, illuminated arch he summoned dignity, and then a cab. There were so many gaps in his memory, stretches of time that he'd efficiently wiped out with vodka over the years, a tidal wave of it sweeping away the substrate. You really could kill time. Killing time drinking was not spending time, was not *whiling* time away, it was serving it up to oblivion. It felt at times like cheating death, playing death at its own game.

At home, dawn already creeping in like the sick joke it was, he rattled four Advil into his palm, downed them with half a glass of tepid tap water, and then looked at her bedroom door. Shut, which meant Inez was home. Good. He stood there for a moment, as if he expected her to wake up, sense him, and open the door, to sweetly welcome her father home at five a.m. He stared at the door a moment longer, turned, and went to bed.

4

The best thing about the apartment, Kate realized quite quickly, was the fire escape. Beyond the bedroom window and above the street you could nest there, held halfway between the inside world and outside world, suspended and sequestered. Today, she'd carefully furnished the space, made a small universe of select things: iced coffee, pack of cigarettes, cushion, book. Things to hold on to, to make you feel you were held on to. Which was a lie, of course. She was catastrophically unheld, and at the same time terribly conspicuous. That, maybe, was the worst thing about being lost: everyone could see you.

She'd had to ask for this iced coffee three times, as if she were speaking an entirely different language. Even before she'd opened her mouth, she had seemed to palpably discomfit the honey-haired barista. When she'd finally made herself understood and Honey-Hair had turned to shovel ice into a plastic cup, Kate checked her own shoes, left and right, and confirmed, definitively, that her soles were unshitted.

Everyone is invincible at eighteen. In that first year

of university, in the weeks before she met George, Kate had experienced the sensation of being at the center of a web that tilted with her as she moved, as if the world were yielding to her, as if she were putting it in motion. Everything was smaller then. Now when she thought of Cambridge, she thought of the city's model, on the raised circular plinth, about half a meter in diameter, on the edge of Market Square, the colleges cast in bronze, blocky and smooth as chocolate. You could loom over the model and put your forefinger on the street you were standing on. Just remembering this brought on a rush of claustrophobia.

She met George when their colleges shared seminars. His college—bigger, grander, more photogenic and famous—hosted. Two dozen of them sat around a huge round wooden table, where dead canonical poets had sat before them, soft January light pouring in through the windows. The second term was the seventeenth century. The first class was John Donne. They'd all bought the same edition, Everyman, handsome in its black-and-white jacket, the thin scarlet ribbon of a bookmark as proper as a Savile Row necktie. Only, the book in George's hands was different. It was the first thing she noticed, his large hands holding that book, a charcoal-black volume with elegant silver lettering down its spine. He read aloud without hesitation, as though he already knew these rhythms. It was at least four months later that she realized the book in his hands was the same version everyone else had. He'd just taken the dust jacket off.

A few weeks ago, before she left, they'd gone to a friend's dinner party. The friend—more George's than hers—had just bought a West London flat, or rather her parents had, and the evening was an elaborate performance of adulthood. There were canapés from Fortnum & Mason, and place cards bearing names in careful calligraphy, a strict boy-girl-boy-girl seating plan around the table.

"Champagne?" the hostess kept saying to people whose flutes had been diminished only by a sip or two. She looked, bottle and eyebrows raised, as if she were about to strike a dainty bell.

George had sat opposite Kate, and as the dinner progressed he seemed to be drawing in the air around him, tightening it.

Who knows how the conversation reached the place it did. But one young woman called Annabelle began talking about pornography. She was petite, fine-boned, and her high voice seemed to undulate erratically, as though subjected to its own tiny weather systems, little breezes and quick currents over which she had little to no control.

"Ugh, it's disgusting," she said. "Just so degrading to women."

And then something rushed into Kate, some renegade idea riding on a red-wine crest.

"Why do you think it's degrading?" she heard herself say. Every eye around the table stared at her face. Her words had been strangely loud. Without looking at him she could feel George watching her. Annabelle frowned, then blanched and reddened, an impressive chromatic succession. With a kind of tremble of refusal, she said, this time to the plate in front of her, "It's *degrading*!" And when she snuck a glance upward, at Kate, it was hot and sharp. She'd been made to repeat herself and sound stupid; she'd been held to her own opinion by another woman. She went on: "It's demeaning to women. To be gussied up like objects and"—her eyes glinted now with what Kate feared were tears—"fucked like animals." And she reached for her napkin to cover her mouth, as if she were wiping away that bad word. The table seemed to shift, in sympathy, unease.

"But isn't it possible," Kate had said, because why stop now, "that some women might like to be fucked like animals? That they might actually want and enjoy that."

Kate saw the eyebrows of the young man to Annabelle's left shoot up in a show of scandalized amusement; he took a large gulp of wine to show he was stifling a smirk. And then, "Oh-*KAYYY*!" the boyfriend of the hostess bellowed, a broad, good-natured putting-to-bed of the entire discussion. "Who wants Eton mess?"

People laughed, relieved. Kate rushed with homicidal urges. Annabelle extricated herself from her chair and walked stiffly in the direction of the bathroom. George issued Kate a deliberate, dark look, then refilled his wineglass.

She stretched her hand across the distance of white linen, reaching for his wrist. His arm jumped at her touch, knocked the wineglass over. A vast, blood-colored puddle spread as the bowl of the glass rolled away from its severed stem.

If the look he'd shot her a moment earlier had been dark, this one was like a black hole. An unequivocal, hateful *Look. What. You've. Done.* They didn't speak in the taxi home. He had to be the first to say something. She would hold out. He had to apologize for that look, which she had then obsessed over with some strange devotion, like a child with a freshly grazed knee. He'd flinched when she'd touched him! As though she were something toxic. She sat up against the chill of the window, the London streets blurred with rain and streetlights, and cried silently and steadily. And when they were home, in bed, they talked in quiet, truncated sentences until hopelessness silenced them and they lay there in the no-light, miserable.

She brought herself back to herself now, and to this day, to this fire escape, to the cat inside that she was supposed to be sitting, to the tiny beads of condensation sheeted over the clear plastic of the cup of iced coffee like some lovely reptile skin, to bicycle bells on the street below. To the sight of a tall woman, with short white-blond hair, strolling down the sidewalk exuding ease.

△▽△

Hot hair-dryer blasts and all the giddy top notes of expensive spritzes greeted her as she entered the salon. The stylist had tattoos of roses up her arms, and Bettie Page bangs, and if she saw fear in Kate's eyes, she was professional enough to ignore it. Buxom, grinning, she hummed along to Rihanna as she calmly twirled Kate's hair into a ponytail at her nape, and then, with no warning, jauntily scissored through its base. Kate felt a lurch. How did hot air balloons come down? How did they land?

Bettie Page held up the rope of hair in the mirror and gave it a morbid little shake as she grinned. It looked thoroughly creepy, a thing neither dead nor alive. And then she tossed it on the floor. Kate saw the mistaken assurance in the gesture. It said, *Fuck him, right?* And the stylist kept working, humming, satisfied in her narrative: boy dumps gal, gal gets fierce new hair. No, that's not it, Kate thought, that's really not it at all. But how do you correct someone who's said nothing?

Months ago, George had told her he thought she'd look good with . . . he didn't have the words, had tried to describe the haircut to her, haltingly, heterosexually, and she'd frowned, picturing a TV news anchor in a royal-blue suit. It wasn't a news anchor who'd given him the idea. It was a woman in one of his seminars. Facebook had thrown her up in a sidebar on Kate's screen one day, announcing that George was now friends with her, and there she was, in a professional-looking photograph, with the shoulder-length bob and side-swept feathered bangs that George had failed to adequately describe.

Kate realized she'd been staring somewhere beyond herself in the mirror with an expression of contempt and she caught it, for a split second, as she came back to her reflection. Bettie Page had tenderly painted each section of her shorn head with a dye-dipped brush and wrapped each little bit in tinfoil as though preparing a series of snacks. Kate was to sit there and wait for them to marinate.

By the time the work was over, her face looked sharper, her eyes wider. She looked older, too, now that she was a white-blond woman. A little frightening, rather than a little frightened?

"Yeah?" said the stylist, and then—the final flourish—she handed Kate a mirror, spun her around, and showed her the back of her own neck. There it was, naked and strange. When was the last time she'd seen the back of her neck? Wasn't there a sort of delicious indecency to it? She paid, tipping too much in her terror and pleasure, and once outside in the thick of the afternoon she kept reaching for it, this bare new neck with the sunlight on it, fingering the point where her short hair finished and her skin began.

5

Inez clocked them as they came in. She recognized their faces from the other week, the same pair, come to fuck with her again, all twitchy grins and limbs springy with their mission as they jounced up to the counter. They had read the café's Yelp entries and had come here on some kind of L.O.L. pilgrimage. She'd become a notoriety. There was a whole thread, Dana had said. The commenters were calling her the Notorious B.I.T.C.H. It was a *thing*.

"Two iced coffees," one of them said now. The shorter one beside him bit his fist and wheeled away and tittered. She gazed at them.

"Uh, hi? I said, two iced coffees?"

"Nah," she sighed.

"Excuse me?"

"We're closing."

He looked around him. There were half a dozen patrons bent into their MacBooks, placid people with their sweating cups of cold brew.

"Uh," he said. "You're literally open."

She folded her arms and let her head slowly fall to one side, frowning, pouting. She hoped that she looked thoughtful.

"Are we?" she said.

The guy spread his palms, exasperated, and Inez now tilted her head to the other side.

"So you're just not going to serve us? Loyal customers?" he said. Then he added, under his breath, *"Fucking bitch."*

"You know," she said. "I hear they play indie rock in Starbucks now. Maybe you guys should go find a Starbucks."

"Burrrn!" said the shorter sidekick, fist to his mouth again. He needed a bigger repertoire of responses, Inez thought.

"You know what? You're not even hot," the tall guy said. "You're just a bitch."

As they walked out the door he raised his middle finger, brandished it vigorously, and a bearded man in a Sonic Youth T-shirt looked up with mild alarm, then glanced at Inez and quickly returned to his screen. She hoped he didn't think she needed rescuing. He looked like the sort, dadlike. Dadly.

She turned and pretended to clean the espresso machine so that no one could see her face. Her stomach felt sour and her brain ran a bitter, rapid monologue of *fuck this* and *fuck this* and *fuck this*.

In the stockroom, Heather was on the phone, seeming stressed.

"Yo, Heather," she said.

Her boss's face flickered with a frown. She indicated *wait a minute* as she bent into the phone, nodding.

Inez whipped off the apron. "I'm heading off early."

And Heather mouthed *No!* while her eyebrows did something extraordinary under the strain of trying to listen to whoever was on the other end of the phone.

Inez flicked a peace sign at the Sonic Youth guy on the way out.

△▽△

Five minutes in, she knew for certain she hated the movie. Hating things: it tended to tell you who you were. Loving things rarely did.

"Come on," Dana had said with her amiable wheedle. "People say it's great. It will be fun and dumb. But good-dumb. Smart-dumb. Also, it will be cool in there. Literally cool."

That had won her over, grudgingly. A downstairs darkness purring with the sound of unwavering AC units. A drastic change of temperature. Delicious darkness, calibrated with artificial cool. Plus a massive Diet Coke, packed with ice, sibilant with effervescence.

"Why are there no brown people in this film?" she whispered in Dana's ear, right into the shell of it, and it elicited a fierce *shush* from the woman who spun around in the seat in front of them. And then, to Inez's irritation, there *were* black characters, including the heroine's love interest. The heroine was an underweight brunette who pulled a lot of faces and was a sex therapist who'd never achieved orgasm. "Achieved"! As if you got a certificate. This was the movie's central joke. The promo poster had testified to it being "the feel-good favorite of the summer," and Inez's hatred was now fortified by the remembered conviction that "feel-good" *always* filled her with hate.

Here's one thing her dad had taught her: walk out. When you think it's bullshit, just leave. You can leave. They'd done that with a Disney film once. Nine-year-old her, small girl sandwiched tidily between her parents in velvety seats, scowling at a twirling and lash-fluttering princess, then whispering, in her dad's ear, *"This is stupid,"* expecting to be scolded, or at least hushed, but instead he'd whispered back, "Yes. It is. Let's go!" and, to Inez's incredulity, and later her guilt, he'd taken her hand and they'd left her mom there. Afterward, she'd watched out the window of a Starbucks as her parents argued on the street, her mother's eyes wet with rage, her father limp and shrugging, his fingers dangling, the shoal of pedestrians moving around and past them, paying an arguing couple no heed.

Right now she was on the aisle seat; to leave would be the easiest thing in the world. The fake sex therapist and her two perky sidekicks grated harder with every frame.

She leaned toward Dana again.

"Dude," she whispered, but an actual whisper this time. "I can't watch this."

Dana's response was to set her mouth, a tiny tightening, eyes fixed on the screen. Inez paused, considering her friend's face in profile, wondering where it came from, this grim resolution to be entertained by garbage. She flicked her on the arm and Dana winced away. Inez stood, walked up the smooth artificial incline of the aisle, through the double doors, and leaped up the escalator in a few strides, giant cup of Diet Coke in hand.

As she stepped onto the street the heat greeted her like some giant shaggy dog determined to fell her with the weight of its body. Her phone said 105°, and she took a screenshot, relishing the fake camera-shutter noise as she did so. An outrageous temperature. But the heat was real, at least. You still couldn't air-condition New York City streets. You could build taller towers, shinier and sharper, but the heat would always stay unassailable. It turned the air yellow with the stink of sweltering garbage, it melted candy bars in their wrappers into formless goo, and it made all the heavy, waiting bodies on subway platforms drip with sweat. She loved this. She loved, too, that it blurred the skyline to mirage, enshrined "stay cool" as a valediction between strangers, and, best of all, made these streets less crowded. Everyone who could afford to be was catatonic in air-conditioned spaces, cowed by the extremity of the day. Here was some "feel-good" then: the heat, in its badness. It *felt good* to know the heat was bigger and badder than you. To know there was nothing that you could do about it.

The ice in her cup was water now and she ripped the

lid off, downed the remaining diluted Diet Coke inside, and lobbed it toward a trash can that was lavish with its own overflow. Flies were so drunk and listless around it that they looked like they might faint and fall.

In Tompkins Square Park she found the bench where she'd first smoked weed, and as she lit up now—removing a natty little spliff sequestered between her cigarettes—her eye was caught by an old guy on the other side of the plaza. Other than she, and a homeless man passed out on a bench, he was the only soul here. He was bent over, all in white, engaged in some task. Inez squinted through the heat haze. He looked familiar somehow. It seemed as though he was tipping out cat food tins on the ground, working slowly, ritualistically, making little piles of them as if in accordance with some kind of map or sign. She watched him. No cats came. Maybe they were all dead from the heat. And yet he kept going. Once every tin had been emptied he straightened up slowly, saw her, and waved, blithe as a kid on a beach.

She remembered now: he'd come to the apartment once, she thought, a year ago, maybe, with a cat in a bag. He'd kept saying to her dad, "Don't let the cat out the bag, Willie!" like this was the funniest joke of all time. She'd been shocked then at how old he was, enough to be her grandfather. And here he was now, feeding nonexistent cats. Another singular freak of the park. She loved them all with a kind of dispassionate decisiveness: Barbie the boxer, forever sparring in pink; Junior the ninety-five-year-old sorcerer with steel-colored dreadlocks; the gender-indeterminate young person who dressed as an angel, cheekbones smeared with glitter, enormous wings of different colors to match each outfit.

As Inez inhaled now, a wave of heat made its way through her. It felt like a vertical worming, like the striated waviness of the screen effect in kids' shows that denotes entering or leaving a dream. And then, coming toward her, crossing the park, another familiar person. The snaggletooth, the braid.

She stood up, weirdly pleased.

He was just steps away now, and from his vacant gaze, even before she saw the earphones, she could tell he was in some far-off auditory world.

She raised a hand. "Hey!" she said. "Martin!"

He looked up and faltered. He had to; she was standing right in his path, and they were facing each other, body to body. She found in his eyes nothing she understood. There was a fright in them. A pause. And then a quick blackening, like a blind drawn with a cord. He went on past her, arcing a wide berth, toward that basement apartment and the familiar closet, and did not look back to see her staring, mouth hanging open a little at his receding back and ratty braid.

She sensed her dad's mad friend with his piles of cat food, watching. He gave her another wave, slower this time, and she looked away, furious.

6

Bill turned onto Broadway, thronged and garish. It was a thoroughly stupid place to live, the main artery of the center of this city that thought itself the center of the world. He and Cara had bought the loft when the neighborhood had been a lovely scabrous wasteland of lawlessness and postapocalyptic potential, when being an artist and a scavenger and an addict were all the same thing. With inevitable sadomasochism, his mind formed a phrase: "A quarter of a century ago." He repeated it, slowly, like fingers tightening around a wrist.

A heavy young woman, maybe she was even a teenager, barreled toward him wearing an oversized T-shirt, fluoro-yellow, which shouted, in black letters ten inches tall, **NU YORK MUTHAFUCKEN CITY**. He let out an unintended "ugh," the kind of sound his daughter unleashed every time he attempted to dispense parental wisdom. This girl heard, and shouted, "Fuck you, old dude!"

These days, on Broadway, he'd find himself thinking of the kind of time-phased shot that seemed to feature in a lot of music videos from the nineties: in the center of the frame, intransigent, there's a stationary figure on a crowded sidewalk and then, in dehumanized streaks of color put in motion, everyone else goes past—time contracted, segmented, and stitched. Except the figure in the center was never quite still; you'd notice fractional shivers, a stop-motion effect. Even if you stood still, time would fuck with you, rattle you.

Home, finally, and he heard female laughter sounding from Inez's room. Hers was one side of the loft, his the other, and as he made his way through the space to the kitchen the laughter burst out louder as her door swung open. There in the doorway was a tall black girl, broad shouldered, who saw him, yelped "Shit!" and slammed the door. She'd been wearing nothing but sky-blue underwear.

"Sorry, sorry!" he shouted, slamming one hand over his eyes, raising the other in apology, even though she was already gone. He heard Inez's cackle. A moment later, the door opened again. She and the girl: clothed this time, or at least as clothed as this sort of heat allowed.

"This is Fran," Inez said.

"Hi, Inez's dad!" the girl said, giving him a goofy little wave.

"Hi," he said. "Sorry about that. Didn't know you were . . ."

She grinned at him.

"Coffee?" he said, hearing something helpless in his tone. "Something to eat?"

The girl brightened even more and opened her mouth.

"No," Inez said. "We're going out."

Fran looked over her shoulder, waved at him, and said, "Bye, Inez's dad!"

He caught a shred of their laughter as they were entering the elevator, cut short by its closing doors, and then that was that, they were gone. Dennis bustled over stiffly, sat neatly at Bill's feet, then looked up at him meaningfully.

"Well," Bill said.

Dennis held his gaze, searching, attentive, waiting for Bill to expand on this theme. And again Bill said, "Well! What to make of that, bud?"

Bill watched him slump down and rest his head on his paws in a dog's pose of resignation.

Did Cara know about this new development? Had she known for ages? Would she say, "Oh, Inez's girlfriend, yes, I know," in that infuriatingly brisk way, as though the life of her child was—as with her many responsibilities at the firm—just another matter on which she was utterly up to speed, fully briefed, impeccably informed? And that clipped response would be a tacit reproach to him, a more junior employee, for not being abreast of things, for dropping the ball. Well, fuck Cara. He wasn't going to consult her. He'd talk to Inez without her.

He went and stood in the doorway of Inez's room as though it might yield some kind of explanation of sexual identity. Her mess was spectacular, and he regarded it with a kind of admiration while leaning against the door frame. The clothes and stuff were ankle-deep and everywhere. He couldn't trespass if he tried. His eyes moved around the room and counted five beer bottles. On the bedside table an ashtray had become a miniature Vesuvius. Beside it, a jumbo bag of peanut M&Ms, ripped open, spewing rainbow pebbles. The one bit of space was the bed itself, an island of twisted sheets, with a few scanty and rumpled garments that his eyes jumped over hastily. A lone blue M&M, crushed into the sheets, had left a small smudge.

Later that day, he was lying shirtless on the sofa, remembering that small blue smudge, the sound of her laughter, when the door clicked. This often happened; he'd be thinking of Inez and she'd appear. But then, he thought of his daughter most of the time, so it was a matter of simple probability.

She flopped on the floor with a slap, spread-eagled, and deftly toed off her shoes so the soles of her turned-out feet made two gray flags pointing toward him.

"Well, hi, sweetheart," he said.

She didn't respond, just panted, tongue lolling in a cartoon of exhaustion. Her outspread limbs claimed so much of the floor's space.

"Inez," he said, this time both meaner and kinder.

It must have been a tone he'd never used with her before, because she propped herself up on her elbows and looked at him.

"What?"

He hadn't prepared anything. He became more aware of wearing nothing but the shorts she'd ridiculed, aware of his handfuls of soft flesh above their buckle, of the sweat on his back. She took in the sight.

"I just want to say," he began, and at this corny and uncharacteristic preamble, she scrunched her face into a frown. He persevered. "That . . . you know, I love you and support you whatever. And . . ."

His voice sounded strange, even to himself.

"Uh. Yeah. That's great. Cool," she said, with the what-the-fuck affect he knew too well, and she made as if to get up, to get out of there.

"I mean, with your friend. Your girlfriend."

The word sounded as though it were wearing its own frame. She stared at him, incredulous, and then hooted a laugh.

"Uh," he said, pointedly.

She kept laughing. He waited, sweating, humiliation and irritation rising. Finally:

"Fran isn't my *girlfriend*!" she shrieked. "I mean, we hook up," she said. "But she's not my *girlfriend*."

She enunciated the word with a mocking lurch.

"I'm going to tell her you called her my *girlfriend*."

"No, Inez, you don't have to do that."

She didn't appear to have heard him. "I'm going to nap," she said, making her way to the freezer. "Can we get sushi takeout later?"

He watched her grab a fistful of ice cubes and press them into her sternum.

"Sushi?" she repeated impatiently.

"Yeah," he said. "We can get sushi."

"From the good place this time, not the shitty one."

"Okay."

He couldn't remember which was the good place and which was the shitty place.

She looked at him as one cube escaped through her fingers and slid across the floor, skidding, leaving a shining trail.

"You're not going to forget and fuck off somewhere?"

"No," he said. "I've got a thing, but it's early, I'll be back."

"Like, nine?" she pressed.

"Fine."

He watched Dennis retrieve the ice cube and begin to crunch it with big, happy jerks of his jaw.

△▽△

There was a time when Bill had believed sex was everything. Some days, he had felt that all he had to do in this city as a moderately famous, passably good-looking man was walk into a bar and a woman would approach him. And not just bars: anywhere, almost. A store, a park— the fucking *street*! It was a miracle. Like an extended wet dream of existence: wet and ready mouths, cunts, endlessly. He'd felt sex to be everything in that it seemed to be driving the world. He didn't mean the forces of capitalism, yada yada—not boobs and billboards—but something, well, almost *supernatural*, a kind of wild current moving life forward that only he'd tuned in to. He'd wanted to fuck the world, felt himself to be an ongoing roar, and for a while—a few years, maybe—it had seemed the world was roaring back at him, that the more he wanted, the more it gave him. He knew this sounded like a textbook example of mania. But even now, from this sobering distance of decades, it felt more like a truth than a delusion.

Porn now was a kind of heartache. He'd summon flesh on his screen and the stirrings would be outweighed by a kind of dull pain in his chest cavity, a mourning of his own desire, maybe. He'd look down at his penis and chivy it, slap it gently back and forth like a person trying to rouse a drunk, but it would stiffen only to subside, some half-hibernating animal reluctant to venture back into daylight. He'd click in a joyless trance, in the hope that some body, any body, would wake him up. To feel *some* desire, and to desire more, was worse than feeling no desire at all. As for *being* desired, it still happened, but less and less: the small light that went on in a woman's eyes when she realized who he was, or who he'd been.

Skimming through clips felt indistinguishable from swiping through the various dating apps he'd installed six weeks ago. The same joyless trance. Swipe right. Swipe wrong. He was "seeing" someone, as the euphemism went. He'd swiped right on a divorcée, a tawny-haired marketing manager retraining as a Pilates instructor; didn't buy books but for the annual beach-read bestseller. Had never heard of him. Good. Fine. It had instantly become an arrangement.

She required a specific method to come and she'd stated it with a directness he found extraordinary, issuing instructions as if she were telling the delivery men where to put the washer-dryer. One finger in her asshole, two in her cunt. Not like that. Like this. She took a long time. And then, finally, his fingers cramping, jaw locking, she usually got there. Whereupon he'd kneel back, tugging surreptitiously at his now-flagging dick, waiting until she was sufficiently recovered for fucking her not to feel indecorous. Immediately afterward, she'd retrieve and wriggle back into her underwear and this irritated him, seemed almost rude. She'd make a sort of murmured grunt as she did so, and he understood that this was intended to sound postcoitally soporific, to signal her satisfaction and her need for instant sleep, but to him it sounded like his dismissal. Time for him to retrieve his pants, wincing as the buckle hit the floor, and creep out.

7

A man was towing a grand piano down the street, and the spectacle struck Kate as reason enough to follow. She watched tourists stop, turn, and smile, vague and stupefied, reaching for their cameras as he passed, tugging the enormous thing along doggedly, as if they were both late for an appointment. She kept her distance. She didn't want him to notice her, she just wanted to follow him. People talked about how perfect Manhattan was for walking. *The grid system!* they said. *Its simplicity!* But it was the simplicity that stymied her, the rigid right angles that quashed the art of wandering by demanding of you the exactitude, the confidence and conviction, of knowing when to turn right and when to keep going. Kate did not know where she was going but the man and his piano did. They were heading north up Thompson Street, straight toward the big arch of Washington Square, where the fountain gushed like some permanent pom-pom exalting the feat of the structure beyond it. Right beneath the arch, the man parked and went through a sequence of precise motions that culminated in the snappy assembling of a stool.

Then he gave a quick, dapper little hitch to his trousers, sat, raised his hands, and began to play.

It was Rachmaninov, and she felt a silly pulse of triumph for recognizing that. If there were someone here beside her, someone that she knew, she could turn to them and smile and say "Rachmaninov!" and perhaps they'd be impressed.

She found a seat on the edge of the fountain. The stone was hot against her thighs and the air was filled with water and light, small shimmers of both. Kids and not-kids were paddling and splashing one another. Young guys lounged with their feet in the water, headphones on, eyes closed, blissed out, some with their forearms flung over their faces, protecting them from the sun. She watched a toddler in a frilly hat run toward the man and his piano and then stop, stupefied. His mother caught up with him, arms outstretched.

Cigarettes smelled so much better in sunlight, she thought, as she lit up. Something had lifted in her. Now it was okay—good, even—to be sitting somewhere, purposeless, watching some man play a grand piano in a park. He was younger than she'd first thought—a graduate student, maybe, dressed in ugly cargo shorts and a short-sleeved plaid shirt. Reddish hair gelled upright into a series of little spikes. Just a normal guy who'd chosen to drag the most cumbersome of all instruments through the streets of downtown New York on an intensely hot day.

"I love this guy," said a voice beside her. "He doesn't give a fuck."

Kate turned, and the world lurched for a moment. It was the girl from the bodega. The one who'd looked at her on her very first day in New York and said, "Happy Fourth!"

The bodega girl had once again removed her sunglasses and now was sitting, just a few feet away, one knee hitched up under her chin, squinting in the brightness, scratching her ankle.

"Yeah," Kate said, and she looked back to the pianist as if to confirm his continued state of not giving a fuck. There he was, fingers running up and down the keys, sound tumbling out.

The girl turned to her and smiled and in doing so ratcheted her beauty into something brutal. But then a gust of impatience passed over her face, taking the smile with it, and she said: "So how many, again?"

"What?"

The girl gave her a look.

"How many," she said. "How many do you want?"

The two of them stared at each other.

"You're Kate, right?"

Again, the world lost its composure. The Rachmaninov sounded frenzied now, and louder, and she wished it would stop for a moment, that he'd just shut up for a second so she could get her bearings.

"How do know my name?"

"Becauuuuse," the girl said, very slowly, cautiously, as though Kate were mentally impaired, yet also somehow tilting her tone on that stretched second syllable into something like a warning. "You texted me?"

"No," Kate said bravely. "I didn't."

She sounded feeble, like an accused child who's so abject in their denial that she only convinces everyone, even herself, of her guilt. *Could* she have texted her? Could she be suffering some kind of selective amnesia? Maybe this was linked to the not-being-able-to-speak thing. Maybe these were the early signs of some rare neurological disorder. She wouldn't know for sure until she dropped unconscious one day. And even then she wouldn't know, because she'd be unconscious.

The girl was still staring but now something was lighting up the edges of her eyes and the corners of her lips.

"Your name is Kate?"

"Yes." Kate nodded. This was true.

The girl looked at her for a beat.

"But you didn't message me, yesterday afternoon, about *tickets*?"

That weird emphasis on the word made Kate feel uneasy.

"No . . ."

The girl kept staring, and then burst into laughter. Freeze-frame, screenshot, sell all the toothpaste in the world. And then she snapped her gaze back to Kate, who wilted, while sweat pooled in what she remembered, uselessly, was called her philtrum.

"So you're not here to buy Adderall?" she said. "You're just sitting here, chilling at the fountain, and your name's Kate?"

Kate nodded, and brushed away the sweat.

"Oh my god. That is so fucked up. Ha. I must have freaked you out. So you're a Kate. I'm Inez."

And she put out her hand. It was surprisingly cool. Kate hadn't expected that, she'd expected hot skin and a hard grasp. Instead, her fingers took Kate's with a kind of detachment. Kate thought of picking up a pebble on a beach—the smoothness and self-sufficiency of a stone. How different Inez's hand felt to George's. How strange that an entire person's being—or, at least, the illusion of it—was there in the touch of a hand.

She took in Kate's expression and laughed again. "You looked so freaked out."

So: she was the wrong Kate. And things came back to themselves, steadied, and the piano music now sounded lighter and more spirited, just some natural and pleasant extension of the fountain's sound and the move-ment of water. She remembered to breathe and then, her thoughts catching a spurt of hysteria, she looked at Inez squarely (an audacious act) and said, darkly, "Where's *Kate*, then?"

They held each other's gaze for a beat, just long enough for complicity to kindle there.

Then Inez snorted. "Murdered? Whatever, fuck her—fuck the other Kate."

And Kate laughed a little, too, repeated it in her mind. *Fuck the other Kate.*

"Do you want some Adderall, though?" Inez added, fleetly.

"Adderall?"

"Yeah," she said, with impatience. "I come here to sell Adderall."

"I don't—"

"To students. They think it helps them concentrate."

"I'm not—"

"They take it and then sit at their laptops all night like fucking zombies writing their essays. You want some?"

Kate shook her head. "Sorry."

Inez. Now that she had a name, the girl and her beauty became marginally less terrifying. And now that she herself had been mistaken for a stranger, had displaced someone, she felt somehow powerful. She'd slightly fucked with the world. Emboldened, she offered her a cigarette. As Inez saw the yellow packet, instant recognition electrified her features.

"Dude, that's my brand!" she said, seizing one.

"Really?" Kate said, hearing her own feigned ignorance, the way it weakened her voice.

"Ride or die for that all-natural nicotine," Inez said, and Kate couldn't tell if she was joking. Then, scrutinizing Kate's face as she pulled a lighter from her pocket: "You look familiar."

The sweet hiss the cigarette made as Inez inhaled.

"Maybe you just have one of those faces," she went on. "People always tell me *I* look familiar. I think I just have one of those faces. You know?"

Inez turned to look at Kate and calmly blew smoke out the side of her mouth.

"Do I look familiar?" Inez said. Before Kate could answer she spoke again: "You blush a lot."

It was a plain statement. An observation, not a judgment.

"Like, *a lot*."

"Yes," Kate said, stupidly.

"Why?" Inez said.

"I don't know."

But Inez kept looking at her, waiting for something more.

"I suppose," she tried, "I just get embarrassed. Things embarrass me. I get self-conscious."

Kate couldn't tell whether the answer had satisfied her. Inez didn't say anything, but flexed her lips in a way that suggested she was digesting the words, then looked to the grand piano man.

"He's not embarrassed," Inez said.

"Nope," Kate said.

Beside him, a couple were now dancing, badly. He was twirling her, or trying, but she was going the wrong way and laughing at the failure of it.

"They're not embarrassed," Inez added, jerking her chin at them.

The man was all loose and playful in the hips, overdoing it in an effort to get his woman to loosen up. She looked stiff, reluctant, finding his sashaying laughable, too aware that people were watching and that Rachmaninov wasn't really the sort of music you could salsa to anyway.

"Even though," Kate said, trying out a switchblade of sarcasm, "he should be."

Inez responded to this small unkindness with a loud laugh, a daylight sound, an unbidden thing, and Kate felt a rush.

"He looks like he just took his first salsa class," Kate added. She was smoking too fast, inhaling too hard, making herself dizzy.

"Yeah," Inez said. "And she looks like she's about to dump him."

Kate ground out her stub on the stone beside her and Inez took out her phone and scooted closer, asking Kate for her last name. She began scrolling through Facebook on her screen with both thumbs, exhaling smoke from her nostrils like a beatific dragon. Kate saw her own face materialize on the small rectangular plane in Inez's hands.

"Baby got a haircut," said Inez, looking down at the image: an already-outdated librarian person. Kate felt the blush rise again, and her hand going to the back of her neck.

"Yeah," she said, and then she felt her phone buzz: *Inez da Souza has added you as a friend.*

"Da Souza," said Kate, approvingly.

"My mom's last name. Feminism or whatever."

Inez looked down at Kate's phone, its screen saver. "Is that your boo?"

In the picture George's face was lit with a small and reluctant smile. She'd directed him into this photograph, on a late afternoon a year ago in his Cambridge room, telling him the evening light was too perfect to miss. It *was* perfect—low and long in the sky so that all the planes of his face were rendered with drama. He'd been grumpy about it, in the way that boyfriends are obliged to be when their girlfriends insist on taking their picture, and he'd held that expression of skepticism on her, the half-raised eyebrow, the moue of cynical reluctance, a photo face that was no good to her, until she'd pretended to give up, and then, as his face fell back to normal, had whipped her phone back out and snapped.

"He's a babe," Inez said.

"He's in London," she responded. Inez seemed not to have heard her.

"Do you get fucked up?" she said.

"What?"

"You know, do you like to get fucked up? Because then you wouldn't feel embarrassed."

She said it so straightforwardly.

"I don't really like coke," she said, feebly, making a guess. "I did it once and . . ."

Inez exhaled smoke and regarded her with a sort of indulgent amusement. "Coke's overrated. That's some dumb rich-bitch shit. It burns your soul out. It's just Adderall for dicks with money."

"I'm not really . . ." she said.

"I'm talking about psychedelics," Inez said.

"Oh."

"You should try some," she said, hitting the side of Kate's knee. Then she was on her feet. "I've got to get uptown." She held out a fist for a bump, and Kate, getting beyond her bewilderment, complied.

She watched Inez go, watched her make that scoop of her hair over her shoulder so that her neck was bare to the sun, watched the currents this caused, the involuntary gazes.

The piano man played on. It was Chopin now. Or it sounded like Chopin. The dancing couple had gone and in their place was a group of teenage girls holding up their phones at him and laughing. Kate couldn't tell whether they were mocking him or delighting in him. Perhaps they didn't know either.

She tried out the sound of Inez's name in her head and the syllables made a rhythm that got stuck there, an upswing and a triple fall: Inez da Souza Inez da Souza Inez da Souza. She looked down at the phone still in her palm and composed a text to George.

think I just made friends with a drug dealer

She paused, looking at the words.

she called you a babe, she added.

She considered the message for a moment. And then held a key down so it gobbled the words away backward, deleted.

△▽△

In the apartment she stripped to her underwear and spent a few ungainly moments positioning herself, the laptop, and the beer on the bed next to the blasting air-conditioning unit. Her old, wheezing laptop's iron-hot underside necessitated a trip to the sofa to source the least cat-haired cushion as a buffer between thighs and machine.

Inez had 673 friends on Facebook. Zero mutual friends, naturally. There were 353 pictures of her on her profile, and Kate began to click through them, knowing, at some level, that she would look at every one. Most of them seemed to have been taken at night; they were blurred and flashed with streetlights, club lights, the whiteness of her teeth and the brightness of her eyes. When she reached the end she began again without pausing.

It was her phone that interrupted her again. From George: *are you awake?*

Are you awake? never meant "are you awake?" It meant "please" or "help me."

She told him to call her, and with the small *whoosh* of the message dispatched she began to feel a dread grow within her.

She answered the call, waited a half second into the connection.

"Hi," he said, and his voice was crushed and dark.

"What's up?"

He didn't speak, she didn't speak. The transatlantic void seemed to make something solid out of the space between them—the sound of the phone line, of its emptiness, had a rough texture, a noise like old carpet being churned.

"George?" she said.

"Yeah," he said, strangulated.

"Grem." His nickname. "Are you okay?"

Another long pause, and the "yeah," when it came, was so unconvincing that she found it funny.

"Talk to me," she said.

And then his voice, still high with desperation. "I shouldn't have called. Go back to sleep . . . I'm sorry."

"I'm not asleep!" she said. And then, more gently: "I wasn't asleep. I'm awake." Guilt scratched at her. "It's like, eight here," she persisted. "It's not even dark outside. Just talk to me. What's wrong?"

She stared at an image of Inez on the laptop screen while she waited for his words. In the picture Inez was sitting on the street at night and her bare legs formed a diamond in front of her. It was taken from above, by some friend or lover standing over her, and Inez had thrown her head back, eyes closed, mouth stretched into an exaggerated faux-punk sneer to meet the camera. Her throat was long and bare, an invitation, or a dare. Finally, George's voice came through. "I couldn't sleep."

"What?" she said. She'd heard him, but she'd not heard him. She'd been staring at the sheen from the camera flash.

"George?" She thought she heard him swallow.

"What are we doing?" he said.

"What do you mean?"

"I mean what are we doing? What are you doing there, with me here? Why aren't you here, what are you doing there? When are you coming back? Are you even coming back?"

"George . . ."

"Don't say my name like that."

"Like what?"

"Like you think I'm a stupid child."

"I don't think you're a stupid child."

"What *do* you think of me?"

"I love you," she said, and the phrase seemed to her like a tiny flag stuck in a sandcastle.

He sighed and then, when he spoke again, his voice was different, worn out.

"So you can't tell me when you're coming back."

"I'm coming back," she said. The statement sounded unsure of itself. She meant it, but as she'd said it, the phrase had seemed to falter under its own weight. "I just don't know when. A month, maybe . . . But I'm coming back." She added, for good measure, "I'm sorry."

"I'm sorry I woke you," he said.

"You didn't," she said. "I was awake. I said that. I told you that already."

They both waited. Kate began examining a hangnail on her left thumb; it seized her attention instantly and completely, this tiny scrap of skin, the raw red shred beneath. She clamped it in place with her forefinger and then, pressing hard, positioned it between her teeth and bit it off, wincing. The phone static seemed almost soothing now.

"George," she said, very quietly.

"What."

"I really need to pee."

He even laughed a bit.

"Go," he said.

8

"Humiliation needed," the posting began. Inez appreciated how terse and precise the few lines that followed this
request were.

Here's what she'd realized: that she wasn't doing it
for the money, but for something *about* the money—the
alchemy of the thing. The way that some thought tucked
all tight and private in a fold of a stranger's mind could
get out into the world, and make dollar bills materialize, wadded into ballast for the butt pocket of her jeans.
She felt a middle-finger-raising kind of love for the idea
of them all—God bless them all and fuck them all—the
perverts and the loners and the weirdos.

Today was leaden, too humid, everything sickly with
heat. Central Park was bleak, the lake the same murk as
a paintbrush jar, hot rain and wind blistering whitecaps
across it. Uptown was another world.

His building was stone, formidable, pillars facing the
park. A man in a gold-trimmed peaked cap, shoulders
quivering with gold-tasseled epaulettes, opened the door
to her. Young black men paid to guard the palaces of old

white people. As Inez slid her headphones off they released a desiccated torrent of Wu Tang into the marble lobby and he winced. She yanked the cord out to kill it.

"Mr. Cavallo," she said. "On the ninth floor."

The doorman tilted his head toward the concierge, another costumed man behind a desk, and he stared at her coldly as she approached. On the other side of the lobby, facing his desk, were two armchairs, angled as perfectly as props on a stage. The thought of anyone actually sitting in them, of denting their turgid cushions with an ass, was absurd.

"Mr. Cavallo," she said again. "On the ninth floor."

"Your name?" he said, picking up the phone with a gloved hand, eyes on her like she might grab it from him at any moment.

"What?" she spat, a bit panicked.

"Your na—"

"Maria."

He tightened his look on her as he said into the receiver, "*Maria* here for you, sir."

A pause.

"Ninth floor."

"I know." *Dick.*

The elevator had wood panels, mirrored panels, and a dim, artificial light that made her face painterly, eerie. She watched her reflection scoop wet strands of hair out of her face, pull the whole lot of her hair behind her neck and over one shoulder. As she squeezed, a few drops of rainwater fell through her fingers to the parquet and formed a shameful puddle. She thumbed a hasty text to Dana: the address, his name. Dana responded instantly with seven question marks, then: *ffs*.

When the doors opened they did so with a kitschy microwave *ting*, straight onto the expanse of his apartment. An L-shaped cream leather sofa was slung beneath long, rain-slicked windows overlooking the park, the treetops like the moss in an architect's model.

There were specificities. He was exacting. In his first e-mail, he'd enumerated the insults she should use, all of which referred to his genitals. Lack thereof, basically. They were vile and ridiculous, and she'd memorized all six suggestions. "Dickless piece of shit," and so on. Before she left home she'd said them softly into the mirror as she plucked a few stray eyebrow hairs.

And *apparel*, that was the word he used: she should wear scarlet shoes, high heeled, and a leopard-print fur coat. She saw now that these were provided, laid out, as he said they would be, on the beige armchair in front of her. She shed her fucked-up Chuck Taylors, made a small pile by the door, and found this other woman's clothes. There were traces of some powdery fragrance on them, an auntly sort of scent that made her think of crystal perfume bottles, plump hairbrushes, the word *boudoir*.

There were two stages. First, she was to stride into the bedroom, shoes clacking, to find him. She was a little stiff and unsteady; the shoes were too big, she had to grip them with her toes so her heels didn't slip out. The action of toe-clenching, though, seemed to tighten and focus her fury. He was where he said he'd be, in the exact pose he'd promised, but even so, the sight of him was a shock. He was old, fifties, and in a charcoal suit, crouched and fetal on the floor. Thinned white hair trimmed close to his tanned skull. Expensive aftershave rising from his thick neck—a scent like cognac, cedarwood, leather; the smell of money and cruelty. The shock was that he was barefoot and that the clean, pinkish soles of his feet were as puckered as baby flesh. He looked like a man at prayer. That, or someone racked with despair. Child's pose, they called it in yoga. Not a pose for a man.

When he twisted his head and looked up at her, she felt beltless in the backseat of an accelerating car. But the words were there, *there*, rude and ready, on the tip of her tongue, and she began to spit them, tripping them out, striding. Would the faked fury start to feel real? She hurled the words, thick and fast.

The e-mail had stipulated that when he bowed his head and covered it with his hands it would be her cue to lodge one of her shoes in his ribs and say, "Get up." But when she saw his hands creep to his skull, she forgot that it meant something. It looked so pathetic, this grown man cradling his own head on the floor. She became more savage in her insults. It was only when he let out a little perturbed grunt of a whine, tightening his hands so the knuckles went white, that she remembered to stop, to push her shoe, the hoofy red point of it, into his side, feeling the softness of his suited flesh beneath.

"At this point you will drag me to my laptop, which

you will find on the black chaise longue by the window. You will demand that I buy you high-luxury fashion items. You will continue to insult me. The items you demand I buy you can be anything you wish but they must be expensive. Say 'buy it for me now' and use the insults I already listed. I suggest you have at least three or four items in mind before our allotted time together. Beforehand please provide me with a postal address to have these sent to you so as not to interrupt the flow. Please reply to confirm you have read and understood. Then kindly delete this e-mail."

She hadn't deleted it. She'd read it several times, stumbling on "so as not to interrupt the flow," a phrase she found embarrassing. hithisiscarlos@gmail.com was, she supposed, just like xmariaforeverx—a parallel universe of an in-box for this purpose only. A thing he kept from a wife or girlfriend who would never know about checks written in lush black fountain pen and encased in stiff cream envelopes (the space for her name blank).

"Dear Maria, yes I understand you wish to keep your identity private, you may fill in your name yourself."

"Dear Maria"! Ave Maria. Full of grace.

△▽△

When the packages started materializing at the café, huge black boxes with their contents cocooned in cream tissue paper and black silk ribbons, Inez stared at them as if presented with something exhumed. The truth was she

hadn't accepted that there might possibly be any connection between the performance of him hunched at the
screen, filling a virtual cart with designer clothes, and
this, her real world, the *clickclickwhir* of the espresso machine and the cloudy faces of the regulars.

Heather—who clearly doubted both Inez's devotion
to quality coffee and her commitment to, or even *awareness of*, customer service, but maybe knew that a skinny
girl of impeccable facial symmetry was good for business,
and rested her palms over her eyes with yogic simplicity
when Inez refused to do a single early morning shift—
handed the packages to her with a long look, and Inez
seized them with a slow and unthanking snatch. It was
pretty obvious that their contents were not coffee-shop-
wages kinds of purchases. Heather probably thought she
was a trust-fund kid. Well, she was, sort of, just not the
Chanel jacket kind.

Inez's personal requirement for clothes was that every item of apparel be, in some way, visibly well-worn.
Laddered and ripped low-denier tights, busted old jeans
with holes for knees to jut through, scuffed boots, soft
frayed cotton. Scorned every girl who tried or looked like
she tried or tried to look like she tried. Like all aesthetics
of artlessness, it required time and attention. She applied
herself to thrift-store racks with professional methodol-
ogy and ruthlessness, steadily flicking through hanger after hanger. The kind of T-shirts that made the grade were
those that had turned and turned in so many wash cycles
that the fabric had been worn almost translucent.

The truth was the pristine clothing in the black boxes freaked her out. The first jacket that had arrived had python-skin lapels. Actual skin, from a dead snake, glossy, stiff. She had touched it and shuddered—repelled, excited.

She didn't keep a thing. Straight to eBay, *Unused, with tags, Buy It Now!*, an outfit for someone else to dress up in. As fake and corny as the red stilettoes, the fur seemed more stuffed toy than coat. It was all, she thought, a mess of so many fictions, the way some men made women— out of the red shoes from a cigarette ad, the coat from a music video in the eighties, not caring that these things were already mockeries. If she performed the performance, if she acted it out while laughing to herself, didn't that exempt her, in some way?

9

When Bill came into the kitchen the next morning Inez was there with some boy, hip-hop tinnying out of the phone on the table. Fran, then, must be last week's news.

"We have speakers, you know."

Inez shrugged. She was cross-legged on the counter, smoking, bare limbs sticking out from a baggy T-shirt. She'd sloppily scissored off the sleeves, the crenellations of her ribs visible through the slashed arm holes. Bill's mind caught on the black-and-white image of a band on its front and stalled, dizzy, senile, struggling to place the T-shirt, to believe in it as a thing he'd once bought, owned, worn. Armless, and hanging loose on a body that had not been in the world when the Velvet Underground had played, it was now some other thing entirely.

And this boy, some stranger in his kitchen. They were always skinny musicians. Pale, from Adderalled days spent bent over their laptops in their bedrooms, building beats. Strange creatures, always something girlish about them. Sometimes—rarely, now, if he was honest—they wanted to shake his hand and call him "man," imagining (and anticipating telling their friends later?) that they were "vibing" with him, famous author dude. They'd read his book when they were sixteen. It changed their life, man, *like seriously.* And he hated them for believing their lives had been changed by something so ultimately vapid, a deficient thing, full of flash and short on truth. Hated, even more, the small, craven part of himself that was pleased and flattered and wanted to hear this and would never not want to hear it. Hated, most of all, the oblivious ones who had no clue who he was, or what he'd been. Who just saw *girl's dad.*

Inez raised her chin at him like a cowboy in a saloon, that nod that seemed more like a kick. Had she unconsciously copied it from him? He felt the movement as his own as he watched. Or perhaps it was instead the stuff of DNA. There was a legacy. God.

"Bill, Xander. Xander, Bill."

Rarely "Dad." He hadn't, of course, been "Daddy" for a decade. Probably never would be again. Maybe not until he was frail and fading. Maybe then sentimentality would finally crack her. This boy—shirtless, lank-locked, bug-eyed, skin the color of old milk—set down his coffee, wiped his hand on his jeans, and thrust it out to Bill with such exaggerated swiftness that the rest of his body had to catch up with it in a slapstick careen.

"Hey, man," he said, "really good to meet you," and he nodded as he said it, not so much a gesture of deference as an effort to will this sentiment into mutuality.

"Hi," Bill said, and took the hand briefly.

Shaking hands at nine a.m. while wearing a dressing gown felt absurd—and, oh god, here it came.

"Hey, man, I gotta say, I like, *loved* your book, like seriously."

"Thanks."

"Yeah. Like, *shit*, that bit when he's running across the roofs? And jumping between them? Still with the cigarette in his mouth?" And then he clapped his hands to the sides of his head, widened his eyes in freak-out, and exhaled an awestruck "*Fuuuuuuuuuuck*. You know?"

Bill winced, grimaced a smile, and Inez snorted so loudly that she keeled over to one side. She rolled flat on her back, legs lolling over the counter's edge, her head inches from an earthenware bowl of bananas, kicking her heels dopily, hooting. Few people, he realized, could inhabit their own amusement so *bodily* as his daughter did. It seemed especially pronounced this summer. He'd made no comment, for example, on this new penchant of hers for shoelessness—for running around downtown Manhattan like some kind of overgrown Mowgli. At moments, this barefootedness endeared him, seemed to him one more sign of her inimitable, anarchistic spirit. But mostly he just thought, *God, what tiresome nonsense*. Nonsense that would end in a bloodied foot and a six-hour wait in the ER. Maybe this was the problem with his parenting. No consistency.

She was still convulsing, and the boy took in this spectacle of hilarity with an easy brightness, a stupid question on his lips.

Bill knew she loved it when people made this mistake. And he loved to watch her laugh. So, in a way, it was worth it. He turned to make coffee. Inez, finally sitting up, let out a kind of whinny of recovery.

"That's not in the book!" she said, making a show of wiping her eyes. "Running across the roofs. That's totally not in the book. They just put it in the movie."

"Oh shit, no way!" said the boy cheerily. And then, undaunted, "My bad!"

How was it, Bill thought, that this kid could invest such complaisance in the phrase, could make *bad* sound good? "Don't worry about it," he muttered, like the kid was worried.

Trent James, running. Give the people what they want.

Inez, relatively composed now, lit a fresh cigarette. He wanted to resleeve her, clothe her in timeworn cotton. Yesterday, when she'd suffered to be grabbed into a hug, he'd caught the smell of her skin, and it was the smell of Cara, and his stupid heart leaped at the lie of his wife in his arms. His wife as she'd been back then, years or even decades ago. Before Inez. Not the stranger that she was now, a heavy-bottomed representative of her past self, pillaring the Connecticut community along with her placid financial-services husband. His wife had a husband! Sometimes that made him laugh. She had become the kind of person they used to mock together.

It was too much, as well, that Inez's body should yield the ghost of her mother but no trace of her own three-year-old self. Nobody had warned him about this, that he would grieve for the small bundled body of her, that portable person who shrieked with glee and wrapped monkey limbs around him. The weight of her lost to sleep on his chest, he ached for that. Had he appreciated those years? Of course not. They were terrible, exhausting. But he remained a diligent custodian of select moments, washed and rewashed in memory so many times that they'd become glassy.

"Nice T-shirt," he said to her. "Thought you were allergic to guitars."

He had never known his daughter to listen to anything other than hip-hop.

"Whatever. I like the image," she said.

"Not a fan of sleeves?"

Cigarette still in her mouth, she stretched her arms straight above her head, straining taut her stubble-shaded armpits. Blowing smoke out her nose she said, from the side of her mouth, "Let 'em breathe!" Loudly she sniffed her underarm.

"Yeah, your lungs would agree with that, too. How are the tar deposits?"

"Oh, I'll kill myself before they get too heavy, don't worry."

"Reassuring to hear. Wouldn't want you growing old or anything."

"Dead at twenty-seven."

"Right. That's always been my hope for you, sweetheart."

In the corner, Xander laughed, nervous and staccato, a rising four-note ha-ha-ha-ha, and glanced between the two of them, rubbing one hand up a tattooed forearm. He looked uncomfortable, now, to be shirtless, and hunched his chest inward as though that would conceal his nakedness, his useless nipples ringed with scant black hairs. Bill enjoyed this. Liked that his daughter was showing off to discomfit a boy who found himself unwashed and half-naked and smelling of sex in her father's kitchen.

"Kettle?" she said, and threw a look at its rattling lid.

He hadn't really slept last night, just skidded along in the shallows. He directed the thin arc of steaming water into the Chemex, made lazy spirals in the grounds, and noted, dimly, that he was running low on beans. He bought them at a place around the corner that had once been a grimy adult video store but was now a temple to the sanctioned porn of scrubbed oak counters, reclaimed subway tiles, and six-dollar cortados in diddy glass tumblers. The young husband and wife owners—whose mutual attraction must have had something to do with them having the same shoulder-length hair, a wheaty blond color that became mussed around the edges of their faces as they bent into espresso steam—had looked out at him coolly, gazing with no recognition, when he'd turned a shiny page of a magazine last week.

He stared at the grounds sinking, at the steady drip of coffee through glass: a fully formed bad joke of a memento mori. Inez had finished high school a few weeks ago. When he dared himself to think about her not being here, about her really leaving, he felt the floor beneath him threatening liquefaction. This was the first summer of the rest of her life. He should be pressing college, job, travel, something, but felt no urgency. Cara, he supposed, would be doing that anyway, more on her case than he could ever be. Not that Inez seemed to require plans. She wasn't like other people. She moved in her own world, or made her own world, or, rather, the world seemed to make itself around her. Or maybe this was just lovestruck parental idiocy. He refilled her cup, raised his eyebrows at the boy.

"Ah, no thanks, man, I've gotta run."

"Run," Inez repeated, with an edge, but it was un-clear whether this was an echo or a command.

God, these poor boys. These poor fuckers. Was he go-ing to have to counsel his daughter in womanly chivalry? He engrossed himself with dishes in the sink so as not to have to witness their parting.

"Don't forget your shirt," he heard Inez say flatly.

He pretended not to hear a perfunctory kiss. Then the youth, wavering, said, "Uh, bye, man, thanks for the coffee." Bill didn't look around, just raised one hand stiffly behind him in manly salute, a gesture both sincere and mocking its own sincerity. Man to man. So long, bro, take it easy, buddy, later, dude who just bedded my daughter. Hand in the air, Bill felt tepid dishwater trickle down his wrist, under his dressing-gown sleeve, right into his elbow crook.

When the door of the apartment had clicked, Bill

turned. Inez was gathering up her hair, sweeping it around her shoulder and beginning to braid.

"You didn't want to see him out?" he said.

She winced and he stood where he was, wet dishcloth in one hand.

When Inez was twelve or thirteen, he had begun to hope the hope of most fathers of daughters: that she might be beautiful enough for the world to smooth her way, but not so beautiful that her beauty might become a morally compromising force. Her cheekbones began to sharpen, her limbs to lengthen, and he'd felt an inadmissible dread. Each Friday evening when he opened his door to her, sullen and slouched, he'd appraise her face anxiously as he silently confirmed that, yes, her features had indeed grown even more exquisite since the week before. How to explain to her that the server in the diner brought her cheesecake with "for you!" written in chocolate cursive on the plate because he was in a kind of trance—enchanted by and a little fearful of this otherworldly creature and her eerily perfect face. And there was, of course, the dog incident a year or so ago. She'd come in with a shih tzu under her arm, red leash trailing at her feet, and said: "A guy on the street just gave her to me. Cute, right?"

He'd pictured it all right away: her exclaiming casually on its cuteness, then some googly-eyed owner looking up at her and saying, before he knew what words had left his mouth, "You like her? You want her? Here, you should have her!" All while staring at his daughter's face like a man seeing God.

Would she remember the shih tzu affair when she was thirty? He failed, as he drank his coffee now, to imagine Inez at thirty, just as, at her age, he'd been unable to imagine his own future self. Had been calmly and completely convinced of dying young. Had believed that he would never, ever, be forty-seven years old, divorced, the more-than-beginnings of a belly on him, in a dressing gown, with delirium tremens, sipping gourmet coffee—coffee made from beans shitted by Indonesian civets at $122 a pound. All in the presence of his teenage daughter, unmoved by the departure of last night's lover.

"What?" Inez said now, as he stared at her braiding her hair.

Bill shrugged. "Seemed like a nice guy."

Pathetic.

"You met him for about forty seconds."

"Inez, I'm just being nice."

She made a noise of dismissal and he turned back to the sink.

"Which I know," he said, "you think is terribly bourgeois of me or something."

"Oh, Bill," she sighed, with all the world-weary extravagance of a mom in a sitcom.

"You know," he said, "sometimes I wish you wouldn't call me that."

"It's your name. What do you want me to call you?"

Why argue, really. He ran hot water, squeezed the detergent bottle into a plangent belch, and thought, as it ejaculated bright green soap, *Here I am again, inhabiting the refuge of quotidian hurt that is the kitchen sink*. Every martyr's best-loved activity, doing the dishes.

But then something astonishing, the soft slap of bare feet on linoleum as she hopped down from the counter, and then her arms were around him and squeezing, squeezing so hard that his dishwashing wrists were immobilized. She rested her head against his back for a moment.

"It's nice that you're nice," she said. Then added, heavily, *"Dad."*

She left him staring down at his dangling hands like some newly freed prisoner in a movie.

△▽△

He was teaching this afternoon, last class of the semester, and he wandered the mile or so there on autopilot. Inez had two sources of income, and he allowed himself to acknowledge one of them: the barista job. She'd told him that if he ever walked through the door of the Bushwick café, she'd never speak to him again. He had laughed out loud—as if he would ever go to Bushwick. But then there was the other thing. *At least it's not crack*, went his feeble mental sotto voce. The business of pretending to himself that he didn't know about this other job of hers was so successful that, truly, he didn't really know about it. If Cara found out, and confronted him, he'd be able to say, *"What?* Oh, *Jesus . . ."* and it would be mostly ingenuous. Inez's Adderall clients—he was pretty sure it was Adderall—could easily be the same NYU students whose parents' money Bill occasionally took in exchange for teaching their offspring. He tried not to think of these channels of exchange, because they made him dizzy: the mothers and fathers who paid the institution that paid his salary, and enabled him to support Inez, who made extra money from selling the students drugs—the very same students who, before or after (or during?) taking these drugs, wrote stories that they gave to him. It seemed an endless loop of pointlessness.

His charges were four boys, four girls, all with parents rich or foolish enough to part with tens of thousands for their offspring's year at NYU. Some of the kids sort of worshipped him, he knew that. Even when he railed at them—*especially* when he railed at them—for how little they'd read, for how fucking shackled they were in timidity or incuriousness or laziness. And he sensed, sometimes, that he was the professor they told their friends about. William Marrero, whose book they'd all read or pretended to have read after watching the film. The version that had Trent James on the cover in his *Vanity Fair*–gracing prime, working his Clint Eastwood sex scowl. Bill had been to the premiere, and for every single frame of that movie he'd been acutely aware that he was watching Trent James, movie star, *acting*. The thing had been a kind of existential agony. He'd had lunch with the guy months before. He'd been charming, inscrutable, and Bill had left not knowing whether he'd been fascinated or bored by him and by their forty-nine minutes of Sancerre, seared scallops, and small talk. He hadn't really been able to compute the words the movie star was saying; it was hard to when that chiseled face was in front of you, doing a perfect impression of its hyperfamiliar self. Above Trent's face on the cover of the reissued paperback was some gold-embossed bombast from *The New York Times*, and below it, that craven addendum: "Now a major motion picture."

Nineteen months after that, Trent had been found dead in a bathtub at the Chateau Marmont. An accidental overdose of OxyContin and Xanax. A too-perfect celebrity tragedy. The finely tempered blend of glamour and abjection. And a tragedy made visible by footage of pretty, tearful girls lighting candles and laying flowers and sending sales of the book soaring, day by day. Those pretty girls had made Bill a rich man.

The people at his publishing house had put on somber voices to clothe their delight as they ordered print run after print run. But not Betsy. Foul-mouthed, lipsticked, eighty-something Betsy, who terrified and awed everyone there and whom he believed would never die.

"Honeybun!" she'd said, slapping him with a baton fashioned from a rolled-up *New York Post*. "The next best thing to *you* kicking the bucket! Fabulous!" Aneurism, no warning, a year ago, and she was gone too. His royalties soared on the death of the movie star—sales peaked, then waned, and then died. He took a teaching job.

He was twenty-four years old when it was published, in 1988. When he looked at his author photo, black and white, sexy frown, leather jacket, he felt both embarrassed and secretly proud. He'd been a handsome fucker then, and did twenty-four-year-olds not seem younger now? His MFA students still seemed to bear the soft, not-quite-formed features of children.

A semester had almost passed, with who knows what private heartaches suffered or revelations made, but here they were, on this hot afternoon—themselves, much the same selves he remembered from their first class.

Kwame Okafour, a sober young man with an erect posture and serious gaze that made Bill, a grown man, feel inexplicably chastened. Kwame was Nigerian nobility of some sort, he'd heard, or perhaps that was just something he'd once assumed—a notion that had accreted facticity over time, calcifying into something like truth. Leila Ryan, a funny, faraway bird with the bad breath of the self-starving who wrote quietly fucked-up fairy stories. Meghan Peterson and Hannah Kulz, Girls Who Liked to Bake, as evinced by their scrupulously updated, surprisingly prolix blogs. Both took notes assiduously, in rounded letters neatly squeezed against each other on pretty stationery that they'd given each other (he supposed) as birthday gifts, apologizing for their own presence in the world with cupcakes and pathological kindness. Tim Chan, who never seemed to question *his* place in the world, or really anything at all. He kept the hood of his thin black sweater up at all times, constantly drumming skinny fingers on his knee, and most weeks turned in anhedonic g-chats that Bill suspected of not being fiction. Dana Matthews, Inez's friend, who wrote spare, angry stories about lesbian heartbreak. Occasionally caustic with her classmates, she had a sharp wedge of dyed black bangs slashed over her forehead. His favorite, probably. And Daniel Edelstein, with his sad brown eyes and blond hair and thrift-store sweaters, who, at the end of the first class, had appeared at Bill's shoulder and softly—so softly that Bill had to make him repeat it twice—asked if he might submit his assignments in person rather than by e-mail; he liked, you see, to type them.

"Like, on a typewriter?"

Daniel had nodded.

"Why?" Bill asked, eventually.

Daniel looked flustered.

"It just feels more . . . proper," he'd said, and gone very red in the face, and Bill had felt bad, so he'd cuffed him gently on the arm: "Oh. Sure. You do whatever you need."

His stories were hopeful. Bill had once thought of them as faux naïf. Now he felt there might be nothing faux about them.

Daniel and Dana sat next to each other today, as always, she grateful to have someone to gently bully, he grateful to be gently bullied. He took them in, these faces arranged around this large table.

Adam Boener—who would have had to suffer not only that surname in high school, but also his manifest gayness, yet seemed unscathed, a bear of a young man, who moved through the world slowly and with an air of semiprivate amusement—had baked! Peanut-butter-banana muffins that Meghan-Hannah cooed over appreciatively, eager to generously cede the baking crown.

"Adam, you master baker," Bill said. But Adam just smiled, passed napkins, and gave a small tilt of his head as if to say, "You know me."

But Bill didn't, of course. He didn't really know any of them, despite the fact that he was the person to whom they offered up their (mostly) made-up shit each week. Did he feel any shame that more of his mind went into constructing his own fictions about them than reading their fiction? No, none. There was nothing intentional about the stories he told himself, they were just unbidden daydreams that unfurled along their own lazy trajectories, and they became muddled with what he knew, or thought he knew, to be the truths of their lives. So Kwame maybe was a prince, Leila perhaps did live in an apartment full of cats.

Bill's desire for a cigarette announced itself with the same cartoon clarity as a lightbulb snapped on. Nothing in him now but a desire to smoke. Last class of the semester, what were they going to do, fire him?

"All right all, just ignore me for a moment," he said, positioning a chair under the smoke alarm. He knew that even when he was claiming not to perform, he was performing. That the most performative things were moments like this, affecting unteacherliness, performing not giving a fuck. How much it delighted them; how he fed on that delight.

There was a little rustle of amusement and anticipation

as he tested the chair, stepped on it, and reached up to the ceiling, aware of the sweat stain on his back, the armpit patches of damp. He had to stretch so much that he felt his shirt lift and expose a section of flank, and he felt this slice of nakedness acutely—pale and hairy—as, hands in the air, he fumbled with the alarm as all their gazes rose to him.

For the second time today he found himself experiencing the sensation of blood draining heavily down his upraised right arm: a goodbye salute to the kid who'd just fucked his daughter, and now, well, a goodbye to professionalism, too. He felt their attention tighten. Their rapture was always at its most intense when they sensed he was a little lost. It excited them, and frightened them. When he finally dismounted, triumphant, there was a tepid noise of congratulation and he put one fist in the air in a desultory pantomime of victory.

Once it was over, once he'd shouted after them to read a load of books this summer, *and no fucking vampires*, it was just him alone in the room, with an unexpected feeling of deflation. He flailed in his mind for some poem about this, grasping at words. Who was it, miserable old bastard Larkin? Something about the sadness after something? He lit the packet's final cigarette, crumpled the box in his pocket, and sat. Light came through the windows in two generous rhomboids, dense with sparkles of dust. The room looked beautiful. As he smoked—the final cigarette, this final class—he stared at those dust motes and thought, *This is exactly the kind of moment in which I am meant to think great, stirring, amber-hued thoughts.* Thoughts befitting a writer in his middle age. *Late* middle age. If someone were to appear in the doorway right now they'd see him, illuminated and solitary, and the whole scene would be filmic in its predictable perfection: a teacher lost in reverie in an empty classroom, on the last day of the semester, a summer day swelling beyond the windows.

And then he felt a sort of inward burp of shock. Dana was in the doorway. How long had she been there?

"I think I forgot my book," she said in a near-inaudible voice.

There was no book.

"Are you okay?" he asked.

The question was so stupid, but what else do you say? As she nodded, her face crumpled with the lie of it and she shrank into a chair. For a moment, he thought she was having some kind of seizure, and his mind scrambled. *Epilepsy? Peanut allergy? Am I meant to have one of those insulin pens?* And then, ah, it was only this: emotion. Not a thing you stabbed and stopped with a pen.

He drew out the chair beside her very gently, and sat down very slowly, like she was a wild animal.

"I've just smoked my last cigarette," he said, very quietly, "or I'd offer you one."

She shook her head, a sobbing half laugh escaping.

"But you're probably too sensible to smoke anyway, right."

She shook her head again.

"Well," he said, conciliatory. "We all need vices."

He wanted to put a hand on her back. It felt unhuman to sit there beside her without touching her. But he knew that touching her would technically be a professional breach, if not a personal one, too. Like she wanted some old guy, her friend's dad, rubbing her back.

Then again, she was here, crying. She'd come here to cry. So.

He put his hand awkwardly on the middle of her back, made two small pats, rubbed very lightly. He felt her body recognize this touch, but whether in appreciation or affront he couldn't quite tell.

He removed his hand and said, "You can talk, or not talk, whichever you need. But I'm sorry to see you so upset. And if you do want to talk, you can talk to me."

This was what teachers were meant to say. They were meant to be wise and sane and patient and caring. She was saying something. He couldn't make it out. The words—already shaken through with tears—were lost in the fabric that covered her arms. He leaned forward to listen harder.

"I think I'm, like, in love with this person . . ."

Well, that was just nothing and everything. What do you say to that? He nodded, but then reminded himself she couldn't see him, with her face still buried in her arms.

"Love can be painful . . ." he offered, and winced as soon as the words were out of his mouth, excruciated by his own banality.

"Duh," she said, shakily, tearily, and he laughed and she laughed, still crying. And then the crying got harder. He put a hand on her back again, gently.

"Well," he said. "Maybe you should . . . talk to them?"

She shook her head emphatically, sat up a little, wiped her face, and stared at the desk in front of her. He removed his hand from her back. She cried for a while, quietly, as though it were simply a task.

Then, finally, in a very small voice: "She totally doesn't feel the same way. I know."

"Well," he began. "Maybe they don't . . . but . . . okay. Well, this is the thing." With relief he felt like he was here now, that he'd finally found some small scrap of something that he could give her. "I don't think," he said, "that love is ever a waste."

She wiped her nose on the back of her hand and fiercely avoided eye contact. She addressed the question to his knees: "What do you mean?"

"I mean . . . it's . . ." He was feeling something, almost a surety now, but he spoke quietly to make his conviction less embarrassing. He was looking at her knees; they were talking to each other's knees, which were an easier thing to talk to than eyes. "You know, loving, feeling love, is a . . . is kind of like a human privilege? It's never a waste. I think. I mean, the thing is feeling it, not whether it's reciprocated. You know?"

This was both total bullshit and totally true. For Dana's sake, right now, he'd choose the latter. A pragmatic sincerity. He didn't mean better to have loved and lost than never to have loved at all. He meant better not to lose. Better to love, never have the person, and never lose.

He didn't tell her about the waking fucking hell that

was the deterioration of a marriage, the bottomless black hole that was the love of your life turning into a stranger, the heartbreak, mind-break, body-break, everything-break of a breakup of that kind, that all that agony was far more intense, dense, and crushingly huge an experience than was the love that had preceded it. Unrequited love, that was a walk in the park. Or, rather, a delicious itch to scratch. Who cares if the itch worsens the more you scratch? Keep on scratching, deliciously.

She didn't say anything. She sniffed deeply, drawing up the trembling globule of snot, nodded a bit, and pulled her upper lip long in an effort to stem her nose. It was hard to ignore.

"I'm just going to grab you a tissue, okay?" he said.

She nodded, bringing her sleeve up to shield her nose. The bathroom was a jog down the corridor. He pulled fistfuls of toilet paper from one of the stalls, and then realized he probably had too much in his hands. That it would look as though he were having a joke at her expense. He unwound half, placed it awkwardly on top of the dispenser as though it might be saved, as though someone might actually come in here and elect to use an already-torn-off bit of tissue in a semipublic bathroom.

By the time he'd jogged back the classroom was empty. He gawked at her absence like a dolt; it took him undue time to process the fact of her having gone. On the desk where she'd been sitting was a torn-out page of her notebook. He picked it up and read, in quite small letters in the middle of the page, "thanks, sorry." He realized he'd never seen her handwriting. Why would he have? It was neat and almost old-fashioned-looking—as though it came from a courteous, quieter world. He stood there, thank-you note in one hand, toilet roll in the other, like some kind of travesty of a Hindu god, giving with one, receiving with the other. Paper to receive shit and paper to bear gratitude.

He pocketed the note and kept it, as a way of honoring unrequited, late-adolescent love. Which she'd look back on in twenty years' time, most likely, with humor and affection. It's never love, as soon as you feel the next love. Because isn't that a prerequisite of the condition? That you tell yourself everything that came before wasn't really it.

10

Kate heard George before she saw him: heard the line open up, heard him rustling about a bit as the little slow-circling ouroboros icon communicated its efforts. She could already see her own face, small and pinched and elvish in the bottom right corner of the screen in a little square. Every time she caught her own image, on screen or mirror, there was the half-second arrest of nonrecognition before she remembered: same face, new hair.

The blue snake circled and circled, forever failing to reach its tail, and she stared, understanding it as the embodiment of her dread, the doomy sense that he was going to hate her new look, and her simultaneous craven desperation for him to love it. She felt like a teenager about the whole thing. It was humiliating. And then his face, tired and crumpled, there on her screen. His eyes came into focus.

"Oh my god!" he said. "Wow!"

"Do you like it?"

She couldn't help herself, blurted the question.

His hesitation juggernauted over her.

"Do *you*?" he said.

"Yes! Of course I like it, I did it. But I asked *you*!"

"Well, if you like it, that's all that matters."

This felt like the most sententious thing of all the sententious things he had ever said to her.

"What made you do it?" He corrected himself: "I mean, what made you decide to get it done?"

A tightening throat, an actual *tremor* in her bottom lip. She bit down. Shrugged.

"Oh god, Kate, please don't be all offended! It's just different!" he said. A patient appeal to reasonableness, rationality. "You just look so different. It's a shock."

She nodded as if he'd accidentally communicated more than he meant to. As if his comment had been grimly illuminating, which it had.

"Kate?" he said. Confusion flickered over his features. "Look, I don't understand, what do you want me to say?"

"A shock," she repeated, lightly.

And then his face clouded. He frowned, looked stricken, and his eyes cast about the screen. She was looking, she realized, at a face that couldn't see her or hear her. He was suddenly alone, it was obvious. It was the first time she'd seen him like this, looking at her with such obvious blindness, so unaware of itself. The video must have died at his end.

"George?" she said to him. And then, to the air: "Fucking Skype!"

He stuttered back into movement, opened his mouth to speak, and then his face froze again, blurred into a

Francis Bacon rictus. She clicked away the window, hung up, folded her laptop shut, and pushed it away.

Ten minutes later, having washed her face, drunk a glass and a half of water, and smoked a cigarette on the fire escape, she tried again. There was a meek and miserable detente while she tried to ignore his furtive little glances at the haircut. His eyes kept flicking upward, as if there were tiny airborne creatures orbiting her skull. She asked him about his studies, dutifully. He responded, dutifully. Small pauses grew longer. These pauses had the feeling and flavor of a sea, slate blue, waveless. And she and he were small white boats, visible to each other at intervals, bobbing so slightly, but with all that wide, dark water between them.

"How's Lauren?" he said, and there was a tinge of accusation in the question.

"I'm seeing her," she promised. "She e-mailed me. About doing something later today. I'll e-mail her."

△▽△

Lauren's e-mail to her, subject line "new york new york!!!!!!!!!!!!!" had begun with "hellloooooooo!!!" and the exclamation points had caught in Kate's eyes like grit. She had wondered, with unkindness, whether there might be some correlation between sexual repression and incontinent exclamation point usage. Lauren had suggested tea uptown. Kate had politely parried with art: an opening in Chelsea that the Internet had recommended to her in some spry, sardonic lines of sidebar.

She arrived early by mistake, but as she turned west onto the gallery's block she caught sight of Lauren, a small figure standing with her back against one of the building's walls, tense, bowed into her phone. There was something planted-looking about her, a fixed quality, with a humility to the posture. It was perhaps her flat shoes, her literal groundedness, thrown into relief by the heeled women who thronged past.

Lauren looked up, startled, at this person standing expectantly in front of her.

"Hi," Kate said at her. Nothing. "It's me . . ."

And then the click of recognition in her eyes.

"You cut your hair!" she piped, hastily adding, "It looks great!"

Kate brought her hand, again, to the back of her neck.

"It's great!" Lauren insisted, mustering more emphasis this time. "I just didn't recognize you! It's very short."

"Yeah," Kate said. "Here I am."

"Here we are!" said Lauren. "In New York!"

They stood there, two short British women in their flat shoes. A far-off despair suggested itself to Kate. It would have been better, almost, to have known truly no one here. Either that or to have one real friend, an actual kindred spirit. The foremost image Kate had of Lauren was of her playing croquet with a weedy mathematician boy on the college lawn. And now she was here, doing a Ph.D. at Columbia on Fragonard.

"So!" Lauren inhaled. "What are you doing here?" She had raised her eyebrows to convey compassionate confusion. "Oh, you don't have to tell me!" she added. "I mean, if you don't want to."

"No, no," Kate said. "No, it's not private or anything. I'm just, well, I'm just sort of taking a break here. And trying to, you know, work out what's next."

They looked at each other.

"How's the Ph.D.?" Kate said brightly, before Lauren could ask anything else.

"Good!"

They smiled and nodded, and then Lauren looked behind her, into the bright noise of the building, and said, "It looks quite crowded in there."

Her tone had been so apologetic that Kate found herself replying, "Oh, don't worry!" As if the crowd were Lauren's fault. As if this had been Lauren's idea. As if she were forgiving her for it.

"Shall we try, anyway?" Kate said. "To go have a look, I mean?"

The show was ten enormous square paintings of video stills of pornography. Ultra-close-up shots of brutally lit pink pudenda that looked surprised and shocked by their own baldness, and monstrously, comically large dicks, engorged and veined—superreal flesh, photorealistically rendered on canvases fifteen feet tall. Running across some of them, in lower quadrants, were meticulously wrought striations and wobbles of static—renderings of the visual interference of the pause button on a rewound stretch of overplayed VHS. The room was crackling with flashbulbs and iPhones raised to one another. There was something religious-looking about iPhones raised en masse, Kate thought, little earnest lights of witness. One spectator had sculpted and lacquered her hair into a giant pair of lips, jaunty on the side of her head, and she moved with dancerly cautiousness, all her vivacity channeled into her eyebrows rather than any movement of head or neck.

Lauren, with teeth clamped together, pulled a quick little grimace somewhere between a valiant smile and the physiognomic equivalent of "eek!" But Kate wanted this pack of bodies now, the noise, the champagne breath of loud conversation. She excused herself, told Lauren she was going to find a bathroom, and then headed toward a randomly selected corner as if she knew the way. The crowd was so dense that within a few seconds of movement, a few elbows passed and shoulders dodged, she looked back and couldn't see Lauren at all. At that moment she found herself expelled into a pocket of space in front of a painting. Everyone around her had their backs to it.

No monstrous dicks in this one. It was a zoomed-in shot of a woman's face, in ecstasy, or in a mime of ecstasy, and it filled the canvas. Kate felt herself blush as she took in the enormous open mouth and then the semen. A mouth with pink-sheened lips and very white teeth. A thin strand of hair fell over the right side of her face, over one heavily shadowed and mascaraed eye, shut so that you could see the crevasses in her eye shadow where the papery skin of her eyelid wrinkled.

It occurred to her that this face belonged, or had

belonged, to a real woman. There'd been a camera there, in the moment, capturing it as film or photograph for the painter to paint. A specific moment, faked or actual, a real woman who was now in the world somewhere, buying dog food or shaving her legs, oblivious to Kate staring at a blown-up image, oil-paint rendered, of her face and some man's come.

And then she became aware of a body beside her.

"The artist," a voice said, in a vaguely Germanic accent, "is always the man who talks to no one, and looks the least pleased to be here."

She turned. He was a white guy, shaved head, dour in the eyes, something criminal in the swell of his forehead. His clothes were black. He looked straight ahead.

"Are you," she said, the question querulous and ridiculous, "the artist?"

Finally he turned to her. His eyes remained void. She could not have said what color they were.

"But," he said, in a slow monotone, "I'm *talking* to you."

She was at a loss. And then, like an automaton, or a cold-blooded reptile, his head swiveled back to face the canvas. A tall, groomed woman thrumming with officiousness burst out of the crowd, clamped her hand on the man's upper arm, said, "Guillermo, I *need* you," and, still expressionless, he allowed himself to be led away.

Kate looked back to the canvas, to the outrageous, obscene mouth, and wondered if the moment that had just happened had really happened. There was no one beside her to laugh with. Lauren wouldn't get it. Not that she quite knew what it was she wanted her to get. On the canvas now she saw not the image but the surface of paint, the tiny ridges of dried oils, all the crests and crusts of matter.

And then she felt it on the back of her neck: someone looking at her. It wasn't alarming, this feeling of being watched. It was arresting and exact.

When she was seven, her mother's friend Clara had shown her the trick with a wineglass. How to pinch it between forefinger and thumb on the stem, right beneath the bowl. And then to dip her other forefinger in the liquid and run it around and around the circumference of the lip. The sweetly eerie flute sound that rose from it. This was what she heard now, a wet finger on a wineglass, but as a sensation rather than sound.

She turned. Only one person was facing her. He was tall, a little unkempt, one hand hanging at his side, his fingers loose around the neck of a bottle of beer.

He smiled at her with a small lift of his eyebrows that seemed intended to indicate some kind of question. As though he knew her already, as though they shared some kind of small private history that he was reminding her of, asking, *Remember?* Only she didn't remember, or she didn't think she did. Who was he? There was a light of familiarity in his eyes but she couldn't place it. So she smiled, hazily, feeling the blood rush to her face yet again, raised her eyebrows a little too, to question his question, or to ask what it was.

He didn't flinch, and her face got hotter. She looked away, waited a moment, and then pushed into the crowd again. She wondered if perhaps he'd watched her the entire time, as she'd craned her neck, the slow movements of her head as she'd stared at that enormous painted face.

She couldn't find Lauren. She craved air. And then, over several shoulders, between two moving heads, she glimpsed her, by the exit, hunched once again into her phone.

"Sorry!" Lauren said automatically.

"I couldn't find the bathroom," Kate explained.

She looked a bit green.

"Are you okay?" Kate asked.

"Oh no, I'm fine! I just get these migraines . . . I'm really sorry . . ."

"Don't apologize."

"I'm sorry, it just came on. Sometimes alcohol . . ."

"Do you want to go? Shall we go?"

Lauren faltered.

"I don't want to ruin your night," she said, a vein in her temple bulging, "but I think I just need to go lie down. But you should stay."

Kate helped Lauren into a cab and waved her away—"Feel better!"; "I will!"—and wondered if Lauren was feeling the same flood of relief she was.

She texted her for good measure—*feel better and get home safe! x*—as if officially signing off on her duty. When her phone vibrated in her pocket a moment later she didn't even take it out to look.

Outside, perched on the narrow lip of the building's long windowsill, she lit a cigarette. Being alone felt like a kind of exultation. In this city she'd seen women, of all ages, drinking on their own. Human beings who thought nothing of taking their place at a bar, ordering the damn drink they wanted, paying for it. And if someone approached them, fine, but beside the point. This didn't really seem to happen in London. She was storing up these differences, saving them as evidence, though of what—for what purpose—she didn't know. She was inhaling long and hard when someone sat down beside her.

"Hi," he said, with a small glance.

It was the same guy she'd felt on the back of her neck, staring at her as she stared at the painting. She made as if to answer, was choked by the smoke, but he didn't seem to notice. He kept going.

"I know this is a thing people say," he said, frowning, placing his beer bottle at his feet. "But I saw you in there and I think I know you. Do I know you?"

He was close enough for her to register that he smelled of sandalwood. An unbelievably good smell. She found her breath, shook her head, and said, hoarsely, like this was her first ever cigarette, "I don't know."

He really did look familiar. Her mind reached in all directions, but she found nothing. And then his gaze fell to the cigarette.

"Can I bum one of those?" he said.

She nodded, held out the packet to him.

"It's your last one," he said. "I can't take that."

No conviction in the statement. She noticed the way his fingers lingered, hungrily.

"It's fine," she said. "Take it."

Only when he'd accepted her lighter, lit up, inhaled, and returned it—only after all this did she realize where she knew him from. Not real life, but a book jacket photo. A much younger version.

"William Marrero," she said, somewhere between a question and a statement. It didn't sound satisfactory to her, didn't seem like a complete explanation.

"Bill," he corrected. And then, miserably: "But yeah."

He turned, took in her blush.

"You love the movie."

"I've never seen the movie," she said, truthfully.

"You've read my book," he said.

She nodded.

"Jesus. You must be the only person who's read the book but hasn't seen the movie. So you read the book and . . . You thought it was overrated. Yes?"

The heat had spread out across her chest, up her neck, to her ears.

"Sorry," he said. "I'm being an asshole."

She took a small drag of the cigarette and then said, in a fumbled rush, "I don't want to be the young woman telling the famous author she loved his book."

She dropped the butt beside her, toed it dead, wiped the sweat off her forehead.

"Well!" he said. "Well, I'm insulted now—I'm insulted

that you've mistaken me for the sort of man who'd mistake you for that sort of woman."

She decided to be amused, even though this whole exchange made her teeth ache in her skull. He seemed oblivious to anything excruciating in his words or manner.

"You're clearly," he said, eyes lit up, "not the kind of young woman who goes around telling older men how much she loves their work."

"How do you know that?" she said, and didn't know whether she was indignant or flattered.

He exhaled, looking out across the road as though it contained subtle mysteries. Her gaze followed his, then drifted upward: a giant blue billboard advertising self-storage for as little as $9 a month.

"Your hair," he said simply. "No sycophant would have that haircut."

She didn't tell him the haircut was only days old, not really even hers yet. She just laughed.

He turned to her and said nothing. It was an inquisitive sort of look, but essentially neutral, as though he were making an objective appraisal of what her face might speak to.

"What?" she said quietly.

11

"Base," said the new guy.

Inez looked at him in the mirror: dark shape, wound tight, fists in his lap, there on the edge of the bed. A streetlight outside the shaded window seeped yolky orange into the room.

"Begin with the base," he said, impatient now as he indicated the things spread out in front of her on the dresser. *"Foundation."*

She squeezed out some tan liquid on her fingertips. Not her shade, too pale for her, but whatever.

"Slowly!" he said as she began patting it on. More gently now: *"Really* slowly. Really take your time. Like you *cannot* do it slowly enough."

He was kind of attractive, she thought. A little soft, a little doughy around the middle, but handsome. Dark haired, light skinned, a thin gold chain hanging over his T-shirt, tiny diamond stud in his ear. He looked like he'd worked out a lot a few years ago, but now, sliding into mid- to late thirties, had finally ceded the elliptical to enchiladas. Weights to weed. His left biceps read "Shayla" in large, shaded-in italics.

Inez thought about how desire sometimes made men's voices weird. She looked at her reflection and, in an action borrowed from an ad, placed her fingertips either side of her nose and drew them outward and downward, streaking the biscuit-colored substance into rays. Making the motion languorous, as if she were in some kind of trance.

She could feel his arousal in the room. Could tell without looking. It was a kind of extrasensory boner perception she'd unwittingly honed these last few months. Put *that* in a college application essay.

She made sure not to meet his gaze now, to just keep her eyes on her own face in the mirror and begin this pantomime of transformation. To sit there, in her torn and worn and gently fucked-up clothes, and slowly apply a whole heavy faceful of makeup in the bedroom of a small apartment in Crown Heights. To give him what he'd asked for—specifically, what he'd paid for. It had taken so little time for her to stop being afraid of these encounters. Or, at least, to be less afraid. It was satisfying, in these moments, to add up all the money she was making in these hours. To compare it with her café wages. It made her feel privately hysterical.

"More," he croaked.

She pretended to ignore him as she began blending the foundation with a little dainty wedge of sponge, along her jawline and the sides of her nose, tilting her face this way, that way, primly. This was stupid, but it was also kind of satisfying to watch her skin change, watch it even out into this blank, slightly paler uniformity.

"Blush," he said.

"What?"

He wanted her to blush, like, on *command*?

She thought of the girl in the park, her amazing sudden reddening, the way it kept happening. She, Kate, could probably blush on command.

"Apply blush!"

Oh.

"Base, blush, bronzer, highlighter, eye shadow, eyeliner, mascara, lipstick."

He reeled it off like a child who was too old to be asked to recite the alphabet.

"Right," she said. And then: "How do you know this?"

"Can you not, like . . ." He sighed. "Look, I don't want to sound like a real dick, but can you not talk? It's kind of better if you don't talk."

"Oh. Yeah."

She swirled the brush vigorously in a bright pink compact.

"YouTube," he said.

"Huh?"

She splayed the brush, dense with powder, into the hollow of her cheek, a space made deeper with the jaw drop of her *huh*.

"I know it from YouTube."

"Oh yeah. Those girls who have, like, fifty million subscribers?"

"Yeah, I guess. I don't know, I don't really look at . . ."

"But wait," she said. And now she turned around and looked at him, face to face, ignoring his irritation. "If there are like a billion videos of girls putting on makeup, if it's like, a *thing*, which it is, I mean, not in the way your thing's a thing, but . . . why am I here?"

He rubbed his eyes, and muttered, *"Jesus Christ."* Then, raising his gaze, steeling himself with an inhalation: "Those girls on YouTube aren't in the room. It's a real-person thing. A real person in the room."

Now he stared intently at the ground between his feet and made a slicing motion, fingers angled downward, as he repeated: *"In. The. Room."*

"Right."

One of her cheeks was a bright, artificial pink. His gaze drifted to it, and then back to her eyes. Something changed in his face.

"How old are you?"

"Twenty-five," she said.

"No way," he said.

She could tell, just from the tone of his voice, that libido had left the room.

He was shaking his head, rubbing his skull. "Nuh-uh. Shit, man. Tell me you're not fourteen or something."

"Oh my god, I just told you I'm twenty-five."

"Nah, you're shitting me." With a kind of desperation he flung a hand toward her face and said: "You don't even know how to put makeup on! You can't even contour! I've never met a woman who doesn't know how to put on makeup! Girls I know see that mess, they'd pass out, I swear. Just tell me I'm not . . . I'm not messing around with a minor. Are you a model? Are you one of those teenage models or something? I swear, if you're . . ."

"Ew. I'm not a *minor*. And fuck modeling."

"You at college?"

"What are you, like, my guidance counselor?"

"Fifteen?"

"No!"

Indignant.

"Seventeen?"

"No."

Less indignant now.

"Nineteen," he said, looking at her.

She blinked. Turned back to the mirror.

"Shit. For real? That's how old my niece is, man. My sister's kid."

"I'm not your niece. I'm not anybody's niece."

He looked at her strangely. "So what's your whole deal, then?"

"What do you mean?"

"You do a lot of"—he made a surprisingly elegant twirl of his left hand—"a lot of this kind of thing?"

A gentlemanly evasion. She shrugged. "What's *your* deal?"

"*My* deal?"

He puffed himself up a bit, indignation dressed as

amusement. "What you see is what you get, man. I was straight with you, right? I'm being straight with you: I just wanna watch women put on their makeup. No lie, that just does it for me."

She considered this, considered him.

"What?" he said, with a half-cracked smile. "You scoping me out?"

"Well, I'm here," she said.

"I swear . . ." he said, and shook his head gently, as if he were threatening something, but didn't know what.

"A real person. Here in your room."

He puffed up again, pulled his tummy in.

"Do you have a girlfriend?"

"Nah." Had he noticed her glance at his arm?

"My kid's mama," he said, angling his tattoo toward her. "We still friends, we're cool."

"Cool."

She picked up the lipstick, brought it to her mouth, and eyed him sidelong in the mirror. Stupid, really, how easy it was. She swept it over her bottom lip in slow motion.

"Yeah," he said.

She smacked her lips gently and pouted. Now she popped open a little pot of eye shadow, blue and iridescent, like it was 1988. Then the mascara. Its wand came out with a soft pop, and as it did so she heard the sound of his belt buckle, then his zipper. As long as he didn't want her to—. As long as he didn't expect—.

She swallowed a small lump of dread and began

swiping on the blackness, top lashes, bottom lashes, then the other eye, from a pink tube that smelled like fake strawberries.

His breathing behind her quickened.

She glanced and wished she hadn't: the pants around his knees already, the fast and frightening movements. He was bowed over but in that second he raised his head and saw her stare.

"Fuck," he hissed. "Don't." He cowered away from her while his right arm, *Shayla*, was still pumping, unrelenting.

She whipped back to the reflection of her overdone, sex-doll face in all its lurid, porny shades. She sat very still. It seemed stupid that a person would plainly state their want, shamelessly, show her into his home, peel off a stack of twenty-dollar bills for her, and then, when it came to the moment he'd wanted and waited for, be embarrassed. A quick, ugly groan came from behind her and made her shut her eyes.

When she opened them, the grotesquery of her reflection was still there. The makeup seemed to have immobilized her features, immobilized who she was. The sound of tissues; the fumble of zipper and buckle. Then a full silence. She held it and held it. And then she broke it.

"Do you have baby wipes?" she asked.

"Huh?" he said.

She lifted a pointed finger to the side of her face like a gun. "Baby wipes. To wipe this shit off."

12

It seemed to Bill that the bartenders all looked Amish. They were lean young men in collarless shirts, wearing suspenders, and all of them had facial hair— bijou mustaches, or bushy whiskers, or ludicrous slabs of beard. They worked the space behind the bar like a stage, joshing and flaunting their homosocial horseplay—snapping damp washcloths at each other's thighs, giving fist bumps.

He was here because he'd overheard some childless adman at that Fourth of July party drop the name and, thinking he should take Kate somewhere fashionable, had thought, *Ah yes, that will do.* Everyone here, it seemed, was twenty-two and exquisitely androgynous: men with long hair and delicate cheekbones and silver rings on their fingers, women with pixie crops and undercuts and wide, handsome jaws, sitting with their knees spread, elbows out.

Perhaps, he thought now, with equal hope and despair, she might not come. He'd wait until eight thirty, take his phone out, and scroll through Twitter—a place where he lurked anonymously behind a blue egg and a handle of random numbers—and then he'd go.

They should have just met in a dive bar. He should have taken her to old Brooklyn—Maxine's, just a block away, with sports TV on too loud and gum-cracking, chronically underwhelmed Donna grimly pouring dollar shots. And Marty, the fixture at the end of the bar, a man who, with geological slowness, had been shrinking inside the stiff carapace of his leather jacket for decades. Old Fort Greene when Myrtle Avenue was still Murder Avenue. Not artisanal Brooklyn 2.0, with its oysters and heirloom-everything menu and fifteen-dollar old-fashioneds.

When he'd watched her fingering the back of her neck in front of that terrible painting he'd wondered how many women in this city had the same haircut. A thousand? Ten thousand? It occurred to him that there was an exact figure, an exact number that existed which, barring some extraordinary folly of a statistical project, no one would ever know. He'd been struck by her fingers, their slenderness and their rounded points, like paw pads. He'd thought about what it would feel like to test each tiny cushion of them between his teeth, with tender bites, *one two three four five*.

She looked like she belonged here. The thought struck him as she walked through the door and he watched her cast her eyes about anxiously, looking for him. She was one of these young people, with her cropped white hair and her mannish clothes. He'd written her off; he'd thought she wouldn't come; and now he didn't know whether it was dread or delight he was feeling. Then her eyes found him, found him already staring, and her face leaped with what he thought was relief, but could it have been chagrin?

"I'm thinking," he said, while she maneuvered herself into the booth, her face red, sweat glistening on her temples, her knees banging his, her mouth apologizing for it, "that I should not have brought you here. That I should be showing you old Brooklyn."

"Oh," she said. She pushed damp hair from her forehead, awkwardly. Then: "Do you . . . want to leave?"

"No!" he said. "No. I'm fine. I mean, do *you* want to go somewhere else? I mean, I'm fine here, if you're fine."

She opened her mouth.

"I'm fine," he said. "We can do pretend-old Brooklyn." He waved a hand at the sepia prints. "Instead of old-old Brooklyn."

"What's old-old Brooklyn?"

"Oh, you know."

She didn't, it seemed.

"Dive bars. Grimy, stinking dive bars with ossified alcoholics who remember the good old crack epidemic days. Grubby old unsexy Brooklyn with people shooting up and shooting each other."

"Unsexy Brooklyn is sexy too, though," she said.

She had arrived a little drunk, perhaps?

"Because you fetishize that, too, right?" she added.

He laughed. "I do?"

"Do you?"

For a moment there rose in him the hope that perhaps this wasn't completely doomed.

A waiter set down menus.

"So," Bill said.

"Hi," she said, and turned a furious red.

"The rarebit's really good, apparently. But it's a bit hot for rarebit."

"Oh, I'm vegetarian, actually."

He chuckled but then looked up at her face. Her slightly startled face.

"Rarebit. Not rabbit. A sort of grilled cheese thing."

"Oh," she said.

"Dish of your countrymen," he added.

What a dick-move of evolution, to render faces more conspicuous at the moment they most longed to be effaced. But as her face blasted heat, he too seemed to warm up. The booth was so small; there was less than an inch between their knees under the table. He caught himself thinking of how pale her skin was, what her nipples might look like, whether they'd rush with color like her face. She seemed, already, to have lost control in some way, and this excited him. This was just so different from how it normally was: women who defined themselves as *having their shit together.* Their blowouts and analysts and green juices and Fitbits.

She ordered a beer, he a glass of sauvignon blanc, and the waiter returned to set the wine in front of her, the beer in front of Bill. They both stared for a moment at these misdirected drinks. Then, unavoidably, at each other.

"Your beer, sir," Bill said, pushing the glass toward her.

She gave a small, tense laugh and pushed the wine toward him. As she took a first mouthful he asked, "Why are you in New York, then?"

She looked stricken for a moment, as if the question had been an affront.

"My aunt," she began. "Well, she's not my actual aunt. She's my mother's best friend. She was. She lives here. Only, she just got divorced and is off on this six-month around-the-world adventure."

"Eat, pray, love?"

"More drink, rant, shag, I think, but yeah. She's in Thailand right now."

"Shag," he repeated.

"That's how English people say 'fuck,'" she said.

"Yeah," he said, exasperated.

"Oh. Anyway. So. I'm house-sitting. Cat-sitting. Because she approves of young women having adventures, you know? So I've left my Ph.D. in England, with my boyfriend."

There was self-consciousness, he saw, in the word.

"Permanently?"

"Which?"

"Either."

"I don't know."

He nodded. "Ph.D.s are made to be abandoned," he said.

"And boyfriends?" she said quickly. Another large mouthful of beer.

"A harder call. Men your age are the worst, though."

"What?" she said, with another nervous laugh, perhaps to cover the shock.

"Young men. The worst. They are. I know. I was one."

"How do you know he's my age?" She said this and then instantly waved it away, reneging on the parry. "No. He is my age."

"I'm sure he's an exception," Bill said. "I, however, was *an abysm of a human*."

"In what way?"

"The usual ways," he said. "Knowing nothing, believing I knew everything. Believing the world owed me my own greatness. When I was eighteen I read everything Faulkner ever wrote and thought that made me smart. Smarter than everyone else. And then a few years later I wrote a dumb novel and thought that made me a genius."

He stared at his hand on the wineglass, then at the bar. Two guys, dishcloths flung over their shoulders, were leaning against each other as one showed the other something on his phone. They both laughed. One doubled over with it, as if in pure pain, like he'd taken a golf ball to the groin.

"No one under forty should write a novel," he said to the table. "Don't write a novel."

She flinched.

"Shit. Are you writing a novel? Jesus. Fuck, I'm sorry."

"No!" she said. "No. I'm not writing a novel."

"That makes two of us."

"I'm not writing a novel and I'm not writing my Ph.D. I don't know what the fuck I'm doing. I've sort of lost the ability to think or write," she added.

"*Tell* me about it," he said.

"No, what I mean is I can't even write a sentence. I don't mean a good one, I just mean any one."

"Well," he said. "We could just sit here sentenceless if you like?"

She made a graceless nod and shrug of assent. He watched her take more beer, letting it swell into her cheeks before she swallowed, as though she were willing herself to look ugly, or coarse. And there they were, back in strained silence. The food arrived, two plates landing in the middle of their wordlessness. He felt the waiter privately take it in, this thick awkwardness between them.

△▽△

At the subway he kissed her on the cheek and then watched her dart down the steps into the dark. He paused for a moment and then, as he began walking the few blocks to Maxine's, these four words of platitude came to his mind: "Well, that's that, then." With them came a seeping, comfortable misery. He yielded to it. It could have been worse, he thought. He could have knocked over a ketchup bottle with his elbow, setting in motion a whole cataclysmic Rube Goldberg machine of an accident across their tabletop, ending in some outrageous ejaculation of condiment all over her. But that would have been better, really; so tangibly disastrous that they would have been forced to bond over it forever.

Inside the bar, all the TVs were screaming the artificial green of Astroturf pitches and the modulated thrum of sportscaster cadences. The place was empty except for Donna, who'd served herself a saucer of maraschino cherries and was eating them, one by one, jabbing them with a toothpick. He took a stool right in front of her and she ignored him.

"Five a day, eh?" he said, eyeing the dish. The cherries looked like bloody eyeballs. Or glands.

She looked up, chewing, and finally swallowed.

"Vodka on the rocks," she said, barely a question.

He nodded and said, "And a Maker's for you."

The skin over her skull seemed to twitch in assent. It was as close as she ever came to thanks. As she set the drink down he looked around him, at the emptiness.

"Where's Marty?"

She didn't look at him as she replied, just calmly speared the last cherry. "Dead," she said. "Heart attack. Last week."

"What?" he said. "Fuck."

There seemed to be nothing more to say.

13

Kate woke up to indifferent darkness, the shock of its quiet after the noise of her dreams, and her phone told her it was five a.m. She was on the sofa, curled up and curdled with dejection, in the same position she'd slung herself into seconds after walking through the door. Her mouth was like cotton wool. She still had her shoes on.

When she woke up the second time she was in bed and undressed, morning light outside, and the flavor of everything was different. She reached for her phone and googled him, scrolled straight to "Personal Life" on the Wikipedia page. Just two arid lines: *Marrero was married to {{citation needed}}. They have one daughter.*

He hadn't mentioned a daughter. She thumbed "Marrero + writer + daughter" into her browser's search bar, watching its innocent cursor blinking, and awaited a little girl's face. What came up was mostly rubbish, search-term flotsam. A local news story from seven years ago about a Florida woman, last name Marrero, and her daughter, caught shoplifting. A tweet by some other Marrero that told her nothing. Then an interview, finally, that also told her nothing. She trawled it impatiently, finding the words, *his* words, "My daughter needs a college fund!" She closed out and put her phone down at a decisive distance from her body.

The attraction, she decided, wasn't in having dinner with him, it was in having *had* dinner with him. As with losing her virginity, all her focus had been on the situation's pluperfect. The act had been awkward, painful, odd, and anticlimactic, but who cared, because afterward came the plain, dull thrill of having done it, of it having been done. And now there was this new fact, that she was a person who had had dinner with William Marrero. It had happened. She didn't want to consider the event itself. She tried to forget, for example, the two beers she'd drunk standing up in the kitchen before she left the apartment, a heavy blanket thrown over the cage of nerves, consumed with the same practical patience with which you'd swallow a couple of aspirin. They had made her stupider. *Rarebit.*

Every time she'd said the words *my boyfriend* last night she'd had a distinct sensation of lying. It was as though she'd made him up. It was a confused guilt—guilt toward George, for her failure to grasp his reality; guilt toward this man, for lying to him about her boyfriend, about whom she wasn't actually lying. She wondered if he, Bill, had felt it too, this sense of falsification. Perhaps he'd suspected her of fabricating a boyfriend as a kind of guard against him. She replayed moments. There was the one when she'd said she had lost the ability to write, and he'd said "Tell me about it"—a rote expression of weariness. It was a thing people said when they meant *I, too, have experienced this thing, so there is no need to explain, because I, too, feel your despond and exhaustion, right now, talking to you.* But from Bill's mouth Kate had heard how the phrase was stale and exhausted, and how he knew this, too, and so used it hopelessly. Every second of silence had been like wet cement, hardening. She'd had a desire for something ugly, an ugly thing that she could pick up while he watched—something that would ooze out between her fingers and stink. When he'd kissed her on the cheek at the subway his smell of sandalwood had stopped her for a moment with something like terror and she'd sprinted down the steps with unnatural speed. A ridiculous exit.

Today, right now, it being done, it having happened, she just wanted to get a look at him. Wanted to be outside, on the streets, where encounters happened.

She looked for him and saw him everywhere. She walked past him coming up the steps of the subway. She saw him reading a newspaper on the train that pulled away as she swiped through the gates. At Delancey and Essex it was the back of his head making its way down the stairs. She even did a double take on a bus poster. It was a famous comedian who looked nothing like him, but the image of the man's face, in its confidence, had winked at her with resemblance. She'd seen it for a second, an uncanny flash as the fixed grinning face glided away on the bus.

As she walked, she imagined him coming toward her,

saw the way she'd smile but not say anything for a moment, as though occurrences like this had ceased to astonish her, as though the world were always delivering gifts of serendipity just like this. And they'd stop in the middle of the sidewalk and, still saying nothing, laugh at the absurdity of this, because what do you do with a coincidence? It's a kind of joke of meaningfulness, meaning nothing.

In one crowded café a guy started sketching her portrait, looking up at her with fake-humble smiles. She left and began walking fast to Union Square, a node into which so many of the city's currents ran and fused. There was a huge cosmetics store at its northern edge, and some part of her actually believed she might find a middle-aged and unkempt man idling through the aisles of eighty-dollar face creams. It wasn't impossible.

She walked in, crossing from hot to cool, into glossy black surfaces and arrays of color. Young and smiling women welcomed her and offered boxy little shopping baskets, which she declined. The air seemed full of vaporized alcohol, and she breathed it in as Top 40 pop pumped through the sound system, boys' voices straining to tell you that you were so beautiful just the way you were. There was something antiseptic about the quality of the sound, as if it had been evaporated, powdered, reconstituted. She found herself walking toward one big plane of cosmetics, felt herself reaching for a lipstick, and her reach was the hand of a small girl drawn to a bright sweet treat.

She handled the object, a matte-black capsule. Decapped it. The coy way the thing rose as you slid its base was so smoothly supreme in its own confidence, saturated with its own fat color. On the minuscule silver sticker covering the lipstick's base, she read HOT LUSTER. Whose job was it to make up names for lipstick shades? How did this person see herself and how had she risen to such a position of authority? Did she take long walks around the city, waiting for the name to suddenly blaze at her with its own conviction, so dazzling that she'd stop in a current of yellow cabs, eyes shining, rapt, deaf to the honking of horns as she heard her own voice-over say, *"And then it came to me"*?

Kate kept Hot Luster in her palm as she picked up another lipstick, then another, and turned each one over to read the name. The campy idiom of 1980s soap opera rendezvous: Meet Me at Midnight; Silk Sheets; After Hours; Mistress. A teenage girl's imagined universe of sexual rebellion: No Panties; Hot Mess; Morning After; Back of the Cab; Sext; Booty Call. And the forced frisson of shameful things: Bruise; Binge; Strike; Bitch.

Each stand was flanked with lit side mirrors, and she leaned in to face her own face in one of these and brought Hot Luster to her mouth, slicking it on slowly. The color was as deliberate as a crayon and the application obvious as pantomime. She gummed a blotting tissue between her lips to print a kiss then stared at herself, a newly emboldened, hot lustered face. The thing in her hand was $29.95, an outrageous amount for a lipstick, for a thing the size of her thumb. She was queasy as she paid for it, lightheaded as she left the store, and blinded as she stepped into the glare of a midday Union Square.

The farmers' market was in full effect: heaps of glowing apples, stands of wildflowers, hand-labeled pots of honey. A black woman in a long white dress walked past her, smooth as a sailboat, carrying an enormous armful of lavender, cradling it tenderly. Kate's eyes went with her, to the crossed straps across her back and then, sidelong, to shop windows and their reflections, wanting to see herself, to catch the red lipstick, but not wanting to be seen wanting to see.

A stocky man, glowering, muttered "gorgeous" as he stalked past, and it sounded like a threat. She stiffened, let him see her wince, but some small pleased part of her throbbed the same color as that thirty-dollar lipstick.

Her mother's friend Clara always wore crimson lipstick, the same shade as her nails. It was reassuring, the constancy of it. Every time she came around to drink wine with Sally in the kitchen, every time Kate saw her, there were her red lips, her red nails, coloring her in, defining her. Once, Kate had joined them at the cramped kitchen table for a glass of chardonnay, recoiling at the chirpy noises of novelty the two of them made at the idea of an "all girls together." She'd stared at the lipstick mark on the wineglass, its fading iterations, while her mother and Clara became looser and louder. As the color of the woman's lips faded, Kate realized she was yearning for the moment when Clara would draw her lipstick out of her purse and reapply it. When it happened, she did so without a mirror, still talking, and a deep satisfaction flooded Kate as the color once again saturated Clara's mouth. She'd practice that, Kate thought, reapplying lipstick without a mirror.

When her phone gave an indecent shudder in her pocket, she started with something like guilt. A Facebook message from Inez, barely legible in the midday sun, artless with typos: *were having drinks tonight, friends roof in bushwick you should come if you want. ill be there from 6. lmk and ill send yuo address. no other kates lol.*

The hot air seemed to be beaten into thickness by the bucket drummers at the southern end of the square, the bells and chants of the Hare Krishnas, and the contrapuntal chorus of a dozen different barks from the dog run. She was sweating. A channel of it on her upper lip threatened to make a hot mess of her Hot Luster.

△▽△

In the apartment, she stood under a cold shower for ten minutes, then dressed, still wet, in underwear. The water had ruined her mascara but the lipstick remained. She was absorbed in making faces of desperation at herself when her phone made its little *chirrup* on the bed.

This time, a text from George: *facetime?*

Thirty dollars seemed to buy you indelibility. Hot Luster didn't let go. In the bathroom, scouring her red lips with disintegrating tissue, some of the stain remained. She licked around the edges of her lips and rubbed harder with her finger. When George's face appeared on her screen he looked like a stranger, and her own face, in its tiny corresponding window, seemed to her incorrectly configured. She was, somehow, askew.

"Grem," she said, giving a smile to him, but the name didn't work this time. She felt like a tourist mispronouncing a word.

"Hi," he said, with a shy, confused frown. "Are you wearing lipstick?"

"No!" she said, bringing her hand to her mouth. "Why? Does it look like I am?"

"A bit."

"Weird," she said. "What time is it there?"

She knew what time it was.

"Nine," he said. And added: "Plus five hours."

"Plus five, I know."

"You asked," he said.

"I know. I just. I was just asking."

His expression hadn't changed.

"I made a friend in the park," she said.

It sounded infantile. He cocked an eyebrow. There was a time when she had found this *Brideshead*-ish expression sweet.

"She mistook me for someone else but we got talking," Kate said. "And she invited me to have some drinks on a roof. Like, now."

"Wait, who is this person?"

Kate didn't want to say her name. George had a habit, lately, of making her feel policed.

"Just this girl I met in the park. She's cool."

"Oh well, as long as she's *cool*."

She ignored this. "What are *you* doing tonight?" she said.

"Annabelle's having a birthday thing at a bar in Clapham."

"Annabelle?" she said, trying to find a person for the name, and struggling to affix any sort of reality to the word *Clapham*. It seemed impossible that this part of London still existed when she was here, with yellow cabs honking on the streets outside, and the Chrysler Building pointing up at a sky bigger than any she'd ever seen before.

"Yeah," he said. "She was at that dinner party."

He didn't say "the one where you spilled the red wine all over that white cloth" or "the one where you suggested some women might like to be fucked like animals," but he couldn't keep a little darkness out of the words.

14

The night was starting up across all these rooftops, sound-checks stuttering, barbecues firing, forties being cracked open, a summertime phenomenon of this second stratum of the city. Inez started her second beer and eyed Dana's. They were sitting in the shade of the roof's water tower, and from here Manhattan was a cutout version of itself, both fake and familiar, unreal in the shimmering heat. Beside the tower, as if carried and then dumped there by a mythic flood, was a large single-story house with neat square windows on all sides, the sort of house you'd draw in kindergarten. And below that, one floor of studios, then six stories of dereliction. The elevator couldn't be summoned from the street, only sent from above. Probably a good thing, Inez thought, what with the sketchy legality of the place—a Bushwick dorm, basically, for young adults.

Inez knew this: that a teenage girl saying "nobody understands me" is a cliché. But she also knew this: that no one understood. Not her dopey, drunk dad whose main activity right now seemed to be buying and sampling imported coffee crapped out by wild cats. Certainly not the tyrant her mother had become, hard and humorless beside the personality void that was the banker nonentity she had, unbelievably, *married*. Not Dana, either, not really. Her friend since twelve years old. And yet here they were, she and she, cold Coronas between them.

Lately, Dana seemed to veer between two modes. One moment she'd be in soft-eyed, belly-up submissiveness, buttery in her passivity, a laughing audience to Inez's outrageousness. And then the next she was all stiff and weird and resentful, strange edges sprung from nowhere.

Inez was bored of all of them, though, not just Dana. Kids from small towns where their weirdness seemed singular, here in New York to find their kin. They were all a little older than Inez and yet afforded her a certain reverence because she'd grown up here. She was aware of this, enjoyed it, and also found it embarrassing. Embarrassing for their sake.

"To the Five Boroughs," her friend Tom had exhaled, awestruck and somber, when it somehow came up that her first show had been the Beastie Boys at Madison Square Garden when she was eleven. It was a mission kept secret from her other parent, which of course had enhanced the whole thing hugely. *Don't tell your mom*: the sweetest words an eleven-year-old could hear.

She looked at Dana, pinched her sullen cheek too hard, and said, "Dude: who put gluten in *your* muffin?" And Dana actually struck Inez's hand away as she said, "I'm fucking celiac, so don't joke."

Inez treated Dana's gluten intolerance with the same amount of . . . well, tolerance she brought to the idea that anybody might pay to be taught *how to make shit up*, let alone by her father.

"Your dad's cool," Dana muttered.

"What does he *teach* you? What does he actually do?"

Her tone was derisive but she did truly want to know. It was impossible to imagine him standing in front of a class, holding forth, professorial.

"He's a good teacher," Dana said. "We all liked him. We'll all miss him." And then, bitterly: "But how's *your* education going, Inez? You learning much from your Craigslist perverts?"

For a moment Inez wondered whether to tell her about Carlos, the way his eyes went black. The less she told Dana, the better, she decided. That was how not to be fucked with. Trust yourself, no one else.

"I don't know why you do it," Dana said. And then, almost to herself, in a kind of incredulous whisper: *"It's so stupid."*

The arrival of a text. It made Inez grin. A stranger would shake them up a bit.

"Where are you going?" Dana said.

"New friend, my friend."

Downstairs, she flung the door open and raised her hand to Kate, who looked at it, bewildered.

"Dude, I'm high-fiving you! High-five me!"

If you put your gaze on the elbow of the person you were high-fiving, your palms met perfectly. Like how to open a beer bottle with your teeth, or where to get a fake ID, these were just things you came to know. Kate, she suspected, had different areas of expertise.

A dilapidated elevator shaft, concrete walls, inscrutable pieces of timber, three bikes in a drunk, half-tangled stack. She felt Kate taking it all in.

"I know, so janky, right?" Inez said. "This building is like basically falling apart."

There was some pride in it—a boast, almost. She yanked the door of the elevator cage shut and said, "I totally didn't think you'd come, by the way."

"Here I am," Kate said. She added, hastily, "Thanks for inviting me."

When they stepped out onto the roof Inez heard a soft, marveling sound come from Kate as the view hit her. Brooklyn was wide open beneath them, Manhattan a visible fairy tale. And tonight the city was going for it, putting on a show like this was its last, the sky outdoing itself in flamingo pinks, all the tiny squares of steel and glass lit into glittering tiles, as if the whole skyline were sequined and shimmying. Evenings like this made Inez want to open her mouth wide and eat the world. She looked at Kate's expression, so daffily rapt.

"You know it's all the pollution and shit that makes the sunsets do that, right?" She turned her back on it all, propping her elbows against the concrete behind her.

Kate shrugged. "I love it."

"That the sunset is nothing but, like, actual shit in the sky?"

"If the air were clean the sunsets would be boring," Kate said. She sounded, Inez thought, like both a parent and a kid. "Less spectacular."

Inez considered this. "*You're weird.* Come meet people."

Fingers tight around Kate's wrist, Inez walked her through the house, a tour of the space and its residents, different music drifting out from different rooms, different faces looking up from beds and hammocks and couches, hands raised in brief waves. The biohazard of a kitchen at one end, crusted cereal bowls in teetering stacks, bristling with spoons. A drum kit, projector, bean bags. Dana was hunched in the middle of a collapsed couch now, frowning at a laptop. She unhooked her earbuds one by one, a gesture meek and precise, and got to her feet. When Dana said *hey*, she met Kate's eyes and shook her hand with a certain deliberation, a grimness to her courteousness, as though they already shared a knowledge of something. Inez couldn't take this, the absurd solemnity of it, a pair of global heads of state meeting at the fucking UN, so she seized Dana in a headlock, pulled a grotesque sad-face at Kate, and said, "Dana's no fun today. I think it's that time of the month."

Dana wriggled free, rubbed her neck, shook her head, and sat back down.

"Let's go get drunk," Inez said, snatching Kate by the wrist again.

Outside, there were thin blankets and fat cushions, and Inez threw herself down on them, stomach first, ankles in the air, as she always liked to do, and poured mezcal into red plastic cups. It tasted smoky and burnt, the way the sky looked, and she watched Kate take greedy little tugs of it, like she was sucking up the dark violet shreds of clouds.

Others joined them, and Inez poured Dana an extra two inches. The bottle emptied and then Gabe was tipping out ashy gray crystals from a baggie onto a tray, delicate and precise, fashioning small bundles of them out of rolling papers. "This is the top-drawer shit," he said, several times, a favorite phrase of his, regardless of the quality. Inez knew there was a whole fifth dimension of difference between a bit of shitty speed plus powdered aspirin, and the real deal, speedless, that granted you a religious experience.

"Here!" Gabe said, making an offering to Kate.

She looked like she'd just been handed a gun and told she had to shoot the president. Inez couldn't help it, she laughed. She flung herself to Kate's side, scooting closer, slamming her body up against hers. "Take it, take it!"

And Kate did. Difficult things to swallow, these paper bombs.

"You've got to take a massive gulp now," Inez urged her, passing her the bottle. "Like, *huge*."

After she'd done this, Kate smiled, suddenly, with her hands empty and her eyes wide. *All gone.* This pleased Inez. She threw her throat back and let out a howl to the moon, wherever it was.

"You're going to be so unembarrassed! And I'm going to be your tour guide! Here begins the unembarrassment of Kate!"

△▽△

By the time she noticed Kate was gone, the sky had turned navy blue and the fairy lights strung everywhere looked soft and blurry—melted, almost. The crowd of friends had multiplied into friends of friends and everyone seemed loose and oblivious, people muddled up in people.

"Shit," she said to Gabe, stubbing out the cigarette. "Have you seen her?"

"Huh?"

Of course he hadn't. He had a stupid vague grin slopping around on his face and his eyes weren't keeping up with his body's movements.

Inside, Inez gave the bathroom door a gentle kick. There she was, sitting on the toilet with her feet tucked under her and her phone in her hands. Kate's eyes looked a little red. It would hit at any moment, Inez thought.

"Sorry. I had to . . . My boyfriend is sort of . . ." and Kate held up the phone to indicate some kind of crisis.

Inez said nothing for a moment. Then: "You're coming out with us tonight."

15

Dennis never failed him. Always got to his feet with difficulty as he heard Bill enter the apartment, and ambled over, head slung low, body stiff, tail wagging faintly to greet his owner's return. Always doggily, indomitably himself. He pushed his muzzle into Bill's hand and gratefully licked the sweat.

"Hey, man," Bill said, closing the door behind him, slinging his keys. "Hot, right?"

Dennis twitched his ears and rearranged his chops in a way that seemed to Bill to be affirmative, and then resumed panting with soulful eyes. Bill swore, sometimes, that this look expressed regret at not being able to parse human words.

The AC units whirred.

It always struck him as a great gender unfairness that women, in temperatures like this, could wear next to nothing and look desirable, but that men in shorts were, unfailingly, considered buffoons. Even a man in a T-shirt was halfway to being a buffoon. Or at least, a man of his age was. With a semifrozen beer in hand and a cold, soaked dishcloth over his head, Bill yielded to the sofa and allowed it—the day, the heat, everything—to vanquish him.

When he parked the beer and pulled off his damp shirt, balling it beside him, Dennis followed the object with intent, his nose twitching.

"No, dude, you don't want to smell that."

Dennis, chastened, dipped his head, doleful-eyed.

Bill switched on his default hate-watch of a news channel. A blond-helmeted Stepfordian in a pink suit was addressing him from behind a desk, manicured hands clasped firmly.

"Record temperatures," she was saying. And now the man beside her—because she was just a woman, wasn't she, and these TV people must think viewers needed "masculine authority"—confirmed it: "One of the hottest summers on record."

Dennis sat at his feet, alive and attentive, his sides heaving. They stared at each other with mutual regard, an old benevolence.

"And now," the female voice was saying, "is this little boy corrupting your children?"

The screen split into two: on the left, her face, immobile save for the infinitesimally raised eyebrows, indicating that *this*, fellow Americans, was not your average story; on the right, a freeze-frame from a video.

"A boy from Fort Lauderdale, Florida, has become a YouTube supercelebrity."

As she spoke, the footage of a hyperanimated tween began. He was wearing saucy little pink shorts and a tie-dyed crop top, mugging for the camera in his bed-room, rolling his eyes with draggy glamour, pouting, and then pushing his butt inches away from the camera and oscillating that butt with remarkable speed, all while cast-ing a look of precocious sexual intent over his left shoul-der. Bill turned to his dog.

"Is this child corrupting you, Dennis?"

Dennis's tail drifted back and forth with uncertainty.

"Going by the YouTube name of *Tiniest B*," the an-chor said, stressing it in a way that made clear she was as leery of this vulgarity and foolishness as you were, "the boy has attracted more than seventy *million* views online for videos that contain sexually inappropriate language and dances."

Bill smiled at the screen. "Sexually inappropriate dances, bud. Watch out for them."

Dennis wagged his tail with a little more enthusiasm.

"Exactly! Butt shaking! You'll end up on the news, pal. Twerking sensation."

The anchor talked on, sternly.

"His real identity remains unknown, but parents across America are demanding answers."

Bill switched it off. "Demanding answers," he said into the silent apartment. Dennis wagged his tail hopefully.

"Walk?" Bill said.

They walked south and then east, toward Tompkins Square, and Bill found himself passing the building where, some months back, he'd had an unremarkable night with a woman who'd gone to high school with him, or so she said. Did they talk to each other, all these freshly divorced women in their forties whom he'd known decades back, old acquaintances who, out of the blue, sent him Facebook messages with winking emoji in them? He wondered if they'd formed a sort of sorority. Then he looked up and a sign seized him. It was—there was no other word for it—*fizzing*. Neon letters descending, B-A-R, but the B sputtering in and out of existence, humming as it flashed and died in the morning, leaving an ar where a bar had been.

Neon, meaning something new. Newness for the permanently new New York, a newness that was now blinking out. Soon these signs would spark the same nostalgia as subway carriages berserk with graffiti, or prostitutes with platinum perms. Were there social media accounts for this, digital mausoleums for images of a dead city, so that its ghosts could live on in virtual permanence?

Dennis shuffled his hind legs to a halt and a squat, then cast Bill an abject glance. He duly looked away, waiting with the little green baggie in hand, as his dog did his business on the sidewalk.

△▽△

Few people inspired in Bill a desire to make offerings. He took a certain splenetic pleasure in showing up to dinner parties empty-handed. But Casey, the oldest person he knew and also the person he'd known the longest, the permanent kid, was a person he wanted to give things to. Cannoli. They'd please him, offer succor to his sweet tooth, cookies for breakfast. And so Bill walked to Little Italy. Down Avenue A and Ludlow, west along Grand, to a bakery that had been there forever, a Proust machine for a thousand old fuckers like him, mooning over the bites of their pubescence. He ordered seven and then carried them, in a bright white box, all the way back, route retraced.

The door from the street gave its haunted-house whine. Casey's doors were never locked. Three flights up, Bill found him in the usual chair, by the window, mouth slack, fingers limp. A cold wash of dread moved through Bill's chest.

"Casey?"

His eyes snapped open, that unnatural blue, full wattage. Snapped open so fast that Bill wondered if he'd been fucking with him.

"You're late!" Casey said.

"I'm surprising you. I can't be late."

"No surprises. You should have been here half an hour ago!"

This was normal, really.

"What did you bring?" Casey said.

"Guess."

"I hate surprises, loathe them, you know that, Willie."

Untrue, Bill thought. Casey loved surprises. Disruptions. Any act of anarchy. He just didn't like to be on the receiving end of any of them.

"What's in the goddamn box, Willie?"

"Sweet things."

"Goody."

"Cannoli."

"Let's eat them."

"You got any coffee?" Bill said, depositing the box and moving to the poky kitchen, opening cupboard doors hopelessly. "Proper stuff, not that vile powder."

"Vile powder!" Casey parroted from the other room. Then, glumly: "I have rum."

Bill opened and shut doors, finding cat food, more cat food, a garish bong, a jar of Jiffy. The fridge was clinical in its emptiness. He gave up. He told himself he hated sweet things, but Casey's ardor was the kind that you had to just go with. He sat in the half-shipwrecked armchair beside him, coffeeless, getting cream and crumbs all over everything, listening to Casey make small grunts of satisfaction as he ate.

"When I walked in," Bill said, "I thought you were dead."

He noticed a smear of cannoli cream on the crotch of his jeans and began scrubbing at it with a fingernail.

"Ha!" Casey said. "Spooked you, did I?" And then, with his mouth full: "Well, will be soon."

It took a moment for the words to reach Bill's mind.

"The fuck?"

"Oh, don't go all Florence Nightingale, Willie! All shocked and tragic! Been dying since the day I was born. We all are."

"You're sick?"

"Sick, depraved, twisted," he said, the words made thick and stupid with cream. He wiped some from his mouth, unsuccessfully, and reached a hand, knuckles cubed by arthritis, toward the box again. His fingers trembled with impatience. "Pass me another."

"Well, I can see you're eating like a bird, so . . ."

Casey just grunted.

"Do you have health insurance?"

He knew the answer to this.

"Let me help, Casey. Medical bills. I'm going to help. You know I can afford it. Especially since my only child seems to show fuck-all interest in tertiary education."

Casey kept gobbling.

"Write down your bank details. Or send me the bills."

"Good for her," Casey said.

"What?"

"College!" he said. "That's one for the sheep. Lemmings."

"Those are two different species. But maybe. Cara definitely doesn't think so."

"Who?" he hooted.

"Her mother. My ex-wife. Remember her?"

Cara had been pissed that Casey had worn white. Two decades ago! A ceremony in her parents' garden in Connecticut, her sweet bump under the lace. And Bill, laughing with disbelief at his new bride, telling her that his friend always wore white, that she couldn't seriously be pissed about this, she had to be joking. Her eyes had become even harder at that, merciless. It would take years for him to learn not to show any amusement in the face of her anger.

"Latinas!" Casey yelped. "Hot-blooded. She was a hot-blooded one."

"Yeah, I don't think you can say that anymore, Casey. Kind of racist. Tepid-blooded now, anyway."

"So you've found yourself a hotter-blooded hottie?"

Bill exhaled something like a laugh.

"Ooh, a *girlfriend*," said Casey.

"Not a girlfriend, no. She's much younger. English."

"You found her on the double-you double-you double-you?"

"No. Real life."

"Oh, what is that, Berto? Real life!"

"Face to face," Bill offered vaguely. "IRL."

"I are what?"

"Never mind."

"Well, you should bring her to my real-life birthday party. Halloween. Weekend before. It's going to be a blast. Bang-bang."

As if summoned by the words, there was a knock at the door.

"Lock it!" Casey hissed at Bill.

The knocking became louder, terrorizing, a you-better-fucking-open-up door assault.

Casey's eyes bugged wild, his fingers spread stiff in alarm. Bill leaped across the apartment, exhilarated. The second fusillade came a breath after he bolted the door.

"You're in there!" the voice boomed. The speaker

sounded late-middle-aged, white, heavyset, bruising—
exactly as Bill had imagined. "I just heard you lock it!"

Casey seemed to have shrunk even smaller in his chair.
"Shh," he whispered. He flapped his hands. "Sit down."

Bill did. They both sat there, motionless, wordless,
listening to the battery of fist on wood. He had an urge
to giggle, like they were hiding from a teacher, caught
smoking a spliff behind the bike sheds. Finally, the foot-
steps receded, with more yelling, more threats. Casey
blinked, slowly.

"Cunting landlord!" he said.

"What's going on, Casey?"

He inhaled, extravagantly, as if summoning a swan
dive: "What's going on, what's going on, Marvin Gaye?
Everything, Willie! Everything, always. What isn't going
on, that's what I want to know. It all goes on, all the time,
and it doesn't stop. All of it goes on and on—and what
our little piss hearts can't bear is that it will go on without
us! No different! Just the same!"

Casey's hands were shaking and now he seemed to be
addressing something in the ceiling.

"Only different all the time, always changing, never
the same. Mother, Mother! *Ongoing.* More and more of
it. Going on, different every moment. On and on. The
world turns, Willie!" He spun to look at Bill, and Bill felt
himself flinch.

"And so does the city, Willie! Turning and turning.
But the center *does* hold! It always has! Always new, never
old. Always come the new bright things and the bigger

buildings and the taller towers. They tear 'em down, build 'em higher to kill us all. *Ay caramba*."

And then, on exhaling: "Oh, Mother."

He took another breath, trembling, the blue of his eyes searing as if with some cold light.

"Go now," he muttered. "Clear out, I want to sleep!"

Casey's manner had shaken Bill a little, but this blunt dismissal was reassuring. Characteristic. When Casey grew bored of you for the day, the process was irreversible. Bill watched his friend shut his eyes, small, pinkish, wrinkled. And did a tear streak down his cheek?

Not something Casey would forgive Bill for seeing, if so.

Quietly, he took out five fifty-dollar bills from his wallet and made a stack of them on the table. He looked for something to weigh them down. A cat skull, stuck all over with rocks and jewels and glitter. He could hardly bring himself to touch the thing. As he swept crumbs into the nest of his hand and tipped them into the box, three cannoli remaining, and stowed it in the fridge, he ignored the feeling of wretchedness oozing up from somewhere inside him. Guilt? He'd left things a little better, hadn't he? Cannoli and cash—that wasn't nothing.

16

Inside the warehouse, Kate lost Inez within seconds.
Sound this loud became embodied. She felt an indecent
rolling of it from the pit of her stomach up through her
chest, jellying her insides. Elbows and knees knocked at
her and the air was jungle-dank with sweat, the taste of so
many bodies in her nose and throat. A man fell into her
and grasped her arms, pawing his way up to right himself, almost taking her down. His goggly eyes looked like
things you'd stick on the end of a sock puppet, one veer-
ing skyward, the other leering to the floor. She yelped,
but it was like screaming in a nightmare; she could hear
nothing at all. Feeling the first stirrings of proper panic,
she began pushing past strangers, hacking at limbs like
they weren't really human. Either the way out, or the
toilets. Whichever she found first.

It was a wall she found, a sallow wall, damp with
moisture, but as she set her back to it the floor started to
tilt, gently, some sick tease. When she blinked, she wished
she hadn't: everything refracted and blurred, trailing
echoes of itself, woozily haloed in gold. She blinked again

but nothing returned to normal. When she crouched, the floor came up to meet her. It was all getting worse—the triple vision, the acceleration of the total physical crisis that was happening and that was her fault. She was going to die and she was on her own. Here. How stupid, how mortifying. Her mum would never forgive her, her mum would kill her. What exactly had she taken? There seemed no way to ask that.

Someone familiar was emerging from the terrifying crowd—dark hair, white dress, the image overlaid with echoes—and now a hand reached out to her hand. Kate went for it. Inez, who was emitting spectacular trails of light with every movement, slid down next to her and then took her other hand, too.

She was saying something, Inez was, very close to her ear. She was saying Kate had to ride it and let it wash over her, to not fight it. She was squeezing Kate's hand with the words and telling her it was going to feel *amazing. Any moment*, she said, and Kate believed her, believed in this imminent *amazing*. She was staring, she realized now, at the straight line of Inez's collarbone, which seemed, in its perfect horizontality, like a tiny monument to indestructibility. Inez was telling her to breathe, but Kate was thinking, as she stared at beautiful human bone beneath human skin, of that lovely word *adamantine*. It seemed edgeless, this breath. This was the first thing, the sensation of something vast and bright and extraordinary suffusing her insides, which now seemed grateful to have been transformed. She felt oxygen coursing through her, alchemical, and she made it slow, this next inhalation.

The second realization was even better: Inez, with her blackened soles and brutal cheekbones, had come to find her! Had made her way through this surging crowd, had come to find her, and she'd found her! And with these facts, a grand, wide certainty: that tonight, all of it, its enormity, belonged to her. She wasn't going to die! And George, his fusillade of text messages—every small and worrisome thing—was like scant ashes blown up into the sky, diffused and vanished. She began to laugh, and laughed more at how easy it was. Laughing was the easiest thing in the world.

"Yeah?" Inez said. Her hands, now, had come alive in Kate's hands, little bright animals, and Kate squeezed, stopped them scampering away.

"Yeah." And for some reason: "Immortal!"

"Who's immortal?" Inez laughed. And then, flexing her jaw. "Now we have to *move*."

Being on her feet was like levitating. Inez said a word that sounded like *honeymoon*.

"Are we on our honeymoon?" she said into the shell of Inez's ear—another miracle!—another extraordinary physical creation, and she kept her lips against it, just to tell it so. This seemed like a kind of sex, a penetration— words as warmth and sound.

"You're honeymooning!" Inez said. "Your first time. Your honeymoon."

And now she was pulling her into the crowd, and

here were the others, who looked to Kate like lesser gods, shouting welcomes as they moved.

"Medicine!" Kate said, the word leaving her easy as air. And this was the funniest, truest, most perfect thing she'd ever said.

△▽△

When Kate woke, her toes were poking through the holes of a crocheted blanket, a homespun thing that you'd wrap an infant in. She was back on the roof where the night had started an eon ago. It was hot, a tremble of skyscrapers in the distance, but it felt early, the sky high and new, a thin disc of moon in the blue, ready to dissolve on her tongue. A few slumbering bodies surrounded her, mouths slack, rib cages rising, falling, rising. Inez wasn't among them.

Last night, phrases had occurred to her like blazing revelations, rising up in her mind as twenty-foot neon citadels before which she'd wanted to prostrate herself. *God*, maybe she had—had there been a moment of her actually kneeling somewhere, delirious? Now, as she tried to grasp the words again in daylight, she saw they were dumb— completely dumb. Bad song lyrics that meant nothing.

She set about a slow negotiation to take her body from horizontal to vertical, coaxing it into standing, an enactment of evolution, knuckle-dragging she-ape to upright woman.

It occurred to Kate that all the definitive images of

New York City she'd accumulated were views from a distance. That it was a place best seen from bridges and water and sky. How might you do that with a person? Specifically: yourself. To find an aerial view of your own being. To reach the kind of vantage from which you might properly survey what had been built, what was under construction, to gain a sense of the contours of the thing. To see where the damn bridges went. The lie of the land, they said, and yes, it was a kind of lie. Because this view, she knew, this lovely hazy morning vision, denied all the bloodstreams of traffic down there. It couldn't tell you the way cabs' side mirrors flashed reflections of fast-walking bodies and street crossings, the way the image of those bodies was doubled again in the mirrored planes of buildings. This was being, too, all the quick currents and charges, synapse flares, unmappable.

No one woke up. She looked around at them, heedless, sleeping, unaware of being watched, and felt a little guilt and thrill—a small clutch of panic that one of them would wake and see her standing, watching them.

The elevator sent her down, and with a shove to that heavy door she was outside, in the world, walking through quiet streets to the subway.

17

Not a smart thing to attempt in this state, after a night like that, but it was never a smart thing in any state, was it, basically. Inez hefted up her bedroom window, the window of her childhood, stepped out, and gripped the iron railings. She'd made it home for once, to Broadway, just before the night softened into morning, leaving Kate sleeping in a pile of others on the Bushwick roof. She didn't want to be there when Kate woke up: she could picture her all bloodless and shell-shocked, asking with her eyes how it was that her mind had been removed, rearranged, and put back again. She'd figure it out. Mornings after: they were for being alone.

A tight column of a courtyard, all these jostled, unseen back ends of buildings, pipes, dirty windows, laundry steam, and the carbuncles of air conditioners, humming their ugly chorus into the hot afternoon. Climbing up to the roof had become a kind of addiction this summer. Today the trance of it took over almost instantly: hands and feet and hands and feet and hot metal grating underfoot. Breeze growing brisker, coming up into more blue,

so that distant water towers emerged and the lower buildings and their noises receded. *Don't look down* was the
well-worn warning. But if you never looked down you
denied yourself the purpose of the ascent. That sweet-
hideous lurch of seeing how far you'd come, how high
you were, the flutter and wash of vertigo. A repetition of
black wrought-iron ladders, zigzagging smaller, nothing-
ness between each tread.

When she reached the roof itself there was the familiar pulse of relief and regret. A relief to be on this vast
solid plane, banked with concrete walls sloped smooth
like skateboard ramps, to have made it here, to lie flat on
the baked concrete, belly up. Regret in the basic anticli-
max of any apex, this flat lack of steps to climb.

Modest little honks and humming and rumbles floated
up from Broadway. She sat up and scanned for the small
green squares of roof gardens, these secret aerial oases of
the rich. Apple trees in tubs, tiny wrought-iron tables and
chairs. And there, a female figure in a sun hat, seated,
reading, oblivious to a teenage girl staring at her from
many rooftops away. Inez willed her to look up and see
her. The figure remained perfectly small and still, head
bowed. Some wealthy arty white lady living her wealthy
arty life. Extraordinary, that you could stand here, in
downtown Manhattan, center of the world, dense with
lives, and no one could see you.

If Inez had a ball, and a throw forceful enough, and
a voice loud enough, she would have yelled "Catch" and
lobbed it across all these rooftops, to land in the lady's lap.

But her own hands were empty. And in her pockets: a half-crumpled packet of cigarettes, one smoke left. If she had a gun, and a bottle, she'd set it up there, right on the edge of the wall, and shoot. God, that would feel good. She lit the last cigarette.

Superstition was bullshit, Inez knew. It was something for girls who thought "the universe" was some kind of wish-granting fairy godmother who communicated her indulgences through inscrutable material signs. But when that girl, the wrong Kate, appeared right there in Washington Square where some other Kate had said she'd be, and when this unwanted Kate had pulled out the same cigarettes as her, and a little lighter the same bright yellow . . . well, it just seemed like something. Like it had to be something. And it had, hadn't it?

There'd been the version of Kate in Washington Square, startled and flustered like something out of a BBC drama full of bonnets and corsets. Blushing like she could be curtsying in one of those swanky old brick houses beyond the fountain. And then, last night, this other girl, transformed.

The universe didn't wave wands, but wasn't there a magic to dispensing molly like wishes, spiriting a posse to a party, all your friends sailing through that door behind you without you even trying, without a bouncer even flicking an impatient hand out for an ID? It had not yet ceased to please her, how much more astoundingly fun drugs made the world. And how much more fun it had made Kate. All of her—not just her pupils—bigger and darker and brighter. There'd been a great satisfaction in leaving her and all of them sleeping on that other roof this morning, a bunch of dopey dwarves under a spell.

She wondered how old the bouncer had thought she was. Whether he knew he was waving through a teenager. Twenty! She'd be twenty this year. It was her last summer as a teenager. Twenty was impossibly old. Two decades old. But still a year away from a legal drink. How boring that would be, a legal drink. The end of something. How *incredibly* boring it would be, a nonfake ID.

She crushed the yellow American Spirit pack into a ball, cellophane scrunched against paper, and threw it across to the other side of the roof, watched it skitter on the concrete and lie there, a sole unsightly piece of litter on this wide unpeopled plain. She realized, with something like fury, that she was starving.

18

When Bill got home he found Inez standing slumped in the light of the fridge's open door, despondent.

"There's nothing to eat!" she said, turning to him with a look so excessively doleful that he laughed. She pushed the door shut with half-assed truculence and whined, "I'm fucking starving."

If an empty fridge were a way to dodge her over-reaching inquiry about *his* night, an early-hours arrival home—the "walk of shame," as people younger than him liked to say (or used to? Language kept accelerating, you couldn't hope to keep up)—then maybe in the future he should avoid grocery shopping entirely.

"My poor little Victorian orphan. There's granola," he said, kissing the top of the head. She made a soft noise of disgust.

"And almond milk. Which might be a bit old. Or we could go out," he added. "Do you want to go out?"

"Yes," she said.

"Great," he said, trying to minimize his delight, buoyant with the novelty of it.

When they stepped out into the street and the hot morning he felt her eyes on him. She was giving him that look, that awful smirk. So: he hadn't escaped.

"What?"

"Just glad you're getting some, Bill."

"What?"

"You totally got laid last night. I'm glad. Hope they're hot. Who are they?"

"Jesus, Inez."

"You fucked the son of God?"

"Yes. Christ and I got it on."

"So is He a top or a bottom?"

He pushed his fists into his eyes. "Inez," he said, "do your friends ask their fathers about their sex lives?"

"I'm not fucking *asking*. I'm just saying. Glad you're getting some."

"It's way too early for this. And by that I mean that it will always, always, always and forever be way too early for this, okay?"

"You're such a prude."

"That's what they say about me, sweetheart—William Marrero, massive fucking prude."

He swallowed revulsion at having said his own name out loud.

"How are the college applications going?" he said, a definitive change of tack, and she drowned out the end of the question with a groan.

"So that's 'still not going,' then," he said, no fight in him now.

"Why would I waste all that money?"

"Education is never a fucking waste. Jesus, I thought we'd taught you that. If we taught you one thing—"

"Said the high school dropout."

"I wish I hadn't."

"I don't believe you."

And neither did he. It was the best thing he did, really. He was always pleased when interviewers brought it up. "So you left school at *sixteen*?" they'd say, and then he could rail on—piratical, swashbuckling!—about self-education and life and experience and the stultification of institutions. Except, of course, the last time he'd done that, the quiet, rather severe-looking woman from that British magazine had asked, in a voice as small as it was accusatory: "Does that not make your tenure at NYU somewhat hypocritical?"

He'd thought about that "somewhat" for some time: a rather quaint word. It only heightened what it purported to soften. "Yes!" he'd cried back at the journalist. "Yes, I'm a total hypocrite." And then with an exasperated, self-lampooning shrug: "But, y'know, my daughter needs a college fund." The piece had run under the cringingly enormous quote, "Yes, I'm a total hypocrite!"

He turned to Inez as they walked.

"Also, *you* wouldn't be the one paying. It would be your loving mother and father wasting all that money."

Before either of them could say anything else, they heard rapid footfalls behind them and he tensed. Fight not flight, preparation for a mugging—an old habit, undying.

He grabbed her wrist and turned, and as she shook him off, exasperated, a young woman, thin, wearing leopard print leggings and a skimpy black vest, hastened desperately and awkwardly toward them.

She waved. "Hi! Excuse me!"

She was carrying an iPad, but it was her coked-up anxiety that identified her before the prop did. Inez seemed to recognize it, too. It had been a while since an encounter of this kind. He'd thought, in truth, that at the tender age of nineteen she'd now be seen as too old for modeling, that the window had passed.

"Not interested," Inez said to the panting woman, as she reached them.

"Sorry?" said the woman, still breathless. "I'm a model scout and I . . ."

"Yeah, I know what you are and I'm not interested," Inez said.

The woman, still panting a little, stood on the spot in her gold platform sneakers. Bill watched a slide of sweat at her temple.

"I . . ." she began. "I just, okay, you have an extraordinary look and—"

"All right, let me break it down for you," Inez said, growing expansive. "Modeling is fucking dumb. I'm not standing around in someone else's faggy, overpriced bullshit that they call *art* and pouting and making my shoulders look even bonier while some douchebag photographer gets a hard-on and asks me to, like, try a few with my tongue out and my top off. And I'm not turning into some fucking professional anorexic Instagram-addict narcissist taking pictures with my *squad* just so I can sell three-thousand-dollar dresses to rich, miserable uptown bitches whose hedge-fund husbands are off boning escorts. And if I want hot pictures of myself I'll just take a fucking selfie, okay?"

The woman blinked. The three of them stood there, Bill feeling himself beaming, Inez trying not to look pleased with this speech, making bored eyes, even as those slight twitches at the corners of her mouth betrayed her satisfaction.

The young woman swallowed, shifted her iPad under her arm.

"We're a very reputable agency," she said, a bit affronted, but perhaps mostly astonished. "And we take the health and well-being of our girls really seriously."

"Have you met my dad?" Inez said.

The woman faltered, looked up at him.

"I don't think my daughter's interested," Bill said to her.

He tried to make his voice kindly. He felt bad for her. She'd just sprinted at least one block, in midday heat, in these travesties of running shoes, convinced she was about to make the signing of the year.

"Also, my daughter's nineteen. So really, it's a little offensive, a little *unfeminist*"—oh yes, how he relished that, a wicked flourish—"when you refer to her as a girl."

"I'm all woman," Inez corroborated, placing one hand on her hip, giving her head a toss like Miss Piggy. "And I'm offended."

The scout wiped some sweat from her forehead and looked as though she might cry. She began fumbling around in a fanny pack sitting on her hip. Bill hadn't seen one of those since the nineties. Cara had worn one on holiday in Maine, one of the very last family holidays, and it had seemed to him the absolute signal of her resignation from the world of sexual desirability, an abject flag of surrender. Like some kind of sagging womb, in shriveled black leather, worn outside the body. A thing that made him always think of the word *prolapse*. And now fashion must have decreed they were Back. Prolapses for all.

"If you give me your card," said Inez, "I swear all I'm going to do is stick my gum in it. So seriously, save a tree, keep your card."

Bill made an apologetic smile, a rueful grimace of helplessness, and followed his daughter. He had a sense that the young woman was still rooted to the sidewalk in those ludicrous sneakers, shell-shocked, trying to metabolize her dismay.

"I'm really glad," he said, slinging an arm around his daughter as they walked away, "that you have no interest in modeling."

"It's fucking cheap," she said.

"Yes," he said.

"And lame," she said.

"Also lame," he confirmed.

"*So* fucking lame."

The brunch place had tables on the street, a green-and-white-striped awning, a patio ringed with wooden planters stuffed with red geraniums. It felt Parisian. She ordered blueberry pancakes, and when they finally arrived she patiently held a tilted jug of maple syrup over them until they were drowned. He paused over his biscuits and gravy, watched her arm remain suspended. The miracle of her.

"Hey, what's your friend's name?" she asked, forking a big piece of pancake into her mouth.

"What friend?" he said.

"Weird old guy. Wears white."

"Casey! . . . Casey?"

"I saw him."

He was so eager for this, for her telling him something, beginning a conversation, that it took a huge effort to pay attention to the actual content.

"Where did you see him?"

"What's his deal, anyway?" she said.

Extraordinary, really, her ability to ignore direct questions.

She added: "I like him."

He hadn't expected that.

"You do? Well, good."

The mutual surprise effected an odd levity.

"I like him too," Bill added.

"So how did *you* meet him, then?"

"Oh god. I was fifteen."

"Is this," she said, her voice fat with pancake, "going to be another one of those stories where you stare into space for five minutes between every sentence?"

"Sorry. We met in Tompkins Square Park. He propositioned me. Half-heartedly."

Should he even be telling her this?

"A few weeks later, the blackout happens. You know about this?"

"No."

"The blackout of 1977. All the power went out. Imagine the whole city in total darkness."

"Sounds wild."

He knew she was using the word approvingly. *Dope* or *rad* or *sick*.

"Wild was, yeah, exactly what it was. Not in a good way. People *went wild*. Mad and bad and fucked-up desperate people who . . ."

He didn't know where to go. Could no longer distinguish between his own memories and accounts of this night in novels, memoirs. The blackout, the blackness, had accreted too much, had been filled with too many stories.

She rolled her eyes. "Cool story, bro."

So much you could forget—the sequence of your very own life. Maybe humans weren't meant to live this long, maybe brains couldn't retain this much life, maybe the natural way of things was to die at thirty, when you could still remember it all, or most of it. And maybe it was right that teenage daughters thought their fathers fools. That was the way of things.

Write a book, lose a wife, raise a daughter.

Casey still being alive, though—that hardly felt like the way of things.

"So many of Casey's friends died in the eighties," he said. "Like, almost all of them. They called it the 'gay plague.' That cunt—sorry—Reagan . . . I don't know how Casey survived. I don't know how he's still alive. I guess sex was never really his thing. Just the occasional blow job from boys in the park. He liked it better in other people. Liked to talk about it and liked to watch, like the little perv he loved to be."

She scrunched her nose to express distaste.

"Who's the prude now?" he said.

Her pancakes were gone, his coffee was drunk. While he was paying and she was in the bathroom, her phone on the table lit up. He had never read her texts, or her e-mails, or snooped on her online. He wasn't that kind of parent. But here he was, picking the thing up and reading it. It was mildly confusing, for a moment, no more than that.

Only when he read the message again did a sick understanding come, a weight over his body that pushed down on him and kept pushing down, as if it wanted to expel every bit of air. By the time she slumped back down opposite him, with the scent of the bathroom's expensive soap rising from her hands, he thought he was going to vomit biscuits and gravy all over their table.

"Woah," she said. "Bill?"

He couldn't look at her.

"Jesus, are you having a heart attack or something?"

"I'm fine. I think maybe the—the gravy was bad."

He could hear the lie. No possible way she'd buy it. But:

"Oh, gross," she said. "If they poisoned you we should totally get this on the house. At *least*."

She was looking around for some poor waiter to berate. He waved away this suggestion. "No, god, no."

"Well, I'm going to Bushwick, then," she said, already up, slinging her backpack over her shoulder.

"You are?"

He felt fresh panic.

"Yeah."

"To the café?"

"Yes!"

"Don't forget your phone," he said.

She grabbed it with a wary slowness and then stood there.

"I'm *fine*, sorry," he said. "Go, just go."

"Well. Feel better, okay? Pepto-Bismol."

And then she was gone.

His hands were sweating and cold.

Maria, his mother's name. Above the text, the sender's name, carlosX, had told Bill it was meant for Inez, that the message came from a person saved in her contacts.

Who the fuck was carlosX and what kind of a fuck-faced name was that? And why the fuck was this carlosX telling his firstborn and only child to arrive at four, and to wear *the* shoes *as always*, and yes, they could negotiate a pay raise. *Why the fuck is this carlosX calling my child by my mother's name?*

He accosted a waiter and ordered, in a voice that didn't belong to him, a double scotch on the rocks. When it came he steadied himself with a mouthful or two and a new thought came like a bright coin in his palm. He actually almost let out a small cry of relief: the possibility that it was a joke. Yes! Some kind of joke, it had to be. Games teenagers played, silly names for each other: "carlosX" was likely a pseudonym for that skinny kid drinking coffee in his kitchen the other day. And this, quite possibly, surely, was just some innocent kink between them, none of his business. That was the main thing, wasn't it? That it was none of his business.

Innocent kink. He should never have read it in the first place, and now he chose to believe he hadn't. He observed his fingers around the tumbler, and tilted the glass in a companionable sort of way, so the drink sloshed gently, the glass slipping a little against the sweat on his skin.

△▽△

She got home late. He heard the sound of the elevator before the door, the old whir and crank of it, and got himself out of bed and into his dressing gown to go see her. She was already lying on her back on the sofa, legs dangling over its end, holding her phone above her, thumbs weaving in the semidarkness.

"'Sup," she said, without looking at him. Her phone cast a greenish light on her face. The word sounded a little slurred.

Here was his moment to say it: *Who's Carlos X, then?* He sat down beside her.

"What've you been doing? What did you do tonight?"

He sounded thin to himself.

She continued to text, or whatever it was she was doing, eyes glazed. He thought, for a moment, that she hadn't even heard him, but then, still engrossed in whatever was on that tiny fucking screen, she began to talk. A flat voice.

"The usual. Shot heroin with some homeless dudes. Mugged an old lady. Stole a car. Y'know."

"Okay," he said, and sat there with his hands in his lap.

Now, finally, she looked at him, cocked an eyebrow, and scrambled up to sit cross-legged.

"Not funny?" she said. "Not laughing?"

His gaze slid to her grubby feet. Blackened soles, pink and clean in the arches.

"Jesus, sweetheart, your feet are *filthy*."

19

For a while, Kate heard nothing from Inez, and didn't care. The night at the warehouse had taken days to recover from. She barely ate for three of them, and marveled at the high of this, indulging the delusion, as she poked at her hip bone in the mirror, that reality was baring its bones. Hours in the bathtub, in its cloudy water. Stretches of time flat on the bed, held in a kind of trance by the drone of the air conditioner, ignoring the cat as it ignored her. It seemed, for a moment, a sort of saintly state that she'd entered. And then, this morning, she ate cereal and checked her e-mail and it was broken. She was just restless and irritable now, willing surprises, invitations, miracles from her in-box. *Downloading 5 of 5.* One from Lauren. Did she want to eat froyo in Park Slope? How about never replying, how about not a sorry and an excuse, but just a nothing. Somehow this was a quietly breathtaking thought. Then with a surge of guilt the thought faded. To Park Slope she went.

The froyo place was all aspartame and artifice, sweet white turds cradled in paper cups, covered with a chaos of candy, harassed mothers failing to hold conversations with each other over their clambering toddlers.

When Lauren got up for napkins, Kate checked her phone again. Her attention snapped to the name in the subject line. *William Marrero in conversation.* A reading, in a church in the East Village.

It seemed possible that he wouldn't even remember that failure of a dinner. There were markers, definite dividing lines, and the night with Inez had been one. It had been a miracle that a pinch of dust had done this, had made the world ten times the size it had been before. There was the before and there was the after, and wouldn't seeing him now, in this new territory, this *after,* be a different thing altogether? A self-dare—and already she was playing out some joke in her mind that she could make to him about "froyo," playing up her British bewilderment, Lauren's maximalist approach to toppings. And then her phone shuddered in the palm of her hand: Inez.

"This was so lovely!" Kate said as Lauren reclaimed a plastic chair. Hearing this obvious euphemism for good-bye, she looked stricken.

"I've got to get to a reading," Kate explained.

"Oh!" Lauren said. "Who's reading?"

She told her. Lauren's eyes shone back a little hungrily.

"Oh, wow! You know, I think he was at that art show we went to!"

"Really?"

"It was so crowded I couldn't really tell! I think it was him, though. Not as good-looking as his author photo." She paused for a moment, abashed. "You know that photo?"

"Yes," said Kate.

Lauren waited expectantly. Kate smiled awkwardly. To make up for this, for the lie of the reading being to-night, for the rudeness of not inviting her, she decided to be emphatically warm in her goodbye words. Lauren's body felt small when she hugged her at the subway steps; her hair smelled of cucumbers. The hug was all arms, no back, as if they might break each other.

"So lovely to see you."

"You, too," said Lauren. Kate caught her eye for only a very small moment, but saw what was there, that flint of knowing that this was it, that there wouldn't be another froyo or anything-else outing.

The train rose upward with casual confidence, curving around and over the canal and past the Kentile Floors sign, red wrought iron against this wide blue, and toward the roofs and fire escapes of Chinatown. Looking out the window you couldn't see the tracks below, only the air all around, *like flying*, and she was abashed with the childishness of her own thought.

And then something was happening here in the carriage. A young black guy was pacing up and down with a vital sense of purpose, as though the very act of walking could do something to the space, clearing it or preparing it in some way. Two other young men—boys, just boys?—were hanging off the rails near the doors, waiting for their cue. And then he clapped and a break beat began, sonic scraps amplified, like a low-res image blown up yards wide. He was bounding now, slapping his palms as he bounced. "WHAT TIME IS IT?" he yelled. His two comrades yelled back, dutifully, smoothly, "SHOWTIME!"

Kate couldn't believe the lack of response: that people didn't look up from their screens, screens filled with cartoon candy, a game that seemed to have claimed the attention of a whole population of adult men and women this summer. The main guy, shirtless and bandannaed, the waistband of his jeans cutting neatly across buttocks clad in Calvins, lunged at the pole and was horizontal, suspended, one leg bent, the other extended with yogic perfection, as though someone had pressed pause. Then he swung, flipped, looped, made the space his playground. His comrade took the stage, flipped his baseball cap, caught it, spun it, kicked it up, and caught it on his head, all while the beat thudded through the car and the train plowed on. The youngest, eleven or twelve at the most, spun with a fluidity that was almost voluptuous, with a movement that carried a suggestion of sex. Kate wondered if the other passengers could feel it, a slightly dislodged quality to things, the unease at the feminine, sensual thing being described in the air of this crowded train.

Only a few faces looked up and then it was over. The dancers were clapping emphatically, rousing passengers to do the same. When they came past her she put a dollar in the hat and the youngest stuck his tongue out at her, bit it with his top teeth. He grinned, and she grinned back.

20

Today was what? Her third visit to him? Fourth? The heat obliterated any kind of computation. Walking outside was like dragging your body through lava. Inez passed some young women catatonic on a stoop, wearing just shorts, torsos slick with tanning oil, and every man that passed too mired in lassitude to react. It was the summer that girls dyed their hair into murky sea-life shades, and it drew her eye each time, these dirty mauve and turquoise and aqua and green streaks on blond, tugged up into messy knots and ponytails. Trashy mermaid colors, washed-up sirens on Lower East Side steps. They'd taste of Coney Island if you sucked a strand of hair: salty and sweet. Maybe fifteen years from now, heavy and settled, they'd look at old photos: *oh my god, d'you remember that summer we all had green and blue hair?*

On days like this Inez relished the subway ride not so much for the chill inside the train, the cold orange plastic of seat under thigh, and the grip of cool metal bars, but for the simple disorientation of it. Uptown, the streets were empty.

The doorman recognized her, of course. It was like walking into a marble morgue. This time the guy behind the desk was new and he slipped his eyes at her, slow and sour. Down her white top to her bit of bare belly, browned from weekends on Fort Tilden Beach, her denim cutoffs with the frayed fringes tickling her thighs. The sweat that had been pooling at the base of her back snaked now into her butt crack. She took her sunglasses off, wiped the moisture from her eyes, upper lip, and forehead, and stared at him, this doorman. She felt a white crackle of hostility as she pushed the elevator button. His face puckered with revulsion as the doors finally opened.

Shaking—why was she shaking?—she stepped inside and willed them to close fast. The floor seemed to rise faster than usual, and then they opened again, onto the familiar bland expanse of his home, and this time the ping they made was like a warning note of arrival that seemed to fade as soon as it sounded. The sweat had gone sickly cold on her skin.

When she saw the coat, that cheap-looking, fusty thing, it sent a surge of rage through her. She grabbed it and threw it. It landed slumped against the wall with its sleeves outspread, slayed, in an attitude of supplication or victimhood. No mercy.

The heels, though. She put them on. She clacked into his bedroom faster and louder than she'd done before. It felt like drugs, this unexpected fury.

There he was, as always, a hunch of him on the floor.

"There you are, you piece of shit!"

She bellowed this with a kind of joy, and as he looked up, she saw alarm pass through his eyes in a shiver.

"Yeah, you fucking should be frightened!" she shouted. "You should *fear* me! I'd fucking fear me if I was you. And you know what? I'm really fucking glad I'm not, Carlos! Does your mommy know you do this?"

And then his look hardened: *too far*. He made as if to get up.

"No, you stay the fuck down!"

She stopped pacing. Her chest, she noticed, was heaving.

He looked at her a moment longer and then, very slowly, bent his head again, returned to that fetal position. She listened to her own panting, to the blood moving inside her, and stared at the sweat stain on his back, an hourglass of indigo on the pale blue fabric of his shirt. It was spreading. Disgust galvanized her.

"I've got something to tell you, Carlos," she said, astounded to hear her own tone. "Not a fucking script! Not your corny fucking clichés. I *truly* think you're fucking pathetic. And I think your stupid little men in their cunty little hats downstairs are fucking pathetic. I think your whole fucking life, your men's mag apartment and your too-tight shirts and your too-much money that you have no fucking idea what to do with and these stupid obvious fucking whore shoes, is all fucking pathetic."

He put his hands over his head, as steady and obvious as a pantomime. The phrase is "losing it"; people say they lost it, but to her it felt more like being found and hit by and raised up by a force, so that she was no longer herself. She couldn't have stopped if she'd wanted to.

"Oh, your hands on your head, yeah? Yeah? Hands on the head equals 'Shut up, bitch'? I'm not shutting up, *Carlos*. I'm shouting for free right now 'cause I just think you're a fucking tragic sight."

And then, just as quickly, she was losing steam.

"Fucking tragic there, on the floor, with your hands on your head . . ." Her voice faltered. She sounded pathetic.

And now this. The way in which he lifted his hands above his head and placed them—one, two—flat on the ground. This was something she'd never shake.

A muscle was clenching and unclenching on one side of his oily neck. The smell of him seemed to have intensified into something sharper and more animal. She took a step back. There was the length of a body between them and he was almost two feet taller than her. Nausea began curdling in her stomach. She moved her eyes away from him, looked past him to the windows, where the park—deserted in this heat—was an unreal green, a mirage, as if, unpeopled, it had begun to doubt itself and dissolve.

"Fucking leave," he said. "Right now."

She removed one shoe, then the next, hobbling, shaking. She crouched to align them so that they were flush and neat, toes toward him. She straightened up and it was his bare feet she stared at. The scraggly black hairs on the tops of his toes. He took a step toward her and she could smell his breath, coffee stale.

"Fuck you," she said, a faint, hoarse noise.

There in his lips—an ugly twitch, a tightening, the opposite of a pout, and it came with a stinging smack to the side of her face. She reeled, her left palm pressed to the pain.

Several full and heavy seconds passed before she understood what had just happened, what he'd just done. There was a lightness to her amazement.

"Get the fuck out of my apartment," he said.

After the detonation of the slap, these words seemed to express nothing more than irritation. A piece of trash lobbed at a can, who cares if it misses. He muttered, more to himself than her: "Stupid little bitch, playing games."

He was already walking away. The slap had knocked the speech out of her, the thoughts out of her, everything.

It was only when she was in the elevator, its doors closing, that she realized she'd left her own shoes behind. That they were still sitting there, her dirty, fucked-up sneakers, beside the slung coat. Two pairs: the whore shoes, primly pointed, and her own battered sneakers, gray with dirt, ripe with a summer of sweat.

In the elevator she primed her body to run. Told her legs that this was what they had to do when she got to the ground. That the opening of the doors was the starting pistol. And then she was sprinting through the lobby, outside into the monstrous day, naked soles slapping the sidewalk, hot against bare skin.

By the time she reached the subway her feet were black and pink, dirty and scalded, small bits of grit lodged into her heels, and she was snatching drags of breath. She touched her face, marveled at it still hurting, and longed for a big mirror to see if there was a mark. On the subway platform a fat white woman, seated on a bench in a fuchsia T-shirt, holding a tiny cheap fan to her fuchsia face, turned and stared at Inez as she hopped from one foot to the other, craning down the tunnel to see the lights of the train as it made its gradual approach. People whined about how the city was too fast, but as passengers waddled on around her, it seemed everyone and everything was screamingly slow.

She sat and cradled a dirty foot in her hand, staring at it, only half-hearing that firm and familiar voice, disembodied and genial, advising, always, to *stand clear of the closing doors, please.*

Bill sat with an ankle crossed over a knee, gazing into the audience. The two Xanax he'd swallowed ten minutes ago had dimmed the world into an inoffensive haze, so that when, for example, he observed that the place was packed, the observation caused him neither surprise nor pleasure, only the knowledge that some combination of the two was probably the correct response.

His conversational partner, a critic in her early forties, author of two respectable but pop books on motherhood, was tripling her chin to squint down at the little black mic affixed to her shirt. He realized he didn't care either way if his own mic worked, didn't mind whether he was heard. Let it be someone else's problem. He had nothing more to say anyway.

Today was the book's anniversary. *Anniversary*. As though it were a marriage, or a war. They were reissuing it, a fancy copy, with four mini-essays of introduction from people his editor had referred to, without shame, as "boldface names." He'd refused a tour, citing fear of flying, which was true, and no one had fought him on it.

He, in turn, fought no one on the "boldface names." It was money, it was attention, it was a dubious efflorescence of online articles larded with the term *millennials*.

As that word left a greasy trail through his skull, he saw her. The name was absent for a moment, just the arrest of her sharp pale face and its white-blond hair. Staring straight out, very still, erect and attentive while the people either side of and behind her were bustling and gossiping, fanning themselves, swigging from water bottles, leaning across one another.

There seemed to be eye contact, a click of it, but at this distance you couldn't really be sure. He waited a beat, then reached for his phone and sent "Kate from gallery" two words: *save me*. It was a joke as he wrote it, just casual flippancy, but then, as his finger sanctioned SEND, it went with some kernel of no-joke. He watched it land, watched her dip her head to read it and glance up and go pink. A little conspiracy, from up here to over there. She was texting something. He waited.

from what

Oh, take your pick. Alcoholism, he thought. Paternal failure. Dissolution. Indolence and oblivion and irrelevance. Better, yes, to stick in the here and now. The manageable short term. With the uncanny quiet that sometimes comes over a crowd, conversations all over the room fell away. People looked amused and surprised at themselves. He watched Kate stash her phone. The critic, startled, began making movements of mannered readiness, as though trying to catch the eye of some stage manager in back. He wondered what her first question might be. He did not wonder very hard.

"Well!" said the critic. She glanced down at her note-book and adjusted her seat and gave him a quick professional smile.

His mind was a synthetic sky: blue, blank, cloudless.

"So, William, here we are, in this historic venue, celebrating the reissue of a book that's also in its own way historic . . ."

Oh, she was nervous. He could sense that some current in the crowd had found its way into her speech.

". . . and so I suppose the first thing I want to ask you is just what it's like to revisit this book and how it is to look back on what it was then and what it is *now*, in our culture, in this city."

He inhaled in a small way, opened his mouth, and began.

This answer, and the next, came on autopilot, with a dissociation not just from voice but from body, too. As if he were floating somewhere above or beside himself, an immaterial wisp overhearing this fleshy lump talking, the familiar cadences of urbane self-deprecation, the well-hewn remarks, while half-wondering who the hell they were—this lump, this voice, saying the same things they had said for decades. How long had he been talking? Were they still all there, those listening bodies who'd come to hear this? He granted himself a drift of a look and saw faces, rows and rows of them, unmoving and watching. There was something very unnatural, really, something plain hideous and frightening about so many human eyes trained on one spot, and the spot was him.

"Well," said the critic in brightening conclusion, and, oh god, had he made it, was this the end? He'd no idea if it had been five minutes or fifty. "Now I think we're just going to open it up to some audience questions."

A hand, quickest off the draw, shot up in front of Kate and obscured part of her face. As people wheeled to look at the person about to ask the question, Bill saw the scarlet flash down one side of her bare neck, a quite gorgeous spill of it. *Oh, Kate.* To be stared at, when you hadn't raised your hand. What a poignant unfairness.

"Yeah, hi," the young man said, taking the mic that was hurried to him, standing up, slinging his weight into one hip in a way that conveyed both his absolute assurance and the fact that what he was about to say would take some time. "So this is less of a question and more of an observation," he began.

Bill shut his eyes for one moment and experienced the feeling of falling in slow motion, seated, arms and legs akimbo, into a well of oblivion. He opened his eyes but every time the young man said "Hegelian" he plunged a fathom deeper. As the grad student kept talking, as the minutes passed—entire, fully formed, interminable minutes!—as the crowd shifted awkwardly, with huffs and sighs, and the critic, head erect, kept opening and closing her mouth in a weak effort to interrupt, Bill began to feel something like joy.

". . . and so ultimately, yeah, I was seeking your

thoughts on that and whether, in the dialectical sense at least, you'd agree that that is in fact the key antinomy of what I think we can unequivocally call the contemporary discourse with regard to this?"

And then, bald miracle, he stopped. The room was a single gelid entity. Bill didn't move; he remained staring at the student. The critic bit her lower lip and looked at Bill, terrified, while a collective breath held, strained and ready to split. He savored it for the smallest moment more.

"I'm sorry," he said evenly. "I didn't catch that: could you repeat the question?"

One beat, alarm in the boy's eyes, and then: an absolute eruption from the audience, a roar of it! Like he'd cracked them open, snapped down the middle, one milligram, a tiny sky-blue pill. The whole crowd laughing, a flood of relief, and then laughing more at the sound of themselves laughing. Bill twisted the top off a water bottle and took a sip.

Sometimes, when you truly and fully didn't give a fuck, when you were psychologically and pharmaceutically incapable of giving a fuck, you could find a pure sort of exaltation in the not-caring, you could let yourself be carried off by it to a place approaching sublimity.

The grad student's legs seemed to buckle beneath him for a moment, as if the command to sit were coming from his body rather than from the brain of which he was so proud. Who dared follow that, Bill thought, but they did, of course, because now the atmosphere was irreverent, lawless. He had them. The questions were loose and funny. One young woman, shiny and drunk and sloppy in a sweet way, took the mic and asked if it was true that he had once joined Debbie Harry on stage to sing "One Way or Another." Sort of, yes, but he didn't say that, he just laughed. Everyone else laughed, too.

"Sing it for us!" the girl pleaded.

"*You* sing it!" he said.

And she did! My god. A few lines of it, and when she did a victory twirl by way of a finale and collapsed back into her seat, hiding her face in her hysterical friend's shoulder, everyone whooped and cheered and a hero had been made, a karaoke queen of the hour. Bill plucked a carnation from the crappy vase on the table and threw it to the girl.

By the time the critic shouted that there was no more time for questions, and even before everyone mobbed the table of cheap chardonnay, it was essentially a fucking party. He saw, in his peripheral vision, that a cluster of bodies had already formed at the foot of the stage steps, awaiting him. The critic opened her mouth to thank him, or shake his hand, but before she could speak, he took her elbow quickly and said, just shading it with something conspiratorial, "Hey, did we get kicked out of Elaine's once?"

Goddamn, he felt like George fucking Clooney. It *could* have been her, couldn't it? The two of them kissing in the corner booth until the grand dame patron herself, Elaine the Eponymous, had decided enough was enough and wielded her weapon of choice.

"What?" she said.

He let go of her elbow. "Elaine's? Fly swat? Was that you?"

One quick shake of her head and she hardened with wariness.

"I don't know an Elaine," she said, gathering up her things, wedding band flashing. He smiled.

Down in the crowd, so many young faces. They wanted to take selfies with him, and he duly angled his face up at their outstretched phones and tried to look a bit quizzical, yet tolerant, likable. He couldn't see Kate and had a sense she might leave before he had a chance to grab her. It took a while; he actually had to prize people's hands off him, pat them off, and fight his way over there.

She was leaning against a pillar, cup of wine in one hand, looking deep into her phone.

"Didn't I tell you?" he said, with a sort of fervor.

"Hi," she blurted. "Tell me what?"

"About young men. That they're the worst."

"Hegel guy," she said. He saw her face shine briefly with relief, and then regret. "I think he actually was the worst."

"He's behind you."

"Shit!"

"I'm teasing," he said. "He's probably gone to jerk off into *The Phenomenology of Spirit*."

"The what?"

"Never mind."

"Oh," she said. "Hegel."

She smiled slightly. He was being too much—he could feel it. Calm down.

"That was quite . . ." she ventured.

"I know."

"Are your readings usually that . . ."

"Yeah, no," he said. "Anyway. I'm really happy you came."

"I worried you might think it was weird," she said. "I mean, just showing up after . . ."

"That dinner," he said. "*Wow*, that dinner. That was amazingly bad. Didn't I ask you if you liked coffee?"

"No," she said. She was laughing now, so he decided to laugh too. "You just announced, out of nowhere, that you were 'really into' coffee."

"Know what else I'm into?" he said.

She recoiled, as if there were some inappropriate threat in the question.

"*Wine*," he said quickly. "Wine. So here's an idea. You and I leave right now and go drink a bottle of stony cold white in a *vigorously* air-conditioned bar."

She seemed to falter. He'd completely misread this. Got carried away.

But then: "Okay," she said. And he watched, pleased, as she knocked back the cheap chardonnay, wiped her mouth, and, with a deft little show of sass, slung the crushed cup to the floor.

Outside, it was baking, all the windows and doors of the bars wide open to the evening, drinks and music spilling out onto the streets, as if there were no more borders, boundaries.

22

In some unlit and unplumbed place, a viscid pit-of-the-gut place, Kate understood that they weren't drinking to get drunk. That they had, instead, agreed upon a mutual seduction. They were drinking to the certainty of fucking.

The marble-topped bar was cool under her forearms, and a barman, with the steady flourish of a magician brandishing cards, dealt them two long menus. Bill ordered, without consultation, a many-syllabled wine.

"It's biodynamic," he said.

She looked at him for a moment.

"I just feel," she said, "like getting really drunk."

She watched a change come over Bill's face. He seemed to not quite know what to say, to be censoring himself, distrusting or testing something in the situation.

"Well," he said, quietly. "I can join you in that. I mean, if I may."

She raised her glass, another cheers. He smiled, drank, set his own glass down.

"So you're not going to tell me, are you," he said, "how it is that I'm with a completely different human being from the human being I was with a few days ago."

"We're all different, all the time, aren't we?"

"Fuck the sophomore philosophy student horseshit!" he said. "What happened to you in between?"

She considered this. She could tell him, of course. Spin a sexy story that might also be true. A striking teenage girl, mistaken identity. Drugs. Rooftop. There'd be, she thought, some kind of power in that. But it was hers and she was keeping it. She became aware of her wrists. They seemed more alive than any other part of her.

"No interest, then," she said, "in the woman who didn't know what a rarebit was."

He tipped his head as if weighing the matter with gentlemanly circumspection.

"Well, she was different. Afraid of asking any questions."

He tried again. "*You* were afraid. Of yourself or what you were getting into."

"And now?" she said. Being told what you were was irresistible, albeit in a slightly sickening way. She was feeling, yes, a little sick.

He shrugged, took another sip, and she saw she wasn't getting any more.

"You were quite bored before," she offered.

"And boring. I'm sure I was boring, too."

A mild sort of cruelty to just let the statement sit

there, to let him accuse himself. So she did, for a moment. Then: "Well, yes. But also odiously pleased with yourself. Which is much worse."

He slapped his hands on the bar, a silent chuckle that shook his shoulders. He was being a good sport. But it didn't quite satisfy her.

"Hey, Bill?" she said, faking urgency.

"What?"

She pointed to her wineglass and smacked her other hand to her heart.

"Tell me, is this . . . ? Please tell me, is this wine *biodynamic*?"

"Uh . . . yeah, it is."

"Oh, thank *god*," she said, pantomiming relief. "Thank god. For a moment I thought it wasn't. Because heaven fucking forfend we drink anything nonbiodynamic."

And now he got it.

"Ah, okay." He laughed. "All right." And again, "Okay, then."

Then he seemed to spot something over her shoulder and the temperature changed.

"Oh, fuck."

"What?" she said.

"Get ready."

"For wh—"

A man was clapping Bill on the shoulder. A fat man, whiskered, jowly, looking at Bill as though he were a chocolate eclair. His linen suit was wrinkled and his belly was revealed in a series of convex windows between the straining buttons of his shirt. The panama hat topping his florid face made Kate think of a boiled egg.

"Marrero!" he growled, tipping his head down, drawing the syllables out, in that way men did with other men's names in moments of salutation.

Kate caught bad breath, a rot beneath the booze. Bill nodded at him and then side-eyed the hand that still lay heavy on his shoulder. The hand's owner hesitated, then removed it, with a surprising delicacy. Now he was turning to her.

"Don't tell me you're of legal drinking age already, dear!" the man said. "I could have sworn you were still knee-high! And all that lovely hair lopped off!"

Bill, with undisguised disgust, said, "This is my friend *Kate*, Bailey."

And Kate watched the man barrel on, amazed, wonderstruck even, at his apparent impermeability to Bill's highly obvious dislike.

Once he was gone she said, "Bloody hell. Who was that?"

"A very rich old cunt," Bill said.

She flinched at the word. He looked quietly furious in his embarrassment, then took a mouthful of wine and seemed to collect himself slightly. "People tolerate him only because he gives a shitload of money to so-called important literary magazines. I mean, the guy's favorite book is *The Great* fucking *Gatsby*, for fuck sake."

She considered this for a moment, made a mental note to work out what was wrong with *The Great Gatsby*.

"He once held a Gatsby-themed party." Bill gave a nasty laugh. "As if he had to make *sure* that no one would go to his fucking funeral."

"Did he think I was someone else?"

"Can you imagine? A *Gatsby* party. What a cretin."

She didn't repeat the question.

"Anyway. I'm sorry you had to encounter him."

"Bill," she said. It felt strangely audacious, to say his name out loud like this.

"What?"

She hesitated, feared this was going to sound odd, or stupid, or both, when spoken aloud.

"You've never been scared of people, have you?"

"Of that old . . . ?" he said.

"No. People. In general. Not scared of what they might do to you. I don't mean *that*. I mean more, just, the presence of a person, their, sort of . . . heat, just how much they are."

This wasn't working, it sounded like nonsense.

"How much?"

"Yes. Like . . . just how *much*," she said, words spinning out of her now that communication seemed a lost cause. "Ugh, like the black hole of it, you know? Does that make sense?"

"No," he said, with no apparent unkindness. "But I'm interested. Keep going."

She thought of him on the stage, casual and kingly.

How he'd held that pause before he'd decimated the grad student; the orchestrated cruelty of it.

"No, that's it, really."

She felt the heat of his look.

"I really wanted you to ask a question," he confessed.

"Earlier?"

"Yeah. I was sort of willing it."

"I could not have stood up and sung Blondie for you," she said. "I'm tone deaf."

"That was pretty amazing," he said.

"So did you? Get onstage with her?"

He flung his hands around, in a way that was both evasive and expressive.

"Oh, you have to know that you can do anything you want!"

"Not true!" she said. Bleated it, almost.

"*True*. No one ever tells you, but it's true."

He was testing her, perhaps.

"Are you serious?"

"To be honest," he said, "I believe I can no longer distinguish between serious and nonserious."

"I think there's a difference."

"Try telling me that in twenty years."

That stunned her, for a moment. She did a quick calculation. To be forty-five—unthinkable. And then, before she could say anything more, he was ordering a round of martinis, dirty ones, translucent brine spinning slow helixes in the glass. The night thickened, its sounds multiplied, and they kept talking. She'd so abandoned herself to wherever the rhythm went that the question he asked next didn't even surprise her: a joke he wasn't joking about.

"What's your opinion on strip clubs?"

"My opinion?"

The bar was loud and crowded now. He was saying something about urgency.

"Urgency?" she shouted.

"No, agency. *Agency!* It fucks me off when people assume strippers don't have agency. What kind of feminism doesn't allow for male desire? Dworkin, go home, you know?"

Kate, with shame, heard herself snort.

"Shall we go, then?" he yelled.

"Home?" she said.

"No! No—here's the thing about strip clubs," he said. He seemed to be lit up now with some kind of avidity, the keenest student in a seminar. "They're the realest place I know."

"Real, like . . . ?"

"*Sincere.* Honest," he shouted back. "You'll see. *Real.*"

And if she'd had time to actually think about it, maybe she would have said no, she didn't really want to go. But this was one of those times that did not seem to allow for *no*; it was a truth she had already digested.

He took her hand, a hard grasp, and then they were out on the sidewalk, in the unremitting heat. His other hand reached out and up into the stream of the road, to summon and stop a cab, and it worked with the clean efficiency of a baseball hitting the hollow of a glove. A cab murmured to a stop beside them. Inside, on ripped black pleather seats, watching him, enraged, stabbing the taxi TV with a finger to shut it up, she felt the slow surprise of actually being in this cab. Its obvious motion, the stop and start in the evening's traffic, seemed to stymie the weird propulsion that had been carrying her, and now it seemed preposterous to be lurching west across the city, to a destination neither of them had foreseen. But maybe he had. Maybe he'd planned this.

Now I'm boring him, she thought, calmly. And as she thought it, she felt him dig his fingertips into her palm, still staring out the window, as though he were doing it unconsciously. She imagined the series of half-moon indents his nails were leaving in her flesh and she tightened her hand in return, happy to be hurt.

△▽△

It was a low, bronze-colored block of a building out on the West Side Highway, facing the lights of New Jersey across the water. A man the size and shape of a refrigerator—suited, headsetted, hands clasped over his groin as if what he was truly guarding were his very own genitals—nodded them in. Bass juddered up the stairs. A mirrorball swept a steady constellation around the black walls.

Bill had a way of summoning drinks at a bar that mirrored his talent with taxis: a chin lift, two fingers raised lightly.

Behind him, women moved around the poles lazily, as

though they'd happened upon them and were idly testing them—housewives from a past generation, considering new appliances in a department store. The same was true of their own bodies, the way they'd occasionally run a hand over and around their breasts with a kind of unconsciousness. Their clothing made her think of childhood toys: the aquamarine and sugary pinks of Polly Pockets, the sweet, plasticky smell of doll limbs. Underwear as costume, ruffles and sequins and flounces, dress me up, undress me. Rounded surfaces that feigned to invite touch, but denied possession.

As though responding to an unseen signal, one of them kicked stacked inches of heel up in the air and spun horizontally, electric with speed, legs wrapped, hair flashing. She thought of the boys on the subway, in daylight, eons ago—*WHAT TIME IS IT? SHOWTIME!*

This is real, she cautioned herself. But this hard-faced bartender, those corpulent men enthroned with their champagne and unlit cigars, absurd and menacing in their sunglasses—all of them seemed like CGI figures. She turned to look at Bill, crackling and unkempt, crumpled over his drink, ignoring the scene behind him.

"What?" he said, smiling at her. Across the room a middle-aged, heavyset white woman, her blond hair an enormous, stiff confection, was dancing with a black guy whose gut protruded coyly, apologetically, over the top of his belt. They moved clumsily, their arms around each other as much from the need for ballast as from an indulgence of affection. Tripping a little, and swaying, and laughing, they stayed afloat, finding brief moments of grace.

Kate thought of the couple she and Inez had watched dancing in Washington Square, in the sunlight, and how they were echoed here, and how there seemed to be a consonance in things, in everything. How tempting to think this. And then she thought of George. The world was not a symphony.

Watching the dancers carried her into a kind of hypnosis. The movements they made were the same, the rhythms constant and recurring, as though all of them were animated by the same algorithm. The squat dip, the hip flick, the pole kick. Different bodies all enacting the same moves, over and over. She stared, drunk.

There were so many things to unlearn. The last room of breasts and thighs she remembered was the swimming pool changing room at school, where counteroffensive lesbophobia, the hysterical vigilance of its pitch, cut through the thick atmosphere and stuck in the back of your throat, sharp as cheap body spray.

He rested his fingers on her thigh, tentative.

"Is this okay?"

She was unsure whether he meant the situation or the touch. Being desired felt like desire. Recently, she'd registered that her sexual fantasies were all about being desired, and she felt bad about this. It seemed fucked—unfeministic. But then how could you call a fantasy fucked? You wanted what you wanted, didn't you?

She remembered the lipstick in her bag, imagined its

tight little capsule. Then she remembered the other thing in her bag, tucked tight between two bank cards.

"You okay?" he said. "We can go if you want."

"No. Let's stay."

The hunger in his eyes looked almost like fear. With some startled reflex, a wish to stamp out that look, she kissed him. He kissed back—surprised, then pleased? He grabbed her hair.

She pulled away and stared.

"Too much," he said.

She looked away, to the stage. *Look at them*, she instructed herself. *Look at their bodies. Like them.* There was a group by the stage's edge, where a woman customer with a dark bob sat stiffly in her chair, knees clamped flush together, heavy-handed and embarrassed while a dancer bounced vigorously on her lap. Men watched.

"Is there someone you like?" he asked.

She knew he meant *want*. But could you want without liking? Didn't they have to go together? Unlearn that, maybe. Her thoughts were bumping into each other.

"I'll be right back," she said.

The bathroom was a tiny red hole, one stall, one basin beneath a dim mirror scuffed and blackened around its edges. Inside the cubicle, she drew the lock and marveled that something as small as this modest rod of metal could seal a space into secrecy and safety. Shining her phone down on the ziplock bag, she keyed out a delicate fingernail. Leftovers, a gift from Inez. She'd gone with her to meet one of her men in black Lincolns, who murmured things like "How we doing, ladies," when they got in, and "Y'all have a beautiful night now" when they left—professional niceties, asinine as "have a nice day," but they made Kate happy. She emerged and angled her face into the mirror to see her pupils widen. It no longer made her feel like her lungs were exploding. They were only growing, church organs to fill cathedrals with sound. Light and noise erupted as the door swung open and belched a woman toward her, then closed, sealing the hush. It was the one with the frosted corona of hair that she'd seen dancing with the paunchy man.

Kate smiled at her in the mirror, and the woman returned the smile and said, "Oh, you're so pretty," as she collapsed a bit against the wall.

"It's just mascara!"

Womanhood, its rules. The nonacceptance of compliments. Kate found the wand in her purse, flourished it, and cried, "Have some!" giddy with her own Maybelline munificence, and the woman joined her beside the mirror in a space hardly big enough for their bodies. They settled into a convivial intimacy, talking to each other's reflection as they primped.

"You having a good night, sweetheart?" the woman asked. She was English, Kate realized. Essex, it sounded like.

"I am," Kate declared, but the woman was talking on, letting out a lovely loose jumble of words.

"I'm here with this feller and he's been buying me drinks all night and says he wants to marry me."

"Oh, I saw you two dancing!" Kate cried, smoothing away some Surrey with a patina of Brooklyn, since it was important, somehow, that she not be revealed as a compatriot. "I saw you dancing and I thought, they love each other!"

She inhaled deeply now because here it came, and to enjoy it you had to go with it, otherwise you'd get left behind. And then the woman turned, so she was right up against Kate, and put her hand heavily on Kate's shoulder. Rum and coke on her breath was rich and sweet. Kate steadied her.

"I do love him, you know? I really love him." She shook her head messily for emphasis, tipping forward so that her hair fell against her half-closed eyes. Kate prized the mascara from her hand.

"Oh, thank you, darling," the woman said. "I love him. You know?"

"I know." Kate nodded. "That's really great."

"It's really great," she repeated, patting Kate's shoulder. Then: "You're a love. You're so pretty. So pretty! Young thing like you. Wait till you get all old and fat like me."

"No!" Kate said. "No! You're gorgeous, really gorgeous."

She was, in a way. Her magnificent hair, her black sequins. Maybe she's born with it, maybe it's made.

"You," the woman began, then caught herself, swallowed.

"You need to be sick?" Kate asked.

"No, no, I'm all right, sweetheart." She looked up at

Kate's face again, her eyes sliding until they fastened into focus. "All right," said the woman. "Time to go in here." She jerked her head in the direction of the cubicle.

"You," she said, "you have a really, really great night, okay?"

"I will," Kate said. "And you, too. Have a really wonderful night."

Here she was, granting benedictions from the ladies' room! And it was sincere. She meant them as truly as she'd ever meant anything: it mattered enormously that this drunk blonde have a really wonderful night. Felt nothing but love for her, and love, too, for all those women outside. She was rushing with it, with generosity and magnitude. As she opened the bathroom door the noise and movement of the club hit her. Brighter, sharper, more alive. All of it—in this grand delusion—made and heightened for her. She moved through it thinking, *The sisterhood of strip club toilets.* A proverb. *The sisterhood of toilets is strongest in strip clubs.* She would carry it to him like a cat with a dead thing to lay at his toes.

He didn't see her. His back was to the room, talking to the bartender, who shot Kate a sour look and moved away the moment she took her seat next to him.

"Hey!" he said, surprised.

"Hi." A blissful purr, stretched out in the sun.

She closed her eyes to him and as the corners of her lips rose, goofy, irrepressible, she felt him lean in and catch that smile with his mouth, hands in her hair again.

She found the small square packet in her bag and pressed it into his palm, squeezing his fingers shut.

"You go now."

He looked dumbstruck. How good it felt—to bewilder him slightly.

"Oh, wow," he said. "It's been a minute."

Once he'd gone, she realized she'd forgotten to tell him the proverb. Something about sisterhood . . . something, whatever. It had faded away. She recrossed her legs on the stool, skin against skin, breathed deeply, and held the edge of the bar quite tightly, now that gravity seemed less sure of itself.

She looked behind her to find him and saw him disappear into the men's room. The way he moved through space was a thing she wanted to watch. Maybe she'd even tell him that—whisper it drunk, in his ear, the moment he was back. But you can ruin an easy thing by putting it into words. Tell a nonactor to just walk across the room and he'll move like he's on the moon, a man doing an impression of a man.

Her eyes found a woman dressed for a carnival—a turquoise thong, a glittering edifice of a bra, offering up her breasts to the world in triumph. The woman was making her way to a trio of seated men who puffed up as she came close, readying themselves, and she saw this and perched on the arm of a chair, whispered something into an ear.

Bill was smoothly taking his seat on the stool next to Kate. He followed her gaze.

"You found someone," he said. The drugs had made his eyes into soft flooded pools.

"I just smiled at her."

"I think," he said, speaking into her ear, "you should have a proper dance with her."

The opening bars of a Beyoncé song, a mighty *wohh-ohhh-ohhh*, came like some kind of summons. It was the same song that had been playing in the bodega that first evening, when she'd stood in horrified rapture in front of that humming cooler cabinet seconds before Inez walked in. When she was not yet Inez, a person, only a captivating unknown with no shoes on, buying cigarettes.

"Let's go somewhere else," Kate said, standing up.

"Yes," he said, both emphatic and dopey.

The natural trajectory was roofward, as if pleasure, like heat, always rose. Perhaps all she'd remember of these weeks was a series of rooftops. The high points. Kissing in a cab, the drinks from the club falling at their feet, rolling around with a clunk, and then they were pulling up beside a hotel, a place that was more a monument to monetized eroticism than the strip club itself.

On one of those very first days, those green and early days, stupefied with jet lag, inebriated with every breath of blue New York air, she'd duly walked the strip of an old elevated railroad spur that had been willed into verdancy. Every young person she passed had been a person pointing, telling their liberal visiting parents, "This hotel is famous for people fucking in the windows." And so now, in the elevator of the same hotel, his body supporting her body, her face in his shirt, the sandalwood-and-sweat musk again, she heard her question, mumbled and messy: "Are we going to fuck in the windows?"

"Do you want to fuck in the windows?" he said.

She closed her eyes.

As the elevator rose, he said, "You know that opening in Chelsea?" he said.

"What?"

"Those porny paintings."

Was he consciously avoiding the phrase "where we met"? The coupley cutesiness of it? She made a soft noise of assent. She felt she was barely there, could barely hear him.

"I realized something," he was saying, with the slow delicacy of the very fucked up. "*Reflective surfaces.* No one cared about the paintings, because they couldn't take their own picture in them. Right?"

He paused; she heard his thick, labored breathing.

"They couldn't see themselves in them. I don't mean figuratively. Actually. Actually see themselves. Their actual faces. All they want to take pictures of is themselves. Galleries should just have shows with reflective surfaces. Or outright mirrors. Give the people mirrors. Give the people what they want."

But then the elevator came to a halt and opened its doors so slowly that it seemed to Kate almost coy, as if done for emphasis. That terrestrial mess of cabs, lights, bar noise was way down below, and now here they were, delivered to an unpeopled altitude where all the colors were blue. No sound but the gentle hum of the pool. He rolled up his trousers and she sat beside him on the edge, calves submerged, kicking at dream speed through warm water that was the same artificially perfect shade of turquoise as the stripper's outfit.

When he lay back he pulled her down with him so that their backs were flat against stone still soaked with the day's warmth. She was thinking of this, of the stone's physical memory of sunlight, as she felt a familiar pain. It occurred to her, dimly, that she was wearing a white dress. She reached back in time blindly and failed to find the putting-on of this dress. Did not know where she'd been or who she'd been when she got dressed this morning. He turned his face to her. It seemed as if his features were dissolving, as though they were losing track of themselves.

"It was my birthday today," he said to her. "Yesterday," he corrected, because the glow at the edges of the sky was definite now; it was already tomorrow.

She concentrated on getting her mouth around the shape of the word: "Really?"

He said nothing.

"How old are you?" she managed.

It was what you asked, wasn't it? Slowly, he turned his face away, back to the sky.

"Twenty-one."

She was falling asleep when he spoke again.

"You want to swim? We should swim."

He sat up, turned to look at her. She shook her head.

And now he got to his feet, there on the edge, looming over her.

Campy and teasing, "*Sure* you're sure?" and then he began to fall, a fall that seemed to happen in slow motion until gravity ruined the illusion.

Surfacing, scowling and gasping and whipping water and hair off his face, he looked the way people always do when they surface from swimming pools: as if they hadn't expected to get wet. He pushed through the weight of the water to take hold of her ankles, run his hands up her calves.

She was not so drunk, she observed, to not be glad she'd shaved her legs. He tugged; she resisted. He stopped; she relented. And then she allowed herself to be pulled in. Cotton got soaked through and clung to her skin, sucked away, clapped back.

"I'm an artist in residence," he said, mockery dancing around the words. She thought perhaps he was quoting someone or something. He persisted. "They give me a room here, for the summer. I'm meant to write in the room."

△▽△

It was a small room, but one whole wall of it was a window, making a perfect square of city—an Instagram square. Their clothes made the sheets wet, imbuing them with the tang of chlorine, a smell she'd always associate with childhood. Drunk fingers finally yielded a common nakedness, the shock of the weight of him, the unfamiliar contours of his skull under her fingers, this great sudden strangeness of a body.

At some point her hand pushed his head between her legs, his sodden hair around and between her knuckles, and she imagined she could taste it, her own body, but then, as if imagining could create becoming, his mouth was on hers, his slightly bloodied lips, and then time was splitting into three: the happening, the having happened, and the comprehending of both, which was its own dimension as her pleasure rose.

She woke with a full bladder, and when she sat, head bowed between her thighs to watch clots of blood fall with her urine into the bowl, it made her skull surge with disgust and beauty. Once she'd flushed and washed cold water over her hands, wrist, and face, she steadied herself in the bathroom doorway and looked at the bed.

The sheets were twisted and falling off the end. On the floor: her own peach-colored briefs, twisted, stained. The white dress was a dirt-streaked, pool-damp crumple of fabric beside an empty bottle. On the bedside table, a pair of plastic cups, which she remembered grabbing from above the basin and ripping from their cellophane. The inches of champagne, effervescence gone.

There was a spectacular crimson stain the shape of Australia, a Rorschach shout, on the sheets. In this moment it seemed like some exultant rejoinder to a red wine spill on a tablecloth, one night in London a thousand years ago. She was wearing just his boxers and enjoying it, a tampon string tickling her thigh. He was flat on his back, arms flung wide in an attitude of surrender that looked both abject and luxurious. His head was to one side, mouth slack with sleep. The fingers of his right hand were trailing the stain's eastern border.

They'd leave it behind, that stain; someone else's problem. A maid, someone she'd never meet, would strip and bleach these bloodied sheets, maybe muttering some perfunctory prayer for a girl's lost virginity. It was discomfiting to think of how many people had slept in this same bed, all their dreams and sex and breath and sweat.

She curled herself under his arm. He stirred, stretched, a lazy stiffening of his dick.

"Who did that man mistake me for?" she said.

There was a pause, and part of her wanted him not to respond. Total silence, absolute peace, complete stillness.

"What?" he said. He sounded annoyed.

"The fat and gross old man last night in the hat who said something about legal age."

He was quiet for a moment, then muttered, "Oh, fuck that guy."

Yes, she thought. Fine. *Fuck him*, he didn't matter.

23

Inez took off her apron and let it fall to the floor. Heather was in the stockroom, sitting on a plastic crate, her hand over her mouth in a quaint expression that seemed to say *Oh my*.

"Yo, boss lady."

Her boss looked up from her screen.

"Oh, Inez," she murmured. She shook her head as she inhaled. She sounded appalled, but sweetly so.

"What?"

"I'm reading these Yelp comments," she said. "Is it true you told a customer he was too fat to have a cookie?"

Inez squinted for a moment, trying to remember. It sounded likely, to be honest. Then he materialized in her mind: the awful guy with the enormous ginger beard who'd swaggered up to the counter talking loudly into his phone, thereby incurring Inez's loathing before she even heard him say, "Nah, dog, she was too ugly to fuck."

"Yeah, but he was a misogynist. And also he *was* fat. Like, super fat. Like, no-more-cookies-for-you fat."

Heather gave her a beseeching look.

"Inez," she began, hopelessly. Then, steeling herself: "We've got to have a talk."

"I'm going, by the way. Like . . . I'm *leaving* leaving."

"You're quitting?"

Inez nodded.

"Oh."

"So now you don't have to fire me. Cool, right?"

"Oh, man." Heather sighed. "Well, yeah, okay, then."

Inez raised her palm for a high five. Heather looked at it for a moment, then weakly complied. "So what will you do?" she asked.

"Everyone seems, like, weirdly obsessed with asking me that. Like I've got cancer or something or I'm going to be homeless. I'm *fine*."

Heather nodded, smiled. "Yep," she said.

An awkward pause. Inez made to go.

"Hey," Heather added, pointing to a large package resting against sacks of beans. "Don't forget that."

Inez stared at it for a blank second before she remembered what was inside: silver high-heeled sandals that cost a hundred dollars more than she made in a month here. The very last of the Carlos spoils. She hiked it up under her right arm.

"Later, Heather. Thanks for being a chill boss."

They were princessy shoes, Cinderella-ish, and she thought of Kate, transformed by the fairy dust of drugs. *She shall go to the ball.*

Inez pulled out her phone. When Kate answered after

four rings it was with an uncertain "hello?" as if she didn't trust the object in her hand.

"Meet me in Tompkins Square in half an hour, I've got a surprise for you."

△▽△

Getting pizza delivered to the park was what Inez liked to think of as a *signature move*, a summertime coup. The delivery boy arrived at the eastern entrance at the same time she did, gratifyingly bewildered as she accosted him, called him "buddy," and pushed a fistful of dollars into his hand. She had successfully claimed a whole bench by the time Kate arrived. The shoes were stashed beneath her, the pizza box beside her. The presence of pizza seemed to make Kate laugh.

"Hope you're hungry," Inez said, flipping the lid open. She watched Kate pick all the curled discs of pepperoni off her slice, one by one.

Kate looked up. "Vegetarian," she said, apologetically. She'd made a little pile of them, a tiny bonfire.

"I die if I don't eat meat every day," Inez said. "Seriously."

She pinched up Kate's pepperoni pile, sprinkled it across her own slice, then wiped her fingers on a nest of paper napkins, streaking them orange with an oily residue.

They ate in silence for a while. Inez considered telling Kate she'd just quit her job. She wondered how long, also, she could keep it from Bill and Cara. Her mother had sent five texts today about college applications. The last one had devolved to all caps: *PLEASE RESPOND I AM WORRIED ABOUT YOUR FUTURE.* Unhinged. What, exactly, was she worried about? What was the Future, in her mind, and why did it get her panties in a wad?

"Hey," Inez heard herself say. "You went to college, right?"

"College? University. Yeah."

"My parents want me to go to college. They won't shut up about it. Which is frankly fucking hypocritical of my dad, because he dropped out of high school."

"What does he do?"

"Good question," Inez said. She sighed, lolled her head backward. "Like, nothing. Teaches rich-kid idiots. Obsesses about coffee beans. Gets drunk all the time. He's kind of pathetic, to be honest." With effort, she lifted her head. "Was it a total waste of time, then, college?"

Kate didn't laugh at this. She looked as if she were at a college interview. She even put her slice down to concentrate, it seemed, on thinking her way to an answer.

Finally: "Some bits, yeah. We had to read a lot of ancient dead poets and stuff. It wasn't really . . . *real*. It didn't really get me anywhere. But . . . I didn't really know—*don't* really know—where I want to go. Hence . . ."

Kate made a vague movement of her hands: *Here I am, aimless, eating pizza in this park with you.* She added: "Why? I mean, why do you ask?"

Inviting Kate to the roof that night had been why the fuck not, whatever, take it or leave it. But since then, it had become important to keep her. Inez didn't know why. It was just a sense that Kate knew things that she needed to know, too. She ignored her question, asked her another instead.

"You know what's funny?"

"What?"

"You're smarter than all of us," Inez said. "And yet you act like . . ."

Inez caved her shoulders inward, widened her eyes into what she hoped was cartoon abjection, set her mouth into a moronic moue—a grotesque of meekness.

Kate winced. "Every time you compliment me," she said, "you also insult me."

"Yeah, well. You can take it."

Kate looked her in the eye.

"You're like this walking dictionary thing," Inez persisted. "But you walk around like someone just shit on your shoes."

And as she said the word, she remembered.

"Oh, hey, do you want your surprise or not?"

"I thought this was the surprise," Kate said.

"Pizza? You're way too easily pleased."

Inez drew the parcel out from under her feet. "Is it your birthday?" she said. "Is it Christmas? Is it Hanukkah?"

Kate shook her head, laughing, as Inez shoved the parcel on her lap.

"So why the fuck am I giving you a present?"

Kate stared at it, speechless, like she'd never been given a gift before.

"Oh my god, *open it*, for fuck sake!"

And she did, slow enough to make Inez want to scream. When she eventually drew out one of the shoes, held it up to behold the spike of its heel and the silver rib cage of its structure, the red of its underside, she said, "Oh my god, Inez. Where did these . . ."

"You think I stole them!" Inez said.

"Did you?"

"I can categorically fucking swear that I did not steal them. They were a gift. Well, a payment."

"Payment?"

"Just try them on!"

She watched her falter.

"They're really amazing," Kate said. "But I can't wear high heels."

"Why not, you got some kind of spinal injury?"

"No, but I'll incur one if I walk around in these."

"'Incur'!" she said, fluting the word in mockery. "Don't be such a pussy. You're going to wear them. You're going to wear them and know that your vagina will destroy any man that comes in your path."

"Oh god!" Kate said, and she was going red, of course, palm over her face to hide it, or to emphasize it. It was still so easy to embarrass her. But here she went, shedding those horrible plastic flip-flops and dutifully maneuvering her way into the shoes, buckling their tiny straps. When she stood up, unsteadily, she was six inches taller. Holding her arms out, she began to revolve, awkwardly, for Inez's appraisal.

"Hot," Inez said. She lit another cigarette. When Kate had dismounted, removed them, and carefully rewrapped them in their tissue paper, unease arrived in her face, as if there might be something awful in the juxtaposition of these two cardboard boxes on a bench—one grease-stained and strewn with crusts greebled with cheese shrapnel, the other holding designer shoes worth a hundred large pepperoni pies.

Well, deal with it, Inez thought. This is how it is.

"Thanks, Inez," Kate said. "They're amazing."

Inez kept smoking. This whole exchange, somehow, had irritated her.

"I'm thinking about getting a new tattoo," she said. "Basquiat."

"Cool," Kate murmured, and Inez could tell she was straining to sound encouraging, or impressed, or approving.

"Stick 'n' poke."

"What?"

Inez made a jabbing motion at Kate. "Like that. Stick 'n' poke. My friend does them. The pain's the best bit. You ever stubbed out a cigarette on yourself?"

A beat.

"Inez," Kate said heavily. "What do *you* think?"

She couldn't help laughing at that.

"I used to do it all the time when I was like thirteen," Inez said. "I *loved* it."

A tart shiver of pleasure ran through her at the memory. The dare, the doing it, the mark it made.

"Why?"

"And then my mom saw it and freaked the living fuck out and sent me to a self-harm specialist. *Self-harm.* Fucking insulting! Like I was some emo loser writing her Live Journal and dyeing purple streaks in her hair."

"So it wasn't self-harm?"

"No!" She realized she was almost shouting. "I was having the time of my life. It was . . . fuck, I can't explain. It was like . . ."

"A turn-on?" Kate said.

Inez smoked some more. "Whatever. Maybe. You're smart. And a perv."

"You liked it because the pain reminded you that you were a body? And the body was yours and you had the power to burn it or do whatever you—"

"I'm going to give you another present." Inez lifted her cigarette hand. She felt like a dancer, in the way a great one can make the body emit meaning before he or she even moves. She took a quick drag, and then, in a manner that felt both tender and procedural, seized Kate's pale arm, turned it over, and smoothly introduced the cigarette's glowing end to the skin. A tiny hiss, a sweet soft sound, and Inez felt the voltage jolt, heard Kate's guttural intake of air, and gripped the arm harder as it happened. Kate's eyes were wide with tears.

"Feels good, right?"

No, Kate mouthed, no sound . . . And then, her voice

high and keening: "No, it hurts like *fuck*. You crazy, crazy *fucking* bitch."

"You're mine now," Inez said. "I left my mark on you."

And when Kate just stared at her, blinking and heaving air in and out of her mouth, Inez grabbed her hand: "Come on, you need a drink."

She flicked the butt across the path as they walked. Then shots of mezcal in the bar on the corner of the park. Kate kept staring at the mark on her arm, could not leave it alone.

"Here," Inez said, setting an ice cube on the flesh. "Keep it there."

24

Seventeen minutes now. Three more and he would have to go. He didn't want to, but there was such a thing as dignity, and waiting twenty minutes on a sweltering stoop had no place in his concept of it. He unfolded *The New York Review of Books*, shook it stiff, and glared at the print, willing it to seize him.

Here was the thing, though: Kate was never late. She was chronically punctual, in fact. Had never, he suspected, stood anyone up in her life. And so now a new sensation: alarm. Might something have happened to her? Anything could happen to a person, after all. Struck by lightning, struck by a truck, struck by freak sudden illness. Things struck people. And, oh god, how awful it would be, to have to present himself to some nurse in an ER, be cast in the role of doting older boyfriend. Horror. To have to sit by a bedside, being appropriately grief-stricken. He put the magazine down, looked along the street at all its pedestrians who were not her, picked it up again, turned the page, and began reading.

A pair of pale knees had materialized. He sensed

they'd been there for some seconds before he'd noticed them.

"Sorry," she said, standing before him, shining, gloriously unsorry. He looked at her and at the large parcel under her arm, and she walked past him, up the steps, unlocking the door, while he gathered himself.

He'd come to think in these last weeks that her sexual boldness had a burlesque quality to it—that semi-stifled smile as she looked up at him before fellatio—an imitation of an imitation of porn? Today, though, there was some authentic black charge in her, and it unsettled him as much as it aroused him. Astride him, claiming him, her palm pushed into the side of his face, she was punitive.

He rose to it, an animal back at her, and it didn't seem like her body he wrestled, not *her* hips that he flipped and then pinned down, her face pressed into the pillow, her fingers clawed on the sheets, but something in him, some element that would overtake who he was if he didn't fuck it harder than it was fucking him. It was only when he'd collapsed into the sheen of her back, warm and pale and heaving beneath him, that he realized she'd come with him.

Dazed, he could sense the afterglow of the sound she'd made, a noise he'd been deaf to in the moment. He rolled away, pulling the sheet over him. He was trembling a little, like he'd just got some bad news. The heat, maybe, from sitting on that stoop in the sun for so long.

He glanced at her. He had a ridiculous, momentary idea that she might be dead. When he saw the red mark now, when it flashed there, livid on her forearm as she rolled away, he went cold with guilt and horror, believing it was his doing. That in his animal state he'd burned her, or bitten her—committed the violence that had left such a lurid mark.

"Jesus," he said, propped up on an elbow. He grabbed her forearm and she yanked it away.

"What the fuck, Kate?"

They never used names. Her eyes opened.

"The thing on your arm."

"Cigarette," she muttered.

"What the fuck. Who did it?"

Because now there was that icy vertigo of time and place: *Inez used to do this.* The same spot, the middle of the inner forearm.

"I did it myself," she said, and there was a lie in it, he could tell. He waited, just him and his heart, a wet pouch pumping in his ribs. She scooted beneath the sheets, pulling them up over her chest.

"I'm freaked out," he said. And then: "You're freaking me out. My daughter used to do this."

"Calm down," she said quietly. "It was an accident, just a mistake. It doesn't mean anything."

"How do you give yourself a cigarette burn by mistake?"

He could hear how hysterical he sounded; screeching, almost. He stood up, yanked on his jeans, buckled them furiously. He could feel her watching him.

"Why are you so worked up about it?" she said.

"Burning holes in one's own flesh is normal? Yeah,

crazy of me to *get worked up*. Excuse me while I take this lighter and scorch a line into my own face."

He picked up the yellow lighter from the nightstand, wielded it weakly, and then flung it across the room without conviction. It skidded into a corner. Kate stared at it. He knew how much she hated losing things, knew she'd be bothered—wanting it, no doubt, back in its proper place. But she didn't move, stayed motionless. There was some melodrama of female vulnerability to her in that sheet, something almost Victorian about the sight.

He sat back down on the bed.

"Why did you come to that reading?" he said.

"What?"

"Why did you seek me out? After that shitty fucking dinner where you just blushed and mumbled things into your kale? Why would you pursue me after that?"

"'Pursue'!" she said. "You make me sound so predatory!"

"Never mind." But of course, he did. "I suppose I just have no idea why you would want to see me after that. Why you'd come see me."

"Well, why did you ask me for a drink afterward, then? If you weren't happy to see me?"

"I didn't say I wasn't 'happy to see you.'"

He winced at the phrase. Words that had no dignity after being so double entendred. *Is that a gun in your pocket or . . .*

"This has all gotten really weird."

"Yeah," Kate said, pointedly, as in, *and it's your fault.*

He brought his hands to his eyes, then let his hands fall, and had a sense, now, of finally pulling over, stopping the car, and switching the engine off. So that they were just here, trip terminated, on the hard shoulder.

"Are you a tourist here?" he said, in a small way.

"A tourist?"

With some difficulty he willed some air into his body. "I mean, a tourist for me."

She said nothing. He could feel her listening as a kind of susurration.

"What I mean is: I'm old. Middle-aged. I live here. I've always lived here."

These were statements and yet they sounded like pleas. He shouldn't have to feel this, he thought, let alone have to say it.

"You're twenty-five. I don't know why you're here. Whether you're on vacation here or what. Or what you want. I don't know what you want. What do you want? I wrote a book people gave a shit about for whatever reason and then it was a movie and the movie star died. That's it, you know? There's nothing else. I've done *nothing* else. And people don't change."

People my age, he thought. Because yes, she had changed. That, in fact, was the fucked-up thing about all this, the way she'd been a series of slightly different people each time they met.

Earlier, moments ago: the palm of her hand spread on his face with force, no affection.

She said something and he didn't hear.

"I said I don't know what I'm doing here." She was miserably hunched, her tone both peevish and full of pity. "I told you that when we first . . . I told you I'm just here."

"You can't just be here," he snapped. Then, more gently: "You know, it's okay to want things."

He saw an odd ingenuousness in her expression now, as if something important had just occurred to her.

"I wanted an expensive lipstick," she said flatly.

He stared at her. She must have known, have seen how incredibly weird he found her in this moment.

"And I bought it," she went on. "It has a stupid name."

He realized he needed to swallow, and doing so proved to be a bit of a challenge.

Cautiously: "What's it called?"

She said nothing as she got up, shuffling off in her absurd bedsheet toga. She still didn't speak as she returned and uncapped the lipstick. Slowly, she drew a bright red line down the length of his arm, while he looked on, saying nothing at all.

25

September came and still the afternoons swelled to split with heat. Slow days turning purple, the charge building, until Kate felt she could strike a match on the air itself and the city might explode. When the sky broke, the sound and smell of rain was accompanied by shrill, ecstatic shrieks rising up from women below the windows, and she loved to watch them holding jackets over their heads and running in heels for cabs or doorways, a tottering that delighted in itself, happily hobbled by glamour. The red mark had scabbed and she'd had to fight the urge to pick at it. She'd replayed the way in which the underside of her forearm, translucent, blue veins beneath, had seemed to no longer belong to her when Inez held it. The second in which Inez grabbed tighter, when her arm was a piece of flesh in the vise of longer, stronger, younger fingers. Bill taking her calves in his hand in the rooftop pool, pulling her in with him.

One night he'd said, incredulous, "You've never seen *Do the Right Thing*?"

She'd refused to corroborate her own ignorance. After

he showed her the scene on YouTube, she smacked her laptop shut, went to the icebox, and returned with one ice cube in her mouth and three in her fist.

Today, the sky above the air conditioner was darkening—another dramatic flush of violent indigo.

"It's coming," she said to him.

Bill had his back to her, inspecting a miniature Tibetan singing bowl. He turned, held it up, unlit cigarette in his other hand.

"Who the fuck is this lady, again?" he said mildly, inspecting its bottom.

"There's a thunderstorm coming," she said.

He put the bowl back.

"She has so much . . . *stuff.*"

"Don't you have stuff?" she said.

He stood there and did that trick of his with bar matches, the bending back and snap that made one flare. She looked away. What a little performance. And then as he walked about the room, smoking, she thought maybe it hadn't been a performance after all.

"I guess by 'stuff,'" he said, grinning, "I mean hippie-dippie middle-aged-lady crap."

"Rude."

He looked out the window, smoking.

"It's going to storm," he said.

It was always at her place, not his, and she'd never questioned this. At first, she'd understood that there would be some kind of transgression, mutually unwelcome, in setting foot in his family home, toys on the floor. But now the request left her mouth like some bird out of a magician's hat: "Tell me about your daughter." She could hear the panicky flap of its wings, the trite surprise of it in the air.

He turned from the window and it seemed to Kate as if he were staring at the question, not at her—as if he and her inquiry had entered into some silent showdown. He smoked, looked away, arms folded, and spoke. When he used the phrase "very beautiful" the imagined toys evaporated.

"I mean, I know every idiot thinks so," he muttered on, drily, "but this is just objective. Model scouts run after her on the street. It's that."

The gloom and weight in his voice made her disinclined to ask him anything else, but now she had to, because she knew the answer already. How it did and did not matter. It was why she'd seen something familiar in his eyes at that gallery. The manic flare of his dread at her cigarette burn. *My daughter used to do this.* It was just a shadow on her skin now, that burn. You'd have to know it was there to see it.

"What's her name?" she said.

△▽△

It felt good, she told herself, to get out of Manhattan, to leave the high reek of hot garbage and take the L to Bushwick. As she stepped into the street to cross, two young men on skateboards swept past her, and she jumped back. They sped down the middle of the road, flying, yelling happily to each other, chased by their own slender shadows, which stretched twice their height behind them. During these weeks, Inez would tell her to come meet her on the roof—peremptory, misspelt texts—and Kate would obey, because she always did. Today, despite summoning her, Inez seemed irritated by her presence. It had been something about the shoes, Kate thought. It had been weird since the shoes. Had she not expressed enough gratitude? It had been weeks ago now; Inez should be over it. As a gift, they had confounded Kate. As an object, in fact—as shoes themselves—they confounded her. Who could walk in them, for one thing? Then she'd looked them up on eBay and the cost had made her actually gasp.

Inez, cross-legged, rolled a joint, hair hanging in her face.

"Did you ever find the right Kate?" Kate said.

"Huh?"

Inez sounded stupid when she said that, dumbly American. Every "huh?" made her beautiful face look vacant, begging for a slap. How could you forget the way you met someone? Maybe the main difference between the ages of nineteen and twenty-five came down to the velocity of time, not its overall accounting. For Kate, each accelerating year upon the next made her clutch flotsam like this—a moment of meeting—as a talisman against her disappearing youth.

Kate said, "You know when I met you, in the park,

in Washington Square." She was impatient. She'd just wanted some small moment of nostalgia, and felt shamed now for wanting it, for trying to orchestrate sentimentality. "You were waiting for a Kate."

"How the fuck," Inez said, "do you remember that?" She passed the joint, which Kate took silently.

"Everyone's being kicked out, by the way," Inez said, hoarse.

"What?"

"Of here! Redevelopment. Condos. It's over."

The doom in Inez's voice cast "it" as an all-obliterating melodrama: the building, the party, the summer, Bushwick, Brooklyn itself. All of it.

"I'm sorry. What are you . . . What's everyone doing?"

"They've all got plans," Inez said, a snarl of bitterness. "Gabe's fucking off to Berlin to play techno to idiots. Dana's going to be a *teacher*. Kim landed some fancy fashion PR job."

"Good for her?" Kate ventured.

Inez took a savage gulp of her beer. "You're probably fucking off back home, too, right?"

Kate found no answer, only a craven kind of dodge. "But what will you do?"

"Jesus fuck, why is everyone asking me that?"

"College?" Kate suggested thinly. "You mentioned college."

"My dad is obsessed with that. Which is fucking hypocritical, since he never went."

It continued to seem bizarre to Kate that Inez should

have parents. Beneath the shock of knowing she was Bill's daughter, a fact Kate had zero inclination to mention in Inez's presence, there was the shock of her being *anyone's* daughter. Some people just didn't seem parented—didn't seem as if they had ever been a kid, had ever been anything other than their fully formed, half-feral selves.

"Hello?" Inez snapped.

"Sorry," she said. Then: "I suppose . . . I suppose that parents always want to correct their own mistakes through their children." And now she heard how teacherly her words sounded.

The look Inez gave her was steady, weighted. There was a black patience to it, as if she would hold out for as long as it took for Kate to wither. Kate felt the unsaid sneer: *Who are you?*

"Whatever," Inez said. "We're having a massive Halloween party. Saturday before. You have to come. One last blowout before it's over. And then—" she paused to take a very slow toke, a stagey calm to her motions "—then we're going to burn the place to the ground."

Kate's laugh was false nerves. The weed was making her feel twitchy, making this roof seem too big, the drop beneath them too far.

"You have to come," Inez said, holding out the joint to her again.

"Okay."

"And you have to come in costume. A good one. Don't even think about pulling some bunny ears shit."

"Shall we go inside? It's kind of cold."

She wished she'd brought a sweater. Wished her legs weren't bare.

"Who did you go meet the other night?" Inez asked. "Don't try and play dumb. Who is she?"

"*She*?" Kate squawked. And then she realized it had been a trap. Inez was laughing at her.

"Don't all the ladies love this hair?" Inez said, giving a tuft a quick yank. "I thought you were having a whole lez awakening. Ditching the Brit boyfriend et cetera. No?"

Kate covered her face.

"Oh, what, you embarrassed?"

"I'm so cold, can we please go in?"

"Not until you tell me who you're fucking. Also, you should bring him to the party."

And now Kate diagnosed the feeling within her. It wasn't the weed, or it wasn't just the weed. It was guilt, the worm of it. Her failure to connect this world, in which a version of her fucked this used-to-be-famous American writer, to the other world, the left-behind world, in which George attended dinner parties in Clapham without her, then went home to sit at his laptop to write her long e-mails describing his night. There was something earnest and self-conscious in these overwritten missives, as if he were penning his aperçus for some future biographer, who'd recall the months in which *a love affair became a long-distance correspondence maintained between London and New York*. He had, she realized, no idea. No idea at all. And his ignorance somehow made her furious.

Inez was snapping her fingers in her face.

"You alive in there?"

"I'm realizing I'm a shit person."

She was shivering quite violently now.

Inez made a noise of exasperation, shrugged off her own jacket, and draped it, inexpertly, around Kate's shoulders.

"No, seriously. I've done a terrible thing. I've cheated. I've been cheating and I just haven't even really thought about it until now."

Inez had a way of rolling her eyes, half-crossing them, and then letting her eyelids quiver as if from impending death.

If Kate couldn't make her understand, if she couldn't make Inez see, then she was all alone with her guilt and her unreasonable anger. So she had to go now, she had to get back to the apartment and get on Skype and tell him everything, tell him how she'd betrayed him and was ending it and he shouldn't forgive her. She wouldn't even give him a chance to say anything, she thought.

"Dude, it's two in the morning in England."

"What?" Kate said.

"Chill, okay? Just chill. I'm making you a cup of Sleepytime."

And, wearing Inez's jacket like a sorry cape, sleeves lolling empty off her shoulders, she allowed herself to be led indoors, where things were smaller, where there was a kitchen, and a kettle, and mugs, and an array of other objects all convinced of their own normality.

△▽△

When it came to telling him, days later, she felt very little. Bill had offered her one of his tiny sky-blue pills and she'd saved it, wrapped in a square of bathroom tissue, and popped it before she did the dishes, wiped down the counters, Swiffered the floor. It felt necessary to put the place in order first. It meant that when she came to her laptop she could feel a cool proficiency. Dishes washed, stacked, dried, and now this, the final task to complete, while seated quite formally at the stranger's kitchen table.

It seemed both impossible and marvelous that you could effect such a breakage with only words, that you could end a relationship just by speaking a phrase, like a magician, or a judge, or an auctioneer. She'd rehearsed certain phrases over and over, tested different permutations, all fake and empty for having been parroted by people real and fictional for decades and decades. The sentence that ended it was purely procedural, less like speaking and more like signing some official paperwork.

Still, it was the realest George had been in weeks. When he began to weep, silently, motionlessly, she could taste the tears, and it was terrible. The more she didn't want to, the more she felt the salty sooth of them. He shut it down, said there was nothing more to say, and she did not protest.

She closed the laptop and looked at the immaculate kitchen in its silence, then walked into the pine-fresh bathroom and went to her knees, to a fetal pose, and pressed her face against the chilly clean tiles of the floor. She was a young person, in an old person's apartment, in a ball on the floor. No one came to stop her, and the realization that no one would, not for months at least—that she could stay here, insane and immobile on the floor—snatched at her throat and she sat up, horrified.

Joni Mitchell was sitting in the doorway, placidly licking a paw, the feline equivalent of a bitch filing her nails.

"You don't care," Kate said, becoming a woman talking to a stranger's cat. And the word *care*, the very idea of not caring, brought back the sight of George's eyes pooling, the way he swallowed, the jump of his Adam's apple, and how this had only sent the tears spilling down his face, and now something broke in Kate's chest and it wasn't her own pain, but his. His pain of her own doing.

She got up and left, and as she walked to Tompkins Square she remembered, not knowing why, the recently bereaved couple who'd come for Sunday lunch when she was eleven, how she'd helped her mum whip the cream for the apple pie but had held the beaters in it for too long, so that tiny flecks of yellow appeared—cream turned to butter—and how, mortified, she'd begged her mother not to tell the bereaved couple what she'd done. The shame at ruining a dessert for adults who'd lost their teenage son. As she'd covertly watched the dead son's mother trying to force one forkful of pie and too-thick cream into her mouth, Kate had understood the phrase "holding it together" as a bodily reality rather than an idiom. It did not mean putting on lipstick and a brave smile. It meant the severe physical effort required to hold on to your body as it roiled with forces that threatened to tear it apart, to send every atom hurling in a thousand different directions, because that was how hard the pain seemed to scream. It meant the will, the force, of holding your physical being in one place, intact. Eleven-year-old Kate, destroyer of cream, Kate the wretched overchurner, had watched the bereaved mother's fingers tremble, had faced the wild flash of her eyes as they rolled and tried to stay still, and had shrunk with fear at the mother's voice, taut as the string of a bow. Beside the mother was the bereaved father, whom grief had made radiant.

Kate was not radiant. She was another sad girl crying alone on the streets of New York City, still weeping when she reached the park and not caring who saw. She walked curving paths through the scorched grass. It was a cooler afternoon now, and she reminded herself that this was the same place she'd been that first night, the night she'd heard fireworks and thought they were bombs. The weight of all that had passed, or all that hadn't, made this memory somehow agonizing: the inadequacy of her tragedy, the unfairness of its feeling so outweighing its facts.

And here was the ancient lady in pink, still sparring, feebly. Kate wanted to sob when she saw her, wanted, specifically, to hold that sob in her rib cage like a fist and see what it could do.

She felt weird today and she did not know why. And not knowing was making her feel insane, twitchy. It was something, Inez thought, about having made Kate tea. Because she kept thinking about it—that tea with the moronic bear on the box, lolling in its pajamas and frilly nightcap. Now she realized that she had never made someone a cup of tea before this moment. That was just a plain fact and it seemed significant. The thing was, it had made her feel much older, suddenly, to do this for Kate, just the two of them, alone in the kitchen, not saying much.

Kate caught it the moment she stepped out the door:
that edge in the blue air, among the leaf dust and bonfire smoke and cold soil—a note of summer's mortality.
Somehow, it was mid-October already.

Later that day, she found herself typing her old post-
code into a blinking search bar, feeling the same faint
mixture of titillation and disgust, an unpleasant sensation of lightness, that her occasional online porn searches
brought her. She hit RETURN hard: *take me there now.*
And there it was, a satellite image of her childhood home,
zoomed in so she was hovering above it at a vulture
vantage. The house looked crouched and, in its slightly
blurred state, a little vulnerable, a little compromised. A
place she no longer lived. There was her childhood sand-
pit, the bright red plastic square of it flat on the lawn. It
was no longer really there. Sally had finally got rid of it
a year or so back, passed it on to some neighbor's kid,
but here, in virtuality, it was permanent, like a small flag
waving to her from her past.

Within a week there was snow in New York, sudden

and freakish. No one was ready for it, but Kate, with her small cheap suitcase of summer things, was more than un-prepared—she was ambushed. She bought dead women's clothes in thrift stores. Tweedish slacks, which bore the label of some long-gone ladies' department store, a cable-knit sweater, a Navajo patterned blanket to wear as a scarf. They smelled sensible, in the way of old paperbacks, or houses with creaking wood floors. Bill had watched her peel off snow-drenched running shoes one afternoon—salt grit ringing the legs of her jeans—and showed up the next day holding something.

"Wanted to drop these off," he said. A pair of large and ugly snow boots, bright red and puffy. It was declara-tive, the way he set them down on the kitchen table.

"My daughter's," he offered. "She never wore them."

She stared at them. Shoes on a table were bad luck. Or did that superstition apply only in England?

"What," he said, all out of patience, all out of charm.

"These boots belong to Inez?"

He whipped his scarf off and frowned.

"How do you know her name?"

"You told me!" she said. And it felt like a lie. The real lie, of course, was the omission. He still had no idea that she knew her.

She'd seen all this before, she thought, the shoes on the table, him whipping his scarf off. Déjà vu was a neu-rological accident of accordance. Someone had explained it to her once, but she'd forgotten the details. Something about different parts of the brain. This seemed, though, like a sick synchronism of people and things, not a science of neurons. Also, it all seemed very boring.

"You want me to just take them back?" he said, flapping his arms.

"No," she managed. "I need them," she said, adding: "For the snow."

"For the snow . . ."

"Thanks," she said. "Sorry, I meant to say thanks."

"Sure," he said, flat with irony. He picked up his scarf, was already opening and out the door, an exit too abrupt for her to find a "Bye."

She sat and eyed the boots, the fat red accusation of them. And then picked them up and put them on.

Far away, academic terms had begun, a new school year. For the first time in her life these periods of time had nothing to do with her. She didn't care. She was here, in dead people's clothes and borrowed boots, out of time, and no one stopped her. Except, as she was coming down the steps outside, for a pair of tourists—an Italian couple?—the woman sweetly beseeching, and her husband stiff and silent and shy beside her, who wanted directions, they were looking for Bleecker Street, and Kate was so pleased to be asked—so giddy to be identified, albeit incorrectly, as someone who knew where she was going—that she told them absolute nonsense, with supreme, emphatic confidence. *Straight on here, and then second right, and then a left, and it's right there*, pointing the way, smiling a big true smile. They beamed back and thanked her and made off happily in the wrong direction.

The subway walls this week were plastered with movie posters showing a New York under destruction. Tidal waves, plagues, explosions. A city being razed. The smashed and sundered wrist of toppled Lady Liberty, severed in the smoking wreckage, stone fingers still grasping the torch. And, striding from the wreckage, a movie star, grim-faced, bowlegged, fists by his sides, buff in a tight black leather getup, the man who will save us all. *In a world*, growled the virile voice-over in her head. *This season*. But which season, what *was* the season? Poor planet, so abused, so confused.

As she walked she became aware of the flash of her red boots walking beside her, reflected in the store windows. She felt a need to be away from all this, from streets and sidewalks, from surfaces that played her moving image back to her. To find grass and trees instead: natural things that reflected nothing.

Prospect Park in the snow was dazzling, full of children in bright clothes, shrieking. She found a bench, took a banana from her bag, and as she bit into it two things happened with perfect and horrible synchronicity. She saw the corpse of a white rabbit, its head clean gone, resting in a kind of poetic surrender beneath the tree opposite her, and there was at the same time the sound and sensation of her phone in her pocket. The bite of banana sat in her mouth like shame. She stared at the dead rabbit, its bloodless white fur, then stared at her phone. Another message from Inez that she wouldn't answer, and then a text from Bill. Both of them were telling her to come to parties tonight.

△▽△

The snow lasted one more day and then, on the Saturday before Halloween, it felt like the first day of summer again. The whole city was melting, dripping, leaves slick and shining, gutters gushing, light catching drips from scaffolding. Kate flung open the windows of the apartment and stuck her head out into the mild air. Everyone in T-shirts, coats over their arms, fanning themselves, amid crusted islands of snow like sponges with all the water sucked out of them. Bill's text had been a summons. *Old friend throwing a birthday/halloween blowout tonight, come.* No question mark.

She decided she'd wear the shoes as a sort of costume. The towering, silvered, fuck-me edifices from Inez, not her other pair, the boots. To step in and strap on was to experience the world from a new vantage. She swore the air was thinner up here. Making her stiff and unsteady way through the East Village, step by elevated step, it seemed to her as if the city had pulled off a feat of time travel, cast itself back into the sweaty streets of weeks ago. Fat pumpkins dozed on dusty stoops, hiccups of time. The sky was burning up the day's dust and smog at its edges.

She watched a young man with a bloody axe lodged in his skull stroll past, alone and purposeful, a businesslike glance at the phone in his hand. She would have liked to capture this moment—just a tiny video, seconds long, of a guy with an axe in his skull, jammy blood gumming its edges, giving his phone a brief sober look. And then a bevy of laughing zombies, elbows linked, hyperanimated and raucous, the hems of their clothing carefully scissored into cartoon zigzags, their cheeks exquisitely purpled, and two young women, their faces masked with glossy pitch-black paint from which eye sockets and the serried white bones of teeth sprung ghoulishly. There were flowers in their hair and they wore cotton dresses splashed with other flowers. She raised her phone to photograph them, and one blew her a kiss at the precise moment the device made its pleasing sound, that mimicry of a camera's shutter.

28

It looked to Inez like footage of germs: so many bodies making the roof, the usually wide-open empty roof, look too small a space. What was a party? Who were these people? Pretend dead celebrities, mostly. Watching from the water tower, she squinted down and picked out individuals in the mass. Lisa Left Eye Lopes, flailing condoms for earrings, grinding on Andy Warhol. Tupac and Amy Winehouse, taking a selfie, photobombed by a leering Frankenstein's bride. Frida Kahlo and Frida Kahlo and a zombie Frida Kahlo—fake flowers, cheap makeup— sizing one another up, comparing and admiring. They were all, to her, intolerably disgusting. Clowns, all of them, painted and babbling in their half-botched costumes, their dollar-store trash, glitter and plastic. A heat rose from the bodies, a vast thickness she could reach out and feel. A text to Kate still went unanswered. She looked for her in the crowd but couldn't think what she might have come as. Couldn't, in fact, imagine her in costume.

She'd yanked the ladder up after her. It seemed

pathetic now, to dress yourself up for other people's eyes. To pretend, when everyone knew you were pretending. The porny Barbie makeup, the trashy red shoes and leopard-print coat: someone had paid her to do that. She wore ripped jeans, cut into haphazard shorts, an old T-shirt. A cut down her left shin, the promise of a bruise.

There was the problem of no place to go. The absurdity of being in a city this big and there being no place for her. Even if she slipped into one of the bedrooms here, full of somebody else's stuff and mess, there'd be no lock on the door to prevent sloppy drunk bodies tumbling in, loud and horny, slurring their questions at her. But to be home, Broadway, alone in her childhood bedroom, dejected with Netflix while everyone else in the city, her father included, was out: that was too pathetic to even think about.

She stared at the mass of bodies as if they were one of those Magic Eye paintings; look at it right, a half-crossing of your eyes, and it would yield up some hidden shape, curved dimensions rising from the flatness to describe a recognizable form. The partygoers below her yielded no shape, no hidden image, but the sight of them provoked a sort of vision: an enormous jet of water, shooting down as if from some enormous aerial hose, like the kind some street workers use to blast lichens of gum from the sidewalks, scouring the whole space, scorching the whole party off this roof in furious tides and showers of liquefied mess, drowned screams.

She blinked and realized how badly she needed the

bathroom, but knew how impossible the line inside would be, all those bonded groups of three and four taking fifteen minutes in there to cut lines on the toilet seat while outside twenty people shifted and groaned and crossed their legs and checked their phones and occasionally nominated themselves as the hero who'd thud on the door and yell, "Hurry up, there's a line." Fuck that. She squatted low behind the water tower, bouncing on her haunches, pulled her underwear to the side, and watched piss stream and pool and run between her sneakers. When she was finished, she ran a hand between her legs to wipe herself, then rubbed warm piss on her shorts.

She stood and looked down at the crowd again, letting her right hand dangle. Someone was looking up at her. Weirdly beautiful amber eyes—that was the first thing she noticed, even from up here. She recognized him vaguely, or thought she did. Someone else's images on social media. He was saying something to her, raising an unopened beer can, offering. She climbed down.

"I literally have piss on my hand," she said, unmoving.

"Wow." He retracted his hand. "For real?"

She nodded, taking in his costume of painted bones.

"*Donnie Darko*," she said, with disappointment.

"Or like, just a skeleton?" he offered. He added, "My sister's studying to be a doctor. I copied it from one of her anatomy books. The human body is insane. Like, check out my manubrium—that's this bit."

He touched a forefinger to his breastbone and gave her a beer.

"Cool," she said, and conceded: "Your ribs are really cool."

The bones were hyperrealistic, beautiful—a literalized nakedness that was both dorkily vulnerable and deathly elegant. Spine, pelvis, tibia. Every part the same in every body. She thought of her own bones glowing inside her, the same essential scaffolding, snappable.

"That film's overrated, by the way," she said. "*So fucking* overrated."

He smiled warmly and his eyes seemed to deepen a shade darker, like tea steeping.

"They said you were kind of . . . harsh."

She looked at him. He told her she was "kind of like a celebrity or something." He added that his name was Dylan.

"That's a nice name."

"I'm nice," he said. A slight shrug in the words, of simplicity and sincerity. His phone sounded.

"My friend Caleb's at a party in the East Village," he said. "Some old artist dude called Casey. I might head there."

He paused, looked at her, patently hopeful.

"Do you want to come?"

"No," she said.

"Oh."

"But I want to stay here even less."

29

On the corner Bill had stipulated, there was a café with its one front window open to the world. Its clientele sat at the bar facing the street, replica sunsets flaring in the corners of their black sunglasses. Kate was staring at them when she felt his hand touch her elbow. She was never ready for him.

"Look, I don't want to alarm you," he said, and she was instantly alarmed, "but I *think* there's been some sort of zombie outbreak."

He had a bottle of champagne in one hand. He rested the other heavily on her shoulder and looked at her gravely.

"Shit. Really?"

She was trying to gauge his mood, to steady herself and find him and catch up and match him.

"Yes," he said firmly. "We're going to have to be *very* careful. Stick close to me."

"Okay."

He took her hand, her pleasure bloomed, and they turned their backs on the sunset and began walking. He glanced down at her feet.

"Woah!" he said. "Louboutins!"

"What?"

"Your shoes!"

He was astonished, as he should be.

"Yeah, I can barely walk in them."

"Where are they . . . who . . . ?"

Kate could tell he was rattled for asking the question, doubly so for having botched it. A Barney the Dinosaur ambled past, holding his head in his arm.

"I'm worried we're not dressed up enough," she said. "Shouldn't we be dressed up?"

"'Dressed up'?" He stopped, spread his arms in supplication, and gave the champagne bottle a waggle. "Not fancy enough for you, Miss Fancy Shoes?"

"In costume, I mean."

He considered his own jeans, his shirt, sleeves rolled. And then he looked to her, in the white cotton dress.

"What shall we be?" Then, instantly: "I've got an idea."

In the drugstore he was pulling her down the aisles, skidding like a teenager. She regretted the footwear deeply. She felt like a person coming off an ice rink, still in skates, all the tiny muscles in her ankles quivering to keep herself upright.

He was triumphant when he found it.

"Fake blood!" he said.

She laughed at him, at his plain joy, his fake blood in one hand and champagne in the other.

"How much do you love that dress?"

She loved it; it was the one dress that worked.

"No love at all, really. How much do you like that shirt?"

"Loathe it. Despise it. Abhor it."

On the street, they splashed the fake blood on each other, daubed it on their faces. It looked more like paint than the product of real suffering, but there they were, stained all over. On any other night it would be just a stained shirt, but tonight, days before Halloween, everyone would know what it was meant to be. She worked a fistful of it straight into his breastbone, scrunching it into his shirt, twisting the material to soak it, the red drenching her fingers. He briefly mimed an orgiastic coronary crisis. Then they admired each other. She took his picture. He clowned for it, but it worked: the champagne bottle still sheltering between his feet, the way a baby penguin hides beneath its parents, his upraised arm holding the emptied vial, his other arm held out to his side, palm up, an accidentally debonair pose that said, *who the fuck knows what this is all about, but I'm laughing, laugh with me or at me.*

He did not offer to take her picture in return.

"So what are we?" he said. "Axe-wound victims? Satanists. Murderers."

"All of them, I suppose," she said. "Any. It doesn't matter. Just bloodied."

They'd turned onto the block and were approaching Casey's door, when something streaked through her vision and burst at her feet, splashing icy water across her ankles, up over the straps. She yelped—a ridiculous, undignified noise—and Bill's grip was so hard that she felt the bones of her fingers creak and her throat catch slightly with the pain. A ruptured water balloon, slick against the sidewalk.

"Strike!" Bill said.

The door's buzzer—gray-beige, with tiny cracked and yellowing windows of plastic over ink-faded names, all its buttons indented and grubbed—looked like an artifact. Inside, it was dark and cool and smelled of decades of dust and smoke. Dust wasn't its own thing, Kate remembered. Not like soil or sand. It was the microscopic flotsam of bodies, inappreciable fragments of people, shed daily and unwittingly. *F'ckin' gross*, Inez would say.

As she followed Bill's back up the stairs—lopsided and creaking and uneven—she saw, in running yellow paint, THIS WAY on one step, and then, on the step above, TO THE DISCO. They followed a series of drippily haphazard arrows.

The door to the apartment was open and a small figure was standing at the window, his back to them. A tang of urine clung around things meekly. This must be Casey, then. A bucket of water stood at his feet, a bobbing canopy of red balloons spread above him. They swayed and dipped, rustling against one another in a way that seemed to communicate a sentience, their strings drifting beneath them.

"*Neunundneunzig Luftballons,*" the old man sang, feeble yet tuneful.

"Casey," Bill said.

The singing stopped and Casey began to turn, effort-fully, while they waited. Finally, he was facing them. The intensity of blue in his eyes was indecent and alarming. The blue had an opaque quality as if, Kate thought, a mind could take in only so much of the material world before it closed over, refused to see any more.

He looked straight at Bill and gave no sign of recogni-tion, his mouth hanging open, a balloon string pinched between thumb and finger. A threadbare T-shirt that must have once been white was stretched tight over his frail, sloped shoulders and the drooping dugs of his chest, the raisins of his nipples. White corduroy trousers were held around his waist with a red satin ribbon. Tufts of downy hair stuck up from his pink skull. He stood with-out moving, still seeming not to see.

Kate realized she'd been holding her breath, had made her jaw stiff with the smile she'd been holding since they crossed the threshold.

"Willie," he said, and let go of the balloon with a jazzy snap of his hand. It was a voice scored with scratch marks. "What the fuck are you doing here?"

"A happy early hallow-birthday to you, too, Casey," Bill said.

"You're early! No one will be here for hours. I told everyone they abso-fucking-lutely have to all be here at midnight. Midnight. Which means none of these fucks will get here until eleven fifty-five at the earliest."

"Well, we're here now. I wanted you to meet Kate before all your fabulous wretched friends got in our way."

Casey seemed to be peering at her ankles. "Did you catch a hit, dear? In those fuck-me shoes! Ooh, my! Cooling, though, no? Freaky hellish hot today with all those ice caps melting. We'll be swimming soon, an underwater city. Atlantis! Want to lob bombs at tourists with me? Willie, get yourself and your double-you double-you double-you girlfriend a drink."

Bill held up the bottle.

"Champagne?" Casey said, with abrupt disappointment.

"Yep."

"Well, I suppose we'll just have to drink that, then."

As Bill began ripping the bottle's gold foil, Casey turned his attention to unknotting a balloon's umbilical nub. Kate, the good student, watched quietly.

"So we do this," Casey said, "and then—" and with shaky fingers he brought the balloon to his wet lips and inhaled.

The champagne cork hit the wall.

"Bang!" Casey squeaked. His heliated laughter disintegrated into coughing and he made a lunge toward the bottle in Bill's hand. As he drank, champagne frothed down his lips and chin and soaked his shirt. Kate looked at Bill. He seemed caught between concern and amusement. Casey burped, breathless.

"Forgive me, child," he said, passing it to Kate. "Ladies first."

It wasn't clear whether he meant her or himself—whether this was an explanation or a correction.

She took a gulp and passed it to Bill, who'd claimed

one of the half-collapsed armchairs by the window. He swung his legs over its side with a proprietorial ease.

"So what are we doing, Casey?"

"Well, isn't it pretty obvious, Willie?" He turned to Kate, lifted a shaking finger to the hollow of his temple, and held it there. "Dim-witted, this one."

"We are," he continued, grandly, "taking these balloons, draining them of their precious helium, then filling them with this precious water, and then surprising these precious young people who choose to congregate beneath my window."

"So the balloons aren't for the party."

"Willie!" Casey said, and raised his trembling hands, "this *is* the party. This is all the party."

"Of course."

"My *birth*day," said Casey. "And this coming *death*day. All the dead and alive in one big party. Spirits walking the earth. Leaving, returning."

"How old are you, Casey?"

"Fucking old, Willie, that's how old. Never ask a faggot how old she is. I'm eighty-fucking-eight. Eighty-fucking-eight today."

Kate sat on the arm of Bill's chair, an uncomfortable and not very stable perch, so that when he knuckled her spine she nearly lost her balance. There was a proprietorial quality to his touch, something more needling than reassuring. As if he were prompting her into saying or being something she was not.

The old man shuffled to the window, water bomb

wobbling in his clutch, then peered into the street, took effortful aim, and with a small grunt launched it. They all heard the shriek from below.

She drank champagne, bubbles curdling in her empty stomach, and, at Casey's encouragement, took in mouthfuls of helium and told him, in a tinny voice, royal and ridiculous, that she was charmed to make his acquaintance.

He had been wrong: guests began arriving early, more and more of them. Their volume appeared almost comic. How many people could you fit in this space? The balloons seemed to become excited by these bodies, transmitting currents back to them and between them, like some kind of sentient shoal. Kate found herself crammed and trapped on a sofa, other people's legs looming above, as an old and grizzled artist talked and talked beside her. About himself, nothing else—like someone had left the tap on, like this reservoir of self-regard would never run dry. When he removed his spectacles to polish them, she risked a glance away and saw the bare back of a woman, the lightest thing in the room, narrow, alive with the movements of small muscles. Kate watched this woman turn, watched her accept a drink, and saw her jaw jut and her face tilt upward into a wide laugh. Teeth flashed. Her dark hair was piled up in an abundant, elegant mess, and her dress was a piece of black silk, with a high horizontal slash at the neck that plunged into a scrap of tight, fine, ass-covering fabric. She had cat ears on. Kate thought of Inez and her scorn and her warning: *Don't even think about pulling some bunny ears shit.* Kate had ignored her messages since their conversation on the roof, and the cups of weak tea that followed. That same roof where right now its last party must be under way. The last text from Inez, sent hours ago, which she hadn't opened so as to avoid a "read" receipt appearing beneath it on Inez's phone: *cant fucking believe ur ghosting me BYE THEN.*

Kate looked again to the woman and saw how, even with those stupid furry ears, with a costume so categorically half-hearted, she and her beauty energized the space around her. The woman leaned in to whisper something to the man she was talking to, and that man was Bill, hands in his pockets, looking at the ground, smiling, nodding as he received these words. As the woman withdrew from Bill she seemed to meet his eye, one of her eyebrows raised, that wide mouth twitched into a smirk, and Bill raised his shoulders into a shrug. Kate drained her glass and fixed her attention on her own feet.

She wondered when, how many times, what kind of fucking it had been. Imagined Bill's hands spreading, hungry, across all those tiny hard muscles of the woman's back. Did men have this, too, this coital sense? Kate wondered. Or only the jealous ones?

Encased in the Inez shoes—the outrageous, sexy six-inch heels—her feet looked trussed and abused. She unbuckled the tiny, fiddly straps, extricated left, then right, and felt the relief of newly freed feet. The straps had left indentations in her purplish flesh, and she rubbed them, trying to erase them away. She shoved the shoes out of sight under the sofa and took in the sorry state of her toes. A couple of tiny black hairs sprouted from her big toe knuckle, oxblood polish chipped into messy, jagged little islands within each toenail, a thin seam of dirt, like a pencil line, running under each one.

She was terribly drunk and hungry. She considered finding a pizza place and stuffing her face with dough and cheese to weigh down the helium and champagne, but the only way out was past Bill and Cat Ears. He was elbowing through the crowd now, moving toward her, ducking through all its fabulous, head-sprouting costumery, with a pantomime grimace to tell her about the difficulty of his progress. Finally he was there, collapsing into the space beside her, flinging his arm around her and biting the top of her ear in greeting.

"So what did Don Riley have to say for himself?"

"Who?"

"Don Riley! Incredibly famous Abstract Expressionist?"

She floundered and then saw the tiny shadow of exasperation run through his eyes. He'd enjoyed the "incredibly" a little too much; it had sounded almost English, aristocratic.

"Old badger-face boring you to death just now," he said, and rubbed her earlobe between his finger and thumb, like a person testing a swatch of fabric.

"Oh," she said. "I didn't realize he was a big deal."

"Didn't he explicitly tell you just how big a deal he thinks he is? Because if not we can get him back over here to tell us both."

He made a pretense of craning around to summon him. Kate couldn't find it in her to laugh.

"I zoned out," she said. "I don't think he was paying much attention to whether I was listening or not. I just kept wondering how his boyfriend stands it."

She'd been introduced to him, a young redhead, sulking, who'd taken her hand limply with a visible wince of reluctance and murmured his name: "Caleb." He'd worn a bowler hat. Black, spidered rays ringed his right eye.

"I expect his boyfriend stands it by listening to the sound of his sugar daddy's pencil doodles going for half a million at Sotheby's."

"Half a million?" she said. "Seriously?"

"Or more, probably. Some idiot A-lister bought one three years ago and that was that."

There was a pause. Bill looked away and began jigging his left knee up and down. The sight of it felt like someone flicking the backs of her eyeballs. She blurted the question.

"Who's that woman?"

"What woman?" he asked, vaguely.

"The one in the backless dress you were talking to." She couldn't keep the acid out of her voice. "Cat ears."

"Oh, Saskia?" he said, as if she should already know that name, and he looked behind him in her direction. Kate didn't say anything, didn't follow his gaze, just watched the side of his face.

"Saskia Poignard," he said, still craning to find her in the crowd. "She runs a gallery."

"Oh."

He offered no more information. So she asked another question.

"What's it called?"

He turned back to her and smiled at her in a way she disliked. He stroked her neck where his thumb lay.

"Saskia Poignard Gallery," he said.

"Well," she said. "That's a good name for it."

He laughed. He was full of laughter tonight.

"I'm going to pee," she said, getting up in her bare feet. But he kept his arm heavy on her; she had to struggle free.

"Don't leave me!" he beseeched.

When she came out of the bathroom, *Clockwork Orange* boy, the sulking boyfriend of the famous artist, was leaning on the door frame, texting while he waited. She couldn't help seeing his screen, right beneath her nose: *lol come see all the factory hasbeens casey reade crazy af*

He did not acknowledge her as she stood aside, just wheeled past her into the bathroom. She stood there, dumb, wondering if this was someone else's dream she'd trespassed upon. A person had taken her place beside Bill on the sofa and she had no wish to go stand there in front of them, gormless. So she looked at the walls, as if perhaps she meant herself to be here, were just waiting for someone to come out of the bathroom. Every surface was covered. Torn pages of glossy seventies porn mags, bursting with big bushes and luxuriant handlebar mustaches; scrawled poetry; bejeweled cat skulls threaded together with string; curling movie posters; a ratty, fuchsia-pink boa, dandruffed with dust; a taxidermy hawk in a glass case, resting on real moss against an inexpertly painted sky.

"You like all my fucked-up shit, child? All my lovely old crap?" Casey was beside her, boring holes with his eerie eyes.

"You can have it, darling," he said, reeling closer. "Take it all. Every bit. Might have to fight the others, but I'm done with it. It's yours. You like this?"

And he was pulling the horrible boa off its nail, looping it around her neck.

"Take it, take it!"

She stared at him, wordless, then the dust from the thing wafted up into her nostrils and she sneezed.

"Achoo!" he yelped. Was he always this manic? "Ring a ring of roses! A pocketful of posies! Bless you, bless you! We all fall down!"

She wiped her nose awkwardly and finally found some words.

"Are you . . . moving away?"

He smiled a slow smile and she felt the familiar panic of not understanding, not grasping other people's secrets.

"Catching on, child!" he cried, and he chinked her drink with his. "Cheers! Bottoms up! *Auf Wiedersehen!* Wish me a bon voyage."

"Bon voyage," she repeated, stiffly, as if she were in French class, age twelve.

And then Bill was there, topping up their glasses.

"Our little secret, dear!" he said to Kate, tapping the side of his nose.

"Are you behaving yourself, Casey?"

"Never have, never will, Willie. Too late for that. Goodbye to all that."

"Something you should know, Kate," Bill said, a gentle hand on Casey's shoulder as he addressed her, "is that this gentleman is one of the last surviving Factory superstars."

"Superstar!" Casey snorted. And he did a stiff and unsteady twirl, glass in the air, champagne sloshing down his emaciated wrist. "Ha! *Suuuuuuperstar.* Look at me, don't I look like a superstar? Last surviving! Last of the fucking Mohicans. Not that I ever had a Mohican, a Mohawk. All those vulgar punks with their Mohawks. I always preferred my locks au naturel, you know? Edie said I had the prettiest hair of any boy in New York City. Not anymore, of course."

"Tell Kate about Andy."

"Andy? Andy who? Oh, we don't want to talk about that old cunt," he said. "Dead 'n' gone. He was so pissed, you know, that he didn't die from being shot, from being murdered, you know? Gallbladder! How galling! The ignominy of that, you know? But it's all ignominious in the end, isn't it? Unless you decide it's not going to be. Take matters into your own hands!"

"What the fuck are you talking about, Casey?" Bill said amiably.

A seven-foot goddess glided past them, crowned in a headdress of plastic leaves.

"Oh, did you meet Dendra?" Casey said. "You should meet Dendra. Dendra is a dendrophile. Meaning she is a lover of trees, the trees' lover. She fucks trees! What have you come as, dear?"

"Why, sweetheart, nothing but myself, always."

Dendra extended a hand to Kate. "And you? What do *you* come as?"

Much later, Kate thought that what she could have said was *a bloody mess*, and, what with her conspicuous British accent, people might have deemed it rather amusing, if not exactly witty. But as this seven-foot human with green and black-swept eyes gazed down at her, Kate couldn't think of anything. Dendra cocked a penciled eyebrow: *Does the creature not speak?* And then, eyeing Kate's butch haircut, she gave it a meaningful stroke, smiled, leaned forward, and in a stage whisper said: "Oh, you'll figure it out, darling, no need to decide now. Enjoy it all, I say."

Bill, laughing too loud, pulled Kate into him, and Dendra drifted on, taking Casey with her.

"I need a cigarette," Kate managed.

"And I need the bathroom," he said. "Meet you over there."

The fire escape was packed with drag queens—Cleopatras and Hindu goddesses, Boudicca, Brunhilde, Joan of Arc—and Kate wanted to take their picture but felt too foolish to raise her phone to them. She smoked awkwardly on the edge, wrought iron beneath her bare feet, smiling at them, thanking them when they shifted to make space for her. Across the street, at the pizza joint, a lone man in a Yankees cap was hunched in the window, stark in antiseptic fluorescent light, his gaze heavy on the street in front of him as he pushed a slice into his face. Kate watched him while the conversation beside her gusted in and out.

"So I said, well at least I can die knowing I'm in the Getty!"

"Oh, honey," said another one, luxurious with condescension. "The picture Mapplethorpe *took* of you is in the Getty."

Bill arrived at her side and pointed to the pizza place. "Let's get a slice."

She made no mention of her shoes; to get to them would mean fighting back through the bodies, undertaking the ungainly business of burrowing beneath people's knees and ankles at the sofa. She'd get them later.

As she followed him barefoot down the stairs, the stairs whose THIS WAY TO THE DISCO was visible only in ascent, she regarded the back of his shirt, taut across his shoulder blades. Of course, it hadn't occurred to them to fake-bloody their backs. Offering up red-splashed fronts to the world, thinking that's enough.

In the interior of the pizza place they sat side by side against the wall. She chewed and looked toward the window, to where the disconsolate customer had sat face to face with his reflection. She wondered, as she ate, if she looked just as bleak as he had.

30

Inez opened the cab door, leaving her companion to pay. She looked up at the drag queens on the fire escape as Dylan came and stood beside her on the street, hands in his pockets.

"Shit," he said mildly, appreciatively, at the sight. Then, with another thought: "Hey, you know Don Riley?"

"Huh?"

"He's this big Abstract Expressionist guy. He's my friend Caleb's boyfriend."

"Are you gay?" she said.

He didn't seem to mind the question, didn't find it funny either, just shook his head. "No, I'm just friends with a lot of twinks. I go to Parsons."

She stared.

"Art school."

"Yeah," she said.

He inclined his head toward the door: "Come on."

Balloons overhead. A pack of bodies. The bed crammed with so many people—an optic confusion of limbs. A small dog, dressed in a tuxedo and a tiny top hat, trotted across them, its eager progress stopped when someone plucked it into the air and kissed it, lips meeting its pink lapping tongue. The dog, legs dangling, looked, Inez thought, acutely embarrassed. She was glad she was not a dog.

Dylan was being greeted by a boy dressed as a droog from *A Clockwork Orange*, and as they began talking to each other she could tell she was going to be ignored from this point on, that there was no place for a girl in their interaction—that at best he wanted her to hang around and wait to be fucked later on. They seemed to expect her to stand here quietly, laughing at the right moments, these boys, as they one-upped each other with bitchy judgments about people she did not know, correcting each other loudly, dropping pronouncements. She weaved away from them, to a sofa, plucking a can from a bucket of ice, shouldering through bodies, shoving past a seven-foot person in a headdress of leaves who snapped, "Manners, madam!"

Inez claimed the sofa, a bubble of space. She sat on her haunches, knees up, as she wondered whose party this was. It was hard to tell. It could have been the giantess's, in the headdress of leaves. Could be the droog's, maybe? Everyone here seemed to exude ownership, ego, too-much-ness. She didn't think she'd ever been at a party where'd she'd known no one.

The can of beer in her hand was sweating its chill all over her palm. She leaned forward to park it on the floor, to half tuck it beneath the sofa, so that for a moment her

head was bowed. Her eyes went straight to a bolt of silver spiked heel. A shoe, lying on its side, as if drunk and
asleep under the sofa where it thought no one would find
it. On its toe, a bright red spot, like blood.

31

Casey grabbed Bill by the shoulders.

"Willie," he hissed. "I thought you'd run off."

"Wouldn't leave without saying goodbye," Bill said. His sick old friend actually gasped at these words, a ragged intake of breath.

"Now listen! Billy. Billy-boy not a boy anymore. Not a man yet either, are you? Willie, I'm telling you this now and you'd better heed it. Shut up and listen," he said, blinking, spitting slightly, fingers tightening on Bill's shoulders. "You're lazy, Willie. Indolent! You always have been. Me, too, but I didn't care and never wanted more. Fucked-up fags like me don't care. But you care, that's your problem. You're a lazy fuck and you know it, and now you're all balding and old you think you can't change and you've given up entirely. Haven't you? Haven't you?"

There was a terrifying force in Casey's grip, but Bill willed himself not to protest. His hands stayed at his sides.

"Give me a break, Casey," he said softly. "Just relax for a moment. Enjoy your party."

"You've had a break! You got a break! And you've

been on a break for twenty-five fucking years! Break time's over, Billy the Kid! You hear me? Try working before you die. Try making an effort! Try trying!"

Casey was very breathless now, shaking, worse than ever, and finally the pincers loosened, slipped away, and he was spent. Bill looked at him, at the blue of his eyes, and thought the word *petrified*, as in ossified. And then Casey blinked rapidly, grabbed Bill's hand, kissed it wet-lipped, violent and tender, and left.

△▽△

Kate had returned to the fire escape. Once again, she had that unwelcome sense of invisibility. Inside the apartment the air would be fractious, staticky: even thicker human weather than before. But out here, looking up, the sky was navy and cloudless, and she opened her mouth to it a little. As if that might make her cleaner; alcohol had made her sluggish and spoiled, a lumpen thing, heavy in her bare feet. Where was Bill? With the gallery woman, probably. He'd disappeared, and actively searching for him seemed like an indignity.

Now a creeping awareness of being stared at—it seemed to happen more and more—made her turn around. For a second she thought it was someone who looked just like Inez. That was the surprise Kate felt at first, the surprise of resemblance more than recognition, the general shock of beauty. Inez was holding the shoe, its spike of a heel pointed at her, and looked crazed, furious.

As Kate watched Inez open her mouth to say something the crowd shifted and she was obscured, swallowed up.

Heads away, Kate could make out Bill, just a cut of him in profile. How long had Inez been here? Had she seen him? Had he seen her? God, the two of them, in the same hellishly hot and overstuffed space.

She craned to look for her, failed to find her, and began fighting her way back inside.

It wasn't Inez she saw now, but Casey, careful and clumsy, as he climbed slowly onto the coffee table in the center of the crowd. This made sense to Kate: he was finding an island, a pocket of space. No one seemed to notice him, no one helped him up, as though he, too, had slipped out of the situation, had crossed its borders to join her in the observing and mostly unobserved world.

She watched him, breathless, trembling, standing now, raising himself up, frail, and then he slid something metallic from his pocket. It was a tiny silver pistol—a toy, she assumed—and he lifted it in the air.

In this moment he seemed to feel her looking, because now he was catching her gaze and smiling, giving the pistol a faint sway. She smiled back in a kind of stupor. Still no one else seemed to be looking at him. She glanced around for Bill, or Inez, or any other person who might see what she was seeing, but then the shot came, and with it an eruption of plaster over one corner of the crowd. A quick, chilly spray of fear went through her lungs, then faded.

A collective shriek, spilled drinks, stumbles, an embarrassment at the sudden hush. Now audible, the voice of

David Bowie telling people they could be heroes. Laptop speakers had stood no chance against the crowd noise.

"Someone turn that off!" Casey snapped, pointing the tiny pistol at the sound, and someone did. Quiet thickened. Kate could hear the soughing of the balloons, their extraterrestrial whispers, animated by a gentle rush of fresh night air through the windows.

"Friends!" Casey said. All eyes were on him. "Foes! Frenemies! Oh, forgive me if I spooked your dear hearts! But how else to get your attention?"

Kate craved Bill, or, rather, the idea of him grabbing her hand again until it hurt. She wanted to feel her own fingers crushing against one another, to be reminded of the solidity of her own bones.

"Hello, everybody," Casey said. He seemed to have become smaller on the glass table, forlorn, marooned there. His body drooped. It was as if this were a punishment from a parent, rather than a performance of his own making.

"Get down!" someone heckled without conviction. "Someone get him down and get that off him."

But there was just weak laughter at this. This seemed to be the sort of thing Casey did, Kate thought. Waving guns around to get attention. You didn't stop him.

"I want to thank you all very, very sincerely, for coming to my birthday party. And I want everyone to take a balloon when they go. Do you hear? Everyone must take a balloon. And then you can let it go, watch it float off, or you can take it home and watch it shrivel 'n'

wilt. Float or shrivel! Your choice, dear friends! I suggest float!"

He wiped the dewdrop from his nose with a trembling hand.

"I am honored to spend this night with you all."

Someone said, half-heartedly, amiably, "Get on
with it!"

"Oh, I will!" he said. "Yes, yes. I will get on with it!
Thank you, that's just the thing."

And then, with exaggerated ceremony, he bowed:
north, east, south, west. There was a shallow noise of humor, of curious confusion. Drawing himself up a touch
taller, he screwed shut his eyes and said, "Thank you all
for coming tonight."

He paused, as if to say something more, but then faltered and instead put the tip of the silver pistol to his chest.
The gesture had the modest delicacy of a person pointing
to himself to ask, "Who, *me*?" Kate saw the gun, heard
the second shot, saw the blood explode huge on white,
but as he fell, as those frail knees buckled and his arms
went slack and his body became a bundle of falling bones,
her thought was *Someone catch him before he hurts himself.* It
took a moment for the sound to become understood, the
crowd screaming in horror. They knew this sound from
TV news but now it surrounded them, as if it had come *for*
them, seeking vengeance for them never having believed
in it. Kate, too, had disregarded death, the real eruption
of it in life.

She tried not to lose her balance in the crush of bodies,

noted that her heart was beating briskly but beneath this she was fine. People said this happened in crises, this lucidity, this confidence.

Ginger Rogers was clutching Fred Astaire to her chest. He'd lost his hat and was barking, over and over, while his owner screamed in blasts.

And then Inez was in front of her, face to face, a shoe in each hand. The whites of her eyes were blazing.

"What the fuck!" she screamed, shoving the shoes against Kate's chest and dropping them there. Kate didn't stoop to catch them. Inez pushed her again in the solar plexus. "You were *using me*? To get to my fucking *dad*? To fuck my fucking dad?"

Kate stood her ground, planted in her bare feet. The calm she felt was extraordinary. Now she knew.

"I wasn't using you," she said, knowing Inez wasn't listening.

"All this time?" Inez said, raking her hands through her hair. "All this fucking time? This is beyond fucked up!"

Was he really dead? Had it been a joke? Kate couldn't see his body now, the crowd still swarming and yelling. She watched Inez blinking furiously against tears—of fright, she thought, as well as rage.

"What the fuck just happened?" Inez asked. "What the actual fuck? Is he dead? Did he just fucking die right in front of us?"

Gently, Kate reached for the shoes. She could hear, streets away, the wail and honk of an ambulance, or fire truck.

△▽△

He'd wanted one last orchestrated drama, Bill thought later. The modest stage of his glass table, his own party, his very blood sprayed magnificently on his friends. Those arthritic fingers fumbled, he missed, the cleanness of the moment botched, and the bullet slid past his heart. They wouldn't let Bill in the ambulance; its doors slammed in his face on the street the second after the stretcher bearing his friend's body had been bounced up and in. *Family only.* No family.

He'd spun backward, flinging an arm into the oncoming traffic to claim a taxi to chase the ambulance to Beth Israel. Oblivious, as he slammed its door, sweating, to the crowd, to everything, to Inez yelling *Dad* from the fire escape of Casey's apartment, where Kate— *Kate*—grabbed her wrist. Oblivious to the one red balloon that had drifted out from the party, wobbled above the heads of the fire escape, and begun to ascend, with serene intent, over the roofs of the East Village, as if it knew exactly where it was going.

He died somewhere on Avenue A, sirens yowling, in an ambulance with two strangers. One of the paramedics, the younger man, twenty-two years old and three weeks on the job, took the old guy's hand and made himself look straight into his eerie blue eyes, which were wide, wide open with shock, or wonder, or terror. But when the man let out a terrible heave, he couldn't quell his flinch, nor his soft *Oh my god*. His fellow paramedic, dad to three teenage boys and two stepdaughters, a man who'd seen it all and had, through no fault of his own, stopped caring a long while back, looked away, made a tiny upward flick of his eyebrows—in weariness, or embarrassment—and checked the time on his watch.

Inez had fallen asleep on the bed and Kate, sitting up-right beside her, took this as forgiveness, of sorts. Not that it mattered now, not that she needed it. She listened to Inez's soft, heedless snores and felt herself wide awake. Which seemed right, somehow, as if it was her responsi-bility to stay here, alert and calm, keeping some kind of vigil until it was time to go.

Earlier, on the street outside Casey's, in the melee of hysterical party guests and angry neighbors and the Dopplerizing effect of the ambulance sirens, Kate had no-ticed a lycraed cyclist, stopped in the street to lift his phone and film the whole scene, grinning. The second Kate saw him, she'd grabbed Inez's wrist hard, told her she was tak-ing her home. And although Inez hadn't fought her off, she'd yelled and cried at Kate as they walked, breaking free only to wipe away snot on her sleeve, after which she took Kate's hand.

There were traces of Bill's smell in the apartment. Even as she'd faced the waning storm of Inez's derange-ment, she'd noticed them, catching, while Inez had begun chucking small objects at her, the fragrance of coffee, paperback books, and beyond that, his clean, dry scent. A few minutes after Inez had flung herself on her bed, fetal, she'd finally got quiet and soft, and her crying faded out to occasional sniffs.

Now Kate rolled over and settled into the enclave of Inez's neck, sheltering there, making her own body very small.

"Are you awake?"

Inez made a sound, a grunt. Kate paused.

"You just found me in a park," she said. "And I was the wrong Kate. That's all."

△▽△

Daylight had begun glowing when she heard him come in. The whir of the lift, the latch, then his whispered words to the dog, whose skittering paws had seemed to greet him, a whine of happiness escaping. When the dog settled, there was full quiet again, and Kate didn't move, she stayed curled with her eyes resting on the back of Bill's daughter's neck.

The sound of his slow footfalls, then the shift of light in the room, so that she knew he was there, standing behind her in the doorway. He must have sensed she was awake, must have heard it, or felt it, taking in these two bodies. She didn't move, but then he said her name, a question, quiet, incredulous. She turned, and he looked awful. Real blood, very dark, rust colored, obliterating splashes of fake. When he glanced beyond her, to Inez's sleeping head, then back to her again, she just blinked back at him, refusing the question. He stood a moment longer and then his face changed and he began to nod slowly to himself. He looked at her one moment more then lifted his right hand, spread his fingers, and closed the door.

When she woke, there was a faint burble of birdsong outside, which seemed a mistake; the wrong soundtrack playing by accident. She listened to the apartment and felt or knew that she was the only one not sleeping. Inez was on her back now, head flopped to the side, and Kate looked at the uncanny, incomprehensible, pure-pointless beauty of her face.

She crept out into the main space and stood there, poised. She opened one door, but got a laundry cupboard. Opened another, and it was a bathroom. *His* bathroom, she said to herself, and she began opening cabinets, poking through jars of prescription pills, reading their labels—Klonopin, Zoloft—then investigating pots of things, aspirational unguents. She wanted to take something of his, find a small item to steal. She unscrewed a sleek black cylinder with LUX in tiny gold letters running down its side, and sniffed. It was him, his smell, sandalwood, and even as she felt a flush of triumph and betrayal—*this was the smell all along*—she couldn't stop breathing him—*it*—in. Nothing human, just some fancy fucking deodorant, a white stick of it in its matte black case.

She looked up at the mirror, at her older face, the dark

roots of her hair, her tired, sore eyes, and then back to the object in her hands. With her thumbnail she gouged dents in the smooth white dome, scoring it into mess, churning, fucking it up. She smeared a gobbet of it across the mirror, a bleary comet leaving its trail across her face as she watched herself. A kind of relief—a weird, deep peace—came from this small and stupid vandalism, and she left this apartment that wasn't hers, left both of them, each in their own room, sleeping.

The streets were quiet, gray, and strewn with small pieces of wreckage from a Halloween that had still not officially arrived: candy wrappers, the occasional guttered wig in shiny pink or scarlet. She wore a huge sweatshirt of Bill's she'd stolen from where it lay over an arm of the sofa. Beneath this was the stained dress she longed to ball up and throw away.

On a street corner, a vertical word: BAR, in enormous letters. Neon in daylight was strange. It was strange in the same way daffodils at dusk were strange: flowers born for bright mornings, bewildered to find themselves in shadows. It meant something new, *neos*, for a city that was always claiming to make itself new. As she passed a newsstand, with all its quaintness of magazines and papers, she found herself scanning headlines with a hungry dread. Would there be something about Casey? Or would that come tomorrow? Or not come at all? It was hard to gauge where people stood in the world, or where they had stood at earlier points in time—and who cared, who still cared? What was old news; what was new news?

There was no mention of a former Factory super-star's suicide party. Instead, the papers shouted the doom of a historic impending weather event, a MONSTER STORM. Of DEADLY FURY. It was coming to WREAK HAVOC.

The headlines reverberated with the same stentorian voice-over she'd heard when she looked at those subway movie posters of New York under destruction. *This season . . . In a world . . .* The excess of it was comic, infantile: a toddler building up a tower of blocks just to topple them.

A man bustling toward her, leering like it was his day job to do so, launched "Keep on smilin', sugar!" with a smirk. As she walked on, away from him, coming closer to her bodega and its bright signage, she saw a scrum of people hauling five-gallon containers of water, bags and bags of chips and pretzels and cookies, saying things to one another with the hearty pluck of those bracing for a shared misfortune. She walked past them slowly, wondering whether she was meant to be buying things too.

In the apartment, Joni Mitchell mewled at her. How weird to hold eye contact with an animal.

"Big storm coming," Kate said finally. "But maybe you know that."

The cat blinked and tensed her small cat jaw.

What was one meant to do in a storm? Go home, was the answer. Go to your home, find your tribe, hold them close, hunker down. But a cat called Joni Mitchell was not her tribe and this stranger's apartment was not her home.

In the city beyond the window, there was never not movement. The stop and start of cabs, honking, doors flung open, doors flung closed. The progress of bow-backed Chinese ladies with their enormous clear garbage bags stuffed full of plastic bottles, like giant speech bubbles in a travesty of consumerism. The darting scooters and bikes of delivery men, the cheerful discord of their bells as they dodged one another. Café owners, wide-stanced, hosing their storefronts, killing their jets, as white people stooped to scoop up shit from their glossy dogs. She could get lost in it, yes, in the way people did with TV: total passivity, meeting animation with your own motionlessness. But right now the screen was dead. No one, no people, just a darkening sky and a mean wind whipping down past storefronts, blind and faceless with their shutters down. The bodega was boarded up too now. Her bodega guy, whose name she had never known and would never know, because it was now, after all this time, too late to ask, must have shut up shop and gone home to his family. The red-and-yellow awning buckled violently, as if in the grip of unbearable pain. It was hard even to look at.

Acknowledgments

For your radiant brain, your dauntlessness, and for sending chills down my spine when you guessed I'd written
most of it while listening to Philip Glass, Marya Spence.
(And thank you, Philip Glass.) For your faith, intelli-
gence, humor, diligence, and patience, Jonathan Lee. For
your support, enthusiasm, and hard work, Andy Hunter,
Erin Kottke, and everyone at Catapult. For your extraordinary wisdom and heart, Emily Stokes. For making the Atlantic not so wide, Lucy Sherwood and Brigid
von Preussen. For your early encouragement, Amy Rose
Spiegel, Osheen Jones, Alexandra Kleeman, Sophie
Smith, Matthew Hammett Knott, Brenda Cullerton,
Zhanna Chausovskaya. For providing a roof over a head,
and pup therapy: Robin Bierstedt and Peter Mayer (and
Harper); Hadley Freeman (and Arthur). For upstate re-
treats, Julia Joern. For a roomba with a view, Maxwell
Neely-Cohen. For being a sensei in the gutter that night,

Katherine Bernard. For New York in the first place, Jon Swaine. For a gift that got me started, Alison Wood. For nothing short of everything, but especially books and words and your great love, Phil Hoby and Jane Buckland. For your heroic sanity, Matt Buckland-Hoby. And, last, for being the reason this got written, and the reason, my love, Michael Barron.